# THE RIDDLE OF
# THE SPHINX

By Ken Warner

# Contents

# THE RIDDLE OF
# THE SPHINX

# Chapter One: Malia

Malia Kwan ran through the forest, her heart pounding, tears streaking down her cheeks. She stopped for a moment, trying to catch her breath and listening intently. The sounds of pursuit had faded; maybe she'd lost them. But an instant later, a ball of plasma exploded against a tree inches from her face—heat and shards of wood blasted her skin.

Malia took off again, focusing on increasing her adrenaline. She could feel the Earth's magnetic field augmenting her power. Taking to the air, she flew farther into the trees, careful to stay close to the ground.

She'd made the mistake of rising too high minutes earlier—this had provided her pursuers with a clear shot, and they'd nearly hit her with their plasma cannons.

Malia crested a ridge and dropped to the ground, hiding behind a rocky outcropping. Seconds later, Bastet flew into view. The woman came to rest, hovering several feet off the ground. She was scanning the area for Malia, her weapon at the ready.

Reaching out with her mind, Malia slammed into the woman's consciousness, overpowering her by sheer force of will and making her drop the cannon. Stepping out from her hiding place, she used her telepathy to compel Bastet to back herself into a nearby tree. But at that moment, the woman rallied, ejecting Malia from her mind and shooting her with a laser pistol.

The shot hit Malia in the chest; staggering to her knees, she struggled to remain conscious. She focused again on pumping more adrenaline into her system and regaining her full strength; she felt the incredible power coursing through her body. But as she got to her feet, she found Bastet standing only feet away, pointing her plasma cannon at her.

Malia took to the air as Bastet fired. She'd managed to avoid the brunt of it, but the fireball had grazed her hip. The pain was intense; Malia again concentrated on staying awake as she flew through the woods, zigging and zagging around the trees. Once her hip had healed and the pain subsided, she turned in midair. Bastet was close behind; Malia focused with all her might on ripping the plasma cannon out of the woman's hands.

This shouldn't have been possible—Bastet's emitter couldn't stop Malia's telepathy but provided shielding against her telekinesis. But Salvatore had explained that Malia should be able to overpower the emitter by tapping into the Earth's magnetic field.

It worked—the weapon flew out of Bastet's hands. Malia penetrated her mind, forcing her into unconsciousness. The woman fell to the forest floor and didn't move.

Malia dropped to the ground and retrieved the plasma cannon. Taking a deep breath, she set off again. But at that moment, Salvatore appeared out of nowhere twenty feet in front of her. Before Malia could react, he fired his plasma cannon. The shot hit her in the abdomen, blowing a hole right through her.

Malia collapsed to the ground, writhing in pain. She fought with all her strength to remain conscious, but the edges of her vision went dark. Screaming, she forced yet more adrenaline into her system. Her wound was healing faster than ever. Within seconds, her head cleared, and she was able to stand. But she found Salvatore standing only ten feet away, pointing his cannon at her head.

"You lose."

"Ugh," Malia said with a sigh, dropping and lying flat on the ground. Though her body had healed, her clothes were riddled with burn holes where their weapons had struck her. Her face and arms were covered with dirt from hitting the earth so many times, and she was sweating profusely. "I really thought I could beat you two this round."

"It was the closest you've come so far," said Salvatore, sitting down next to her. "And you managed to overpower the emitter this time. You should be proud."

"I guess."

In truth, she *did* feel accomplished—this skill could prove invaluable in combat. But she found herself wanting to contain her reaction in Salvatore's presence; he was always so composed. And she was exhausted; they'd been training for hours. Bastet had dragged them to this remote island somewhere in the South Pacific to practice. She'd insisted that live battle simulations were vastly superior to practicing individual skills in an isolated manner.

"We should revive your tormentor," Salvatore suggested. "Then it's your brother's turn."

Malia nodded. She got to her feet and followed Salvatore through the trees. Kneeling next to Bastet, Malia reached out with her mind and returned her to consciousness.

"Well?" Bastet asked, sitting up and gazing back and forth between Malia and Salvatore. "Who won?"

"Salvatore," Malia told her. "He went invisible and ambushed me."

"You must use your telepathy to maintain an awareness of your surroundings," Bastet told her as she regained her feet. "He should not be able to take you by surprise. We'll try again on your next turn."

They flew back to the beach where Jaden was waiting for them with Sydney, Miguel, and several Othali soldiers. Malia knew the flying saucer was hovering nearby, but it was invisible.

"How'd it go?" asked Sydney.

Malia recounted the story for them.

"Man, I still don't understand how we're supposed to be able to use our telekinesis through the emitters," said Jaden. "They shield against that."

"Yes, but we can overpower them," Malia told them. "It's like if you were talking, and I spoke over you with a bullhorn. Your voice would still be there, but nobody would be able to hear it over mine."

"Precisely," Salvatore agreed. "The emitter protects its wearer against normal levels of telekinetic energy. But once you tap into the magnetic field, your power will exceed its capacity."

Jaden had learned how to stimulate his adrenal glands only hours earlier. Malia didn't know if he'd be able to use that to overpower the emitters so soon.

"I want you to work on that technique this time," Bastet told him. "And your sister was able to remain conscious after a plasma hit—you'll need to work on this as well."

Jaden nodded, his expression grim. So far, they'd knocked him out every time they hit him with the cannon.

"Malia, there's another skill I'd like you to attempt during Jaden's turn," said Salvatore. "Plasma is nothing more than superheated, ionized gas—it is still matter. You should be able to control it with your telekinesis."

"Yes—she should be able to deflect it," Bastet agreed.

"Or stop it—or even redirect it back at her attacker," Salvatore told them. "Could you help Malia work on this while we're gone?" he added to Miguel.

"Sure can," he replied. "But, uh... we don't exactly heal like these two, so I think I'd prefer if she *didn't* try the redirecting part of that if you catch my drift."

"Don't worry," Malia told him with a grin. "I'll stick to stopping and deflecting."

"That wouldn't work on someone with an emitter, though," said Jaden. "Unless we overpower it with the magnetic field."

"It should work regardless," said Salvatore. "The emitter shields only the person and anything they may be carrying. The fireball loses that protection the moment it leaves the cannon."

"Alright, Jaden," said Bastet. "We'll give you a thirty-second head start—go!"

"Whoa, okay!" he said, suddenly launching into the air and flying off into the trees.

"I wish I could do that," Sydney said with a sigh.

Salvatore and Bastet waited thirty seconds and then went after Jaden.

"You ready, kid?" said Miguel, hoisting his cannon onto his shoulder.

"Yeah, let's do it," Malia replied. "But I'm going to need a little space—I'll try it from the other end of the beach."

"What good is that?" Miguel said with a chuckle. "Them hybrids are gonna be firing at ya from close range."

"I know, but I'll work up to that," Malia replied. "I'll never get it if I start up close—you'll just keep shooting holes in me!"

"That makes sense," Miguel said with a nod. "But my aim ain't gonna be so good at that range."

"Good!" Malia said with a grin. "I may heal fast, but those things hurt *bad* when they hit!"

Malia flew high into the air, enjoying the view of the island and the ocean for a moment before landing at the far end of the beach. The Othali soldiers were hanging back behind Miguel, looking bored. Boosting her adrenaline again, Malia focused on Miguel.

"*I'm ready,*" she told him telepathically.

Moments later, he fired. Luckily, his shot went wide—Malia hadn't been able to affect its course. The fireball was too fast.

Miguel fired again before she was ready—the shot hit her in the foot. Malia dropped, screaming in pain. She managed to stay conscious, but the pain was excruciating. Sydney ran over to her, arriving as Malia's wound finished healing.

"Oh, my God!" said Sydney, dropping to her knees next to her. "Are you alright?"

"Yeah, I'm fine," Malia said with a sigh. "I wasn't ready that time. But it happens too fast—I can't react that quickly!"

"Well, this is way too dangerous—he could hit your head by accident, and then..."

"Yeah, I didn't think of that," said Malia, suddenly realizing how risky this was.

"I'm gonna tell him to aim *away* from you," said Sydney. "You should still be able to work on it that way."

Malia nodded. Sydney ran back to Miguel, and Malia prepared herself for another attempt. Miguel fired a couple more times, hitting the sand off to her left each time. But Malia found it impossible to act quickly enough. There had to be another way.

"*Give me a minute,*" she said to Miguel in her mind. "*I gotta figure something out...*"

"*You got it.*"

Malia reached out with her mind, trying to sense the air between her and Miguel. It worked—she could feel the breeze coming off the water over that length of the beach. Next, she tried to imagine stilling the atmosphere within that same area. This seemed successful as well—it was as if she'd created a bubble, and she could feel the wind from the ocean blowing against it.

"*Okay, I'm ready.*"

Miguel fired. This time, the fireball hit Malia's bubble and froze in midair.

"Whoa!" Sydney yelled, jumping up and down excitedly.

The fireball dissolved a few seconds later.

"*Again,*" Malia said to Miguel.

He fired another shot. It came to rest inside Malia's bubble, and this time, she launched it into the sea. The water sizzled into steam where the fireball hit.

"Yes!" shouted Malia.

She flew back to Miguel and Sydney.

"That was damn impressive," Miguel told her.

"Maybe, but now let's see if I can do it at close range," she replied.

"Alright—you ready?"

"Hold on," said Malia.

Malia formed a bubble around herself this time, holding the surrounding air in place. She nodded to Miguel. He aimed at her abdomen from only ten feet away and fired. The shot entered her bubble and froze. Malia hurled it into the sky, and it disappeared.

"Well, I'd say you've got it," Sydney noted with a smile. "And I can tell you that your mom is going to be thrilled—even though she knows you heal, she *hates* it when you get hit with these things!"

They tried it several more times, and it worked like a charm. As long as Malia maintained a bubble of stillness around herself, the fireball couldn't touch her. By the time Jaden had returned with Salvatore and Bastet, Malia felt confident she could use this skill in battle.

"How'd you do?" Sydney asked Jaden.

Malia noted that Jaden was no longer wearing a shirt and felt like she had a pretty good idea of how it had gone.

"Well, I lost, but I'm getting better!"

"He remained conscious after a plasma shot and managed to overpower my emitter," Salvatore told them.

"Jaden, you will practice deflecting plasma shots while your sister takes her turn," Bastet told him.

"You say that as if I have any idea how to do it," Jaden retorted.

"It's actually pretty easy," said Malia. She explained how she'd done it.

"Oh... yeah, that makes sense, I guess," he answered pensively.

"Malia—thirty seconds. Go!" said Bastet.

Malia took a deep breath and flew into the forest. She raced across the island, then rose high into the air, far above the trees. This left her exposed, but she had a plan. Coming to rest in midair, she reached out with her mind. She formed a bubble around herself, stilling the atmosphere within. Next, she extended her awareness in all directions, silencing her thoughts and opening her senses to any conscious minds coming close.

Only seconds later, though she could see nothing, she felt Bastet flying into range. Malia penetrated her mind and forced her to become visible. Bastet fired her plasma cannon before Malia could do anything else, but the fireball entered her bubble and froze. Malia overpowered Bastet's emitter and ripped the weapon out of her arms telekinetically, sending it soaring into her own hands.

At that moment, she sensed Salvatore flying toward her, also invisible. Malia held Bastet in place while simultaneously overpowering Salvatore's emitter and taking his weapon before he could fire. She entered his mind, forcing him to become visible, and moved him next to Bastet. Hoisting one cannon over her shoulder, she fired at them, careful to aim off to one side—unlike her, they would be unable to heal from such a shot.

"You lose," Malia told them with a grin.

"Well done," Salvatore replied, nodding appreciatively.

"Yes," Bastet agreed. "I think that's enough for today."

"Thank God," said Malia, releasing them from her control. "I'm exhausted, and I need a shower."

# Chapter Two: Sydney

The next morning on the Othali warship, Sydney woke early to a knock on the door. Miguel went on snoring—she was pretty sure the man could sleep through anything. Climbing over him, she got out of bed and threw on her shorts and a T-shirt. Answering the door, she found Brian and Salvatore standing in the corridor.

"I'm sorry, did we wake you?" said Brian.

"Maybe," she replied through a yawn.

"Would you have a few minutes to take a walk with us?"

"Sure, where are we going?"

"The medical bay."

"Oh—is everyone okay?"

"Yes, it's not that—I've been wanting to have a conversation with Melissa... about the twins."

"Ah, right. Yeah, sure—should we take Miguel, too?"

"No, let him sleep," said Brian, peering into their quarters over her shoulder.

Sydney closed the door and followed them down the corridor. They found Melissa Kwan sitting behind the desk in her office.

"Good morning," she said with a smile. "You're all up early today!"

"Do you have a few minutes?" asked Brian, his expression grim.

"Sure, what's wrong?" said Melissa, suddenly serious.

Brian sat down across the desk from her, and Sydney took the seat next to him; Salvatore stood behind them, crossing his arms.

"I've got some concerns about Malia and Jaden that I wanted to bring to your attention."

"Oh, no—what have they done?"

"It's nothing like that," Brian assured her. "Did they happen to tell you about their training session yesterday?"

"Not exactly," said Melissa, rolling her eyes. "Teenagers—I asked them how it went, but their report was pretty light on the details."

Brian let out a long sigh.

"From what I hear, it went extraordinarily well."

"Then, I don't understand... how is that concerning?"

"Melissa, at this point, Malia is practically invincible—and Jaden is not far behind."

He and Salvatore took turns describing their latest achievements.

"Their abilities worry me for two reasons," Brian concluded. "First, of course, is the fact that as long as they remain on Earth, people will try to control them for their own purposes. Lucifer may be gone, and for now, perhaps, they're out of the CIA's reach, but we both know it will never end.

"But also... I fear what they could become. They're good-natured kids now, but who knows what the future might hold."

Melissa nodded slowly, considering his words.

"Power corrupts, and absolute power corrupts absolutely is what you're saying."

Brian took a deep breath.

"Yes, exactly."

"So... what are you suggesting? How do we ensure my children don't grow up to be monsters?"

"Take them away," said Brian. "With the Othali, I mean—to the new planet. Life will be simpler there; you'll be pioneers, living off the land. You won't have world governments vying against each other or powerful corporate interests trying to control your lives. It would be a much more wholesome environment for Malia and Jaden to grow up in."

"They'll be much older than you are now by the time we get there," Melissa reminded him.

"Still, you know what I mean."

"I do. And I am still planning to take them on that journey with my people."

"Malia and Jaden are hellbent on convincing you to stay on Earth," Sydney told her. "And they've enlisted me in the effort. They've hatched a plan to talk the commander into remaining here with all of the Othali, too."

"Yes, they talk to me about that constantly," said Melissa. "But making the voyage has been the plan since the invasion, and I don't intend on changing that. Once Commander Anhur is ready to set out again, we'll be going with him."

"Good," said Brian. "Don't misunderstand me—I'd love to have the three of you stay here. You're the only family I have left. But that's my self-interest talking."

"I believe you could remain here if you wished," said Salvatore, "without any worry for Malia or Jaden."

All eyes turned to him.

"They've been working on you, too, haven't they?" Sydney said with a grin.

"Yes. But I do think it would work out for the best. I spent many years with Lucifer and Isis, and I am familiar with the personality traits that feed into megalomania. Malia and Jaden have not exhibited those qualities."

"Yet," Brian pointed out.

"True," Salvatore conceded. "And I did not know my brethren as youngsters. But I remain convinced that with the proper guidance, Malia and Jaden would fare well here. It is their home; the humans are their people."

"Thank you," said Melissa. "I think so, too. My mind is made up, but I think they will need guidance no matter what planet they're living on. Building a society on a new planet will be hard work, but I think it will help develop good character."

"Agreed," said Brian. "And I'm sorry for playing devil's advocate with this."

"No need to apologize," Melissa replied. "Your concerns are valid. And I appreciate your bringing them to my attention."

# Chapter Three: Brian

Brian felt better after speaking with Melissa. He'd gone into the conversation expecting much more resistance—from what Sydney had told him, he suspected the twins might have swayed Melissa's thinking. And he'd anticipated Sydney taking the children's side, too. It was a relief that they both remained committed to the original plan.

Later that morning, he and the others headed up to the conference room behind the bridge to meet with Commander Anhur and some of his staff. The twins and the rest of the Martians were there as well. Only Babcock was missing. He was enjoying the relative safety of life on the warship with his granddaughters and wanted nothing more to do with the conflict with Majestic.

"Good morning," Anhur said as everyone took a seat. "Thank you for joining us. I wanted to discuss our next steps and get a sense of our timeline. Hathor, have you had a chance to evaluate our production facilities? Will they suit your needs?"

Hathor opened her mouth to reply, but Venus interrupted him.

"Commander, I'm afraid the situation is a complete disaster. Your technology is not compatible with ours. I've spoken with your engineering staff at length, and while it may be possible to modify your equipment to provide the capabilities we need, that could take months. And even then, it may not work—we won't know until we try."

"An obstacle, perhaps," Anhur replied, "but hardly a disaster. It will take us several weeks to construct our shuttles, so you do have some time—and we can wait a little longer if necessary."

"That's all well and good—and I thank you for that," Venus said with a sigh. "But the other issue is that we no longer possess the schematics for our saucers. Or our weapons."

"What?" said Brian. "Why not?"

"There was that small matter of Majestic nuking my compound, dear," Venus told him. "I had some of the data on my saucer, but that's gone, too. I can probably reconstruct much of what we need from memory, but I'm not sure my recall will be complete."

"Sounds like you'll be reinventing the wheel," Miguel told her. "But you've done it once; I'm sure you could do it again, right?"

"Yes, yes, I suppose," Venus replied. "But another problem is that we have no base of operations. Even if everything goes perfectly, and we're able to build a couple of new saucers before you folks leave this star system, then what? We cannot defeat Majestic and stop the Sphinx with two saucers. We'll need to establish a new compound somewhere, complete with our own production facilities—"

"And by that time, Majestic may have already carried out their plans to exterminate humanity," Bastet pointed out.

"Exactly," Venus agreed.

"What are they waiting for?" Anhur asked. "Why haven't they done it already?"

"That is a good question," said Salvatore. "I have been wondering this myself."

"I have a theory," Brian told them. "Hathor, do we have any idea how many hybrids are out there?"

"Around fifteen hundred worldwide, I'd guess," Hathor replied. "They lost quite a few retaking the twins and more in the latest battle. I only had access to the North American data, but I think that's a solid estimate."

"And they're all based in the compounds? The information we found in the data center indicates there's one per continent."

"No, not all of them—they've got operatives working in the field all over the world, too."

"Okay. And what's the average life expectancy for a hybrid?"

"Well, Majestic believes it's around one hundred fifty years, but none of them have been alive that long yet, so it's hard to say."

"They're not immortal like your people?" asked Sydney.

"We don't live forever, either," Salvatore told her. "Our life expectancy is roughly twelve hundred years."

"Hold on," said Jaden. "I thought you guys were like millions of years old?"

"Yes, but we spent the vast majority of that time in cryostasis," Salvatore explained. "We would have been long-dead by now were it not for that."

"And only twelve of you came to Earth?" asked Sydney. "How could you have continued your species with so few?"

"We brought genetic material from over ten thousand Martians that we could have used to repopulate our species," Salvatore explained. "But reproduction has proven impossible for us on this planet. We were never able to determine the cause of the problem. Whether it is the Earth's strong magnetic field, the radiation levels, the chemical makeup of the atmosphere, or some combination of those factors, we do not know. It's also possible the extremely lengthy cryostasis played a role. But I believe Lucifer viewed the hybrids as the only way for our people to continue as a species."

"Then I'm pretty sure we know what Majestic is waiting for," Brian told them. "They need more hybrids. Fifteen hundred is not nearly enough for the genetic diversity required to ensure the survival of the species. They'd need closer to ten thousand, at least. Think about it—they're be building a new civilization with a whole different species.

"And my understanding is that Lucifer told Malia and Jaden on several occasions that they're planning on exterminating only 99.9% of humanity—is that right?"

"Yes," Malia confirmed.

"And they also told you that only a tiny percentage of humans have DNA compatible with the Martians, correct?"

"That's right," said Malia. "So, those must be the people they're planning to let live."

"My thought exactly," Brian agreed. "I believe they will wait until they have the minimum population of hybrids necessary to guarantee the survival of the species, and even then, they will spare the compatible humans to continue improving their genetic diversity."

"Wait a minute, then," said Miguel, with a puzzled expression. "How long have they been abducting people, now?"

"The program started in the early 1950s," Hathor replied.

"They been abducting people that long and only managed to make fifteen hundred of them hybrids?" Miguel asked incredulously. "That don't seem right. There should be way more than that, no?"

"He's right," said Brian. "By a couple of orders of magnitude, I think. Have they been conducting abductions from all of the compounds?"

"Yes," replied Hathor.

"Lucifer's operation averaged ten abductions per night," said Salvatore. "Even with only one-tenth of one percent of those people possessing compatible DNA, with five facilities processing people for seventy years, there should be more than 100,000 hybrids by now."

"Sure, but first of all, only Lucifer's compound existed for the first couple of decades," Hathor pointed out. "The one in Africa came next—they built that in the 1960s. But they didn't construct the one in Australia until about ten years ago. On top of that, the actual compatibility rate is more like a hundredth of one percent."

"Alright, but that still yields over five thousand hybrids," said Brian. "Far more than your estimate—and much closer to the required number."

Hathor considered this for a moment.

"You're right; I never ran the actual numbers before."

"So, where in the hell are the rest of them?" asked Miguel.

"I have no idea," Hathor admitted, shaking her head.

"And we've got nothing but estimates for every variable," Brian added. "They could be very close to ten thousand by now—it may be only a matter of weeks or even days before they're ready to execute their plan."

"Which takes us full circle back to the original point," Venus said with a sigh. "Time is not on our side."

"I've been thinking about this," said Brian. "Why don't we sack one of the Majestic compounds? We could establish our base there, take over their saucers and weapons, and utilize their production facilities."

"The complex in Africa is solely responsible for fabrication," Hathor replied. "The others don't possess such facilities. And we don't know any of the compounds' locations."

"That's no longer true," Salvatore told them. "I've analyzed the radar data worldwide, and we now have precise coordinates for all of them—or, at least, their *likely* locations."

"I don't understand," said Anhur. "What radar data?"

"Our saucers show up on radar when their shields are down. Analyzing historical data for all signatures exceeding the sound barrier and filtering out known military installations, five locations stand out as having significant activity—one per continent, excepting North America and Antarctica. We already destroyed Lucifer's compound, which accounts for North America. And although such radar data does not exist for Antarctica, we have no reason to believe Majestic has a compound there."

"But again, Africa is the only one that would provide us with production capabilities," Hathor reminded them. "And it's also the most heavily fortified, by far—their entire saucer fleet is based there. How do we sack that with our current resources?"

"That's a fair point," said Venus. "We've got only the warship and one saucer. They have a hundred saucers there—they could overwhelm us by sheer force of numbers."

"Couldn't you just use the warship's weapons to blast through their doors?" suggested Miguel. "You folks probably have enough soldiers to take the place in a surprise attack—move the ship into their hangar bay and offload everyone."

"Blowing through their blast doors would be fine if our objective were to destroy the place," said Venus. "But we want to sack it— we're going to *need* that barrier to stop Majestic from retaking the compound."

"We could build new blast doors," said Salvatore. "But the other issue is that this warship won't fit inside the hangar bay. From what Malia has seen inside the hybrids' thoughts, their docking port is wider and deeper than Lucifer's was, but not any higher. We'd be able to enter with the saucer only."

"Which means we can get about fifty soldiers inside the compound," added Venus.

"Would that be enough?" asked Sydney.

"Maybe," said Hathor. "At that point, the problem is that we'd need to take control of the facility's systems. And to do that, we'd need to get bio-scans of their commander and use an emitter to take on their identity. That's going to be tough in the middle of a firefight."

"So, round 'em all up first, or shoot 'em—whichever happens first, and then get the leader's bio-scan."

"This is messy," said Venus. "There's way too much room for error. Once they realize what we're trying to do, the commander would probably initiate protocols to prevent us from taking control."

"Or they might remove the commander from the facility to protect them," said Hathor. "And bring in reinforcements from the other compounds."

"What about this," said Brian. "We go in by stealth. Hathor could use her emitter to infiltrate the place, assassinate its commander and assume their identity, and override the security protocols. Then you can reassign their entire command hierarchy to our people, lock them out of their ships, and open the hangar bay doors for the Othali strike team waiting outside. We move in, imprison the hybrids, and take over."

The rest of the group stared at him in silence for a moment.

"This could work," Salvatore said finally. "Take control of the systems before the fight even starts."

"Sure, as long as they haven't found a way to detect imposters using emitters yet," said Bastet.

"*We* haven't," Brian pointed out. "Although we do need to work on that, we have no idea how to do it."

"Other than having the kids use their telepathy," said Miguel. "And they don't work for Majestic."

"Forgive me, but Majestic has a lot more experience with the emitters than we do—they invented the things," said Hathor.

"Well, they couldn't detect imposters during the battle over New York, and that was only two days ago," said Sydney. "What are the chances they've got something ready to roll out this soon?"

"Point taken," Hathor replied. "But if they *are* working on it, they won't need very long, I'm sure."

"Which means we should act on this as soon as possible," said Venus. "This is a good plan. It could pretty much solve all of our problems. *They* certainly have the schematics for the saucers—and they stole the ones for my weapons. And for all we know, they might have information regarding the Sphinx and their extermination plan that wasn't present in New York or the North American data center."

"With the number of saucers they have there, you wouldn't need to worry about building any," Brian pointed out. "In fact, we could let the Othali take a few, and then they wouldn't have to bother with building new shuttles."

"This whole plan is extremely dangerous," said Hathor. "I know—I'm the one who infiltrated the North American command center. But that took time—lots of it. We don't have that luxury in this case."

"Speaking of which," said Brian, "do the other continents separate the abduction facilities from the headquarters and data center like North America did?"

"No," Hathor replied. "It only happened that way because we started out in what eventually became Lucifer's compound. Lucifer operated independently of the rest of the Majestic command structure in large part. They built the New York facility for the command center as the organization expanded. And eventually, the needs of the data center outgrew that space, so they constructed the complex behind Mount Rushmore. The other facilities are unified—everything happens under the same roof."

"Would our people be able to control your saucers?" asked Anhur. "It was my impression that you've got neural interfaces for them."

"We do, but we can equip your people with neural implants," said Venus. "That's easy compared to the rest of the plan. Are you willing to provide support for this operation in exchange for a few saucers?"

"I'll consult with my staff, but I believe so," Anhur replied.

"Are we set on this course of action, then?" asked Hathor. The others nodded their assent. "Alright. Let me review our data on the Africa facility. Find the easiest way in."

"While you're doing that, I'll get to work on detecting imposters," said Venus. "I do have a couple of ideas for that."

"Malia and Jaden—I'd like to resume our training this morning," said Bastet. "I've got another exercise in mind that could help take you both to the next level."

"Great," Jaden muttered, rolling his eyes.

"Very well," said Anhur. "Let's adjourn for now, and we'll reconvene tomorrow morning."

# Chapter Four: Jaden

After the meeting, Jaden and Malia went with Salvatore and Bastet to the hangar bay. Sydney, Miguel, and a group of soldiers joined them again. The Othali had a crew working to repair the area; restoring the shielding at the entry was the first thing they'd done. With that in place, they could use the port to board the saucer while the warship was in orbit. The landing platforms had not been rebuilt yet, so they had to jump off from the end of the corridor. Jaden and Malia used their powers to transport the humans into the saucer's airlock.

Once inside the vessel, Jaden and Malia joined Salvatore in the cockpit. As they moved out of the hangar bay, Jaden took in the view of the Earth below. Despite its increasing familiarity, Jaden always found the vista awe-inspiring.

"We'll return to the same location, I think," said Salvatore as they raced into the atmosphere.

"Which is where exactly?" asked Malia. "I know we were somewhere in the South Pacific..."

"An uninhabited island in Fiji."

They reached their destination minutes later. Salvatore took the saucer over the beach, and everyone transported down to the surface.

"So, what's this new exercise we have to do?" asked Jaden.

"First, I want to see you deflect a plasma shot," said Bastet.

"I did that yesterday," Jaden replied. "Ask Miguel!"

"He did," Miguel confirmed.

"Good. Then you should have no trouble showing me," Bastet told him.

In truth, Jaden didn't feel confident he could do it again. But he moved a few feet away, reached out with his mind, and focused on stilling the air between him and Miguel.

"I'm ready."

Miguel hoisted his plasma cannon onto his shoulder, aimed at Jaden's midsection, and fired. Sure enough, the fireball stopped halfway between Miguel and him; he held it there until it dissipated.

"See? I told you I could do it."

Jaden heaved a sigh of relief.

"Excellent," said Bastet. "Now, the two of you will battle each other."

"*What*?" Jaden blurted.

"This is going to be fun," Malia said, giving him a smug smile.

"How is this fair?" Jaden demanded. "She can use the magnetic field—of course, she can kick my ass!"

"You possess the same skill," Bastet reminded him.

"I've done it *once*."

"So, do it again," said Bastet, handing him her plasma cannon. Salvatore gave his to Malia. "Jaden, you will go first. I will give you thirty seconds, and then Malia will follow. Whoever remains conscious wins."

"What, but how—" Jaden stammered.

"Go!" said Bastet.

"*Dammit*!" Jaden yelled, strapping the weapon over his shoulder. He launched into the air and took off into the forest.

This was ridiculous. Malia was way stronger than him—he'd been making solid progress, but she'd been ahead of him since the very beginning. Her powers had manifested before his, and he'd been two steps behind her ever since.

But he *was* getting sick of living in her shadow. Salvatore always chose her over him for the toughest missions. Maybe this could be his opportunity to shine. But how the hell was he supposed to beat her?

Jaden flew deeper into the forest, then stopped, turning to face back the way he'd come. He had to tap into the Earth's magnetic field again—this was the only way he'd have any shot at defeating Malia. Focusing inside himself, he imagined his adrenal glands going into overdrive. It worked—seconds later, he felt the power surging through him. This was much easier this time than it had been the previous day.

Next, he reached out with his mind in all directions, senses alert to anyone coming near. Malia was smart—it was unlikely she'd simply rush headlong after him. She'd probably try to sneak up on him and take him by surprise.

Finally, Jaden concentrated on suspending the air around him, wrapping himself in a cocoon of stillness. He was ready; he hoisted the plasma cannon onto his shoulder and waited.

Seconds later, something tickled his awareness—someone was behind him. Turning, he fired a shot into the trees, but there was nobody there. It had to have been Malia. She must have sensed his extended consciousness and backed away.

Suddenly, he felt Malia penetrating his mind. She was trying to knock him unconscious—God, she was strong. His vision growing dim, Jaden fought back. Though he felt himself weakening, he drew on the power from the Earth's magnetic field and focused on expelling Malia from his mind. It worked; his vision cleared, and his strength returned.

"*Ain't gonna be that easy,*" he told his sister telepathically.

"*Yes, it is,*" came her reply.

A plasma shot hit his cocoon from directly in front of him and came to rest only inches from his chest. Jaden hurled it back the way it had come; an instant later, he heard Malia scream.

"*Gotcha!*" he taunted, flying directly ahead to find her.

"*That hurt, you jerk!*"

Malia had been cocky—she hadn't shielded herself from plasma shots the way he had. She must not have believed he could hit her; this knowledge only increased his desire to beat her.

Jaden reached out and penetrated her mind. He could feel the wound in her abdomen the fireball had created and Malia's body healing. Sensing her surprise at his intrusion, he imagined extinguishing her consciousness, like water putting out a fire. But Malia's power surged, and she ejected him from her mind.

He spotted her up ahead and increased his speed. But she

must have seen him, too, because she took off. Jaden kept catching glimpses of her between the trees and continued his pursuit. He fired a couple of shots with the cannon, but it was too hard to hit a moving target.

Instead, he reached out with his mind and tried to arrest her movement. He wasn't strong enough to stop her, but he managed to knock her off course. Malia sideswiped a tree and screamed again.

"*Hah*!" he called out telepathically.

"*Shut up*!"

Malia led him on a wild chase across the island, weaving between the tree trunks. Jaden tried stopping her telekinetically a couple more times, but she shook him off. Finally, she stopped in midair, rounded on him, and fired her plasma cannon. Jaden grimaced, but he had nothing to worry about—his cocoon was still intact, and it stopped the fireball. But the distraction had cost him—he'd lost Malia. Jaden frantically scanned the area, reaching out with his mind to sense her presence, but she was gone.

"Damn!" he said out loud.

Malia had underestimated him, and he'd nearly turned that mistake into a victory. If he'd been able to press his advantage a little longer, he felt confident he would have had her. Well, there was no point dwelling on the loss.

Jaden flew farther through the forest, staying alert for any sign of Malia and fortifying his protective cocoon. Before long, he emerged from the trees on the far side of the island. He flew along the waterline for a while, eventually finding a creek leading back inland. Jaden followed this for a minute; it led him to a ridge. There was a waterfall here that fed the stream. Behind it, he spotted a hollow in the rock—not quite a cave, but a space large enough for him to stand. Jaden had an idea.

Touching down next to the stream, he stepped behind the waterfall. There was just enough room for him to stand here without getting soaked. This was perfect.

Jaden waited, his awareness extended in all directions. When Malia approached, he'd redirect the waterfall to knock her out of the air. Then he could penetrate her mind and knock her out before she had a chance to recover.

But the minutes passed, and there was no sign of his sister. Jaden tried to expand his awareness farther out, but still, he sensed nothing. Had she given up? He was about to leave his hiding place and head back to the others when he felt Malia fly into his vicinity.

A second later, a plasma shot came through the water and stopped only inches in front of him. Jaden felt Malia penetrating his mind. Focusing with all his might, he expelled her from his thoughts and hurled the fireball back the way it had come. He fired two more shots with his plasma cannon in the same direction. Staring through the curtain of water, he spotted his two fireballs floating in midair above the stream, Malia just beyond them. Jaden focused on the waterfall, redirecting it toward Malia. She dodged in the nick of time.

Jaden reached out telepathically, trying to penetrate her mind. But at that moment, she shot her cannon three times in rapid succession, hitting the cliff face above him. Rocky debris fell from the ridge, landing on Jaden and distracting him. He tried to fly through the waterfall, but his foot slipped on the wet surface, and he landed face-first in the water instead. And in the chaos, he lost his concentration; the cocoon of stillness around him disappeared.

Scrambling to his feet, he turned to look for Malia just as a plasma shot slammed into him, blowing a hole through his abdomen. Jaden fell again, screaming and writhing in pain. He fought to remain conscious as his wound healed.

Finally, the pain subsided. But he sat up to find Malia standing nearby, pointing her cannon at him.

"Surrender?" she said with a self-satisfied grin.

"No way."

Jaden reached out telepathically to penetrate her mind. But at that moment, Malia fired again at the cliff face above him. This time, Jaden used his telekinesis to stop the debris from hitting him. But with him distracted, Malia entered his mind and started pushing him into unconsciousness. Resisting her and simultaneously holding up the debris was too much; Jaden released his control and focused on ejecting Malia from his mind.

Rocks and dirt showered down on him as Jaden pushed her out. But then the entire cliff face collapsed, burying him under a massive pile of rubble. A rock hit his head, and Jaden's vision started going black.

"Jaden!" Malia screamed.

Struggling to breathe through a mouthful of dirt and fighting to stay conscious, Jaden felt something inside himself snap. Rage overcame him, and suddenly he could sense the full power of the Earth's magnetic field flowing through him once again. Fully alert now, he gathered all his strength and then released it with an almighty howl. His power exploded, hurling the rubble pile off of him.

Getting to his feet, he found Malia staring at him, her eyes wide with terror. Reaching out with his mind, he flung her face-first into the remains of the cliff face. He could feel her resisting with her own telekinesis, but it wasn't enough. Next, he used his power to rip a nearby tree out of the ground, hurling it at Malia. She managed to turn and face toward him just as the trunk slammed into her, pinning her against the rock.

As Malia fought telekinetically to push the tree away from her, Jaden penetrated her mind, extinguishing the light of her consciousness. Finally, her eyes closed, and he could sense her body going limp.

It was over: he had won.

# Chapter Five: Darius

Darius and Sybil gazed out their cockpit windows as the people disembarked from the enemy saucer. He spotted two Martians, two humans, the two anomalies, and a group of alien soldiers. They gathered on the beach for a few minutes, and then the boy took off into the forest. Seconds later, the girl chased after him.

Darius wondered what they were up to this time. The previous day, he and Sybil had watched as the anomalies took turns combatting the Martians. Their heat signatures made them easy to track; he brought up a holographic image of them in the cockpit center.

"They're dueling each other today," Sybil noted. "My money's on the girl."

"I'll take that bet," Darius told her with a grin.

"You're going to lose. The girl's more advanced."

"We'll see."

Finding the alien warship had been a stroke of luck. The control center had noted small perturbances in their satellites' orbits. In itself, that wasn't strange; slight variations in the planet's gravitational field and interactions with other orbiting bodies always necessitated minor course corrections. But the odd part was that these new perturbances occurred with such regularity—every ninety minutes since the battle over New York.

Something massive had to be causing them—and whatever it was, it didn't show up on their sensors. Command had sent Darius and Sybil to investigate the previous day. Locating the object hadn't been complicated; they'd used the satellites' telemetry to calculate its position. But after spending hours tracking it, they still hadn't been able to achieve direct detection; their shields were formidable.

But suddenly, they'd observed a disturbance as the enemy's sole saucer left the warship's damaged docking port. Staying in close range, they'd been able to track the ship using its engine output. They communicated their findings to command, but they'd ordered them to limit their operation to reconnaissance. So Darius and Sybil had covertly observed the training sessions and then followed the saucer back to the warship.

Today, they had different orders.

# Chapter Six: Malia

Malia's eyes fluttered open. She found herself lying on her back on the beach with several concerned faces staring down at her. It took her a few seconds to remember what had happened. But as the memories surfaced, Malia grew angry. Sitting up and getting to her feet, she advanced on Jaden, despite Sydney's admonitions that she needed to rest.

"You tried to kill me out there!" she shouted, poking her brother in the chest.

"Only after you did the same to me," he retorted.

"*What?*"

"You brought a freakin' mountain down on top of me—I couldn't breathe. That was totally out of bounds, and you know it!"

Malia opened her mouth to respond, but Bastet spoke first.

"Take it easy—tell us what happened."

Malia and Jaden told the others the story.

"And then I brought her back here," Jaden concluded. "Which I *wouldn't* have done if I was trying to kill her," he added, glaring at Malia.

Sydney looked worried, but Bastet regarded them with a satisfied expression.

"You have done well. Both of you."

"I think they got a little carried away," Sydney told her. "One of them could have sustained a serious injury."

"But they didn't," Bastet pointed out. "And they both displayed superb improvisational skills utilizing environmental weapons. Malia, I believe you underestimated your brother. I hope you will never repeat that mistake—with him or anyone else."

"Trust me; I won't," she muttered, staring daggers at Jaden.

"That is enough for today, I think," said Bastet. "You have both made tremendous progress in a short time."

They returned to the saucer and headed back to the warship. Malia didn't say one word to Jaden for the whole trip. In truth, she felt guilty. She knew she'd gone too far when she saw the cliff face collapse on Jaden. And she would have apologized had he not responded in kind. But thinking it through, she realized she couldn't really blame him. She probably would have done the same thing if he'd brought an entire hillside down on top of her.

"What's the point of having us fight each other?" Jaden asked Bastet. "Nobody else has our powers, so it's not like we'll ever have to deal with that in a real situation."

"That's precisely the point. The only way to improve is to train against someone stronger than you—but there is nobody stronger than the two of you. Without your powers, Salvatore and I will never be adequate sparring partners. So, the only way for the two of you to continue progressing is to push each other, as you did today."

Malia nodded; this made sense. And if they were going to do this again, she'd need to make up with Jaden first. Otherwise, he might actually try to kill her next time.

Once on board the warship, Malia and Jaden said farewell to the others and headed to their quarters. Jaden had his own room, and he pointedly closed the door to the cabin Malia shared with her mother. She knew he wouldn't be ready to talk for a while.

Malia showered and got dressed, then headed to the mess hall. She ran into Jaden in the corridor, but they didn't say a word to each other. They ended up sitting across from each other while they ate, but only because the room was so crowded and there were no other seats. By the time their mother returned to their quarters that evening, Malia and Jaden still hadn't spoken.

"Hey, mom," Malia said when Melissa walked in. Sitting up in her bed, she realized her mom looked worried. "Everything okay?"

Melissa knocked on the door to Jaden's room without replying. "Jaden, can you come in here, please?"

The door opened, and Jaden walked in.

"Yeah, Mom?"

"Sit down."

Jaden sat in one of the chairs with a sigh, rolling his eyes and staring at the floor. Malia could tell he knew what was coming just as well as she did.

"Would one of you care to explain what the hell happened today?"

They both sat in silence.

"I'm waiting."

Malia started recounting the events down on the island, but Melissa interrupted her.

"Sydney already gave me the play-by-play. I want to know what you were thinking."

"Ask Malia!" said Jaden, looking up at their mother for the first time. "She started it—it was supposed to be a contest, but then she took it too far."

Malia didn't know what to say.

"I... I'm sorry."

"Oh, you bet you're sorry," said Melissa. "Do I understand correctly that you buried your brother under a giant pile of rubble? Why would you do such a thing?"

Malia said nothing, her eyes welling up with tears.

"I'll tell you why she did it—because she couldn't stand to *lose*," said Jaden. "She didn't think she'd have any trouble beating me, but then all of a sudden, when I got the upper hand, she couldn't handle it."

Malia said nothing; he wasn't far off the mark. She *had* gone into the exercise expecting to beat him—but with good reason. Jaden had lagged behind her ever since their powers had first manifested.

"You aren't guiltless yourself, young man," Melissa admonished, pointing a finger at him.

"What is that supposed to mean?" Jaden demanded, looking affronted.

"You threw a *tree* at me," Malia reminded him.

"Yeah, because I had to defend myself!"

"Oh, please—I already beat you, and I was about to apologize for going too far."

"Enough!" Melissa yelled, staring back and forth at the two of them. "You know, your uncle is right—this is exactly why we need to leave Earth."

"*What?*" Malia and Jaden said at the same time.

"But we want to stay here!" Jaden added, his expression aghast.

"And what happens when you're adults, even more powerful than you are now?" said Melissa. "What should I expect when you find yourselves in a situation where your ego might be threatened? That you will do whatever it takes to win regardless of the consequences to those around you?"

They both stared at her without replying.

"I didn't think I'd have to worry about this, but I can see that I was wrong. Once we're done with our work here, we will be leaving Earth with the Othali."

"But, Mom—" said Jaden.

"Don't you understand? With the power you both possess, you could become a bigger threat to the humans than Majestic. I have to make sure that doesn't happen."

"Mom, we just got a little carried away," said Malia. "It won't happen again!"

"You're damn right it won't," Melissa told her. "I'll be speaking with Bastet—your training program is canceled."

"Mom!" said Jaden.

"Not another word," Melissa replied. "I've made my decision. Now, go to bed—both of you."

Jaden got to his feet, shaking his head, and retired to his room, slamming the door shut behind him. Melissa left their quarters without saying a word. Malia got ready for bed in silence and then climbed into the top bunk and lay down under the covers.

"*You think Sydney ratted us out?*" Jaden asked in her head moments later.

"*Oh, you're talking to me now?*"

"*I'm still mad at you. But we gotta work together if we're gonna convince Mom to change her mind.*"

"*I'm sure Sydney talked to her,*" Malia told him. "*But let's be honest, we* did *mess up. Can't blame Sydney for that.*"

Jaden was silent for a minute.

"*Yeah. You're right. Sounds like Brian talked to her, too.*"

"*Well, you said yourself it seemed like he was afraid of us that day in Venus's compound, remember?*"

"*Yeah. He was.*"

Melissa returned only a few minutes later. She prepared for bed herself, got into the bottom bunk, and turned off the lights—without one word to Malia.

Malia lay awake for a long time, staring up at the ceiling. She knew their mother had good cause to worry. Malia and Jaden were growing more powerful by the day. But did she really fear they'd go down the same path as Lucifer? That they'd grow up to become evil, somehow? Malia could never imagine herself trying to commit mass murder. Today had been nothing more than sibling rivalry gone awry... she hoped.

But something Jaden had said earlier kept nagging her thoughts.

"Mom?" she whispered.

There was no reply. She must have fallen asleep. But a moment later, she said, "Yes?"

"Were there... Did you ever have any other kids? Besides your first set of twins in ancient Egypt, I mean?"

"No. Just you and your brother."

"What about Bomani? Did he ever have any children?"

Melissa sighed.

"What is this about?"

"I'm just curious."

"Bomani did father a handful of children over the years. In every case, they aged rapidly and lived very short lives, just like Rashida and Nour."

"Did they have powers?"

"No."

"None of them?"

"Where are you going with this?" Melissa asked.

"It's nothing," said Malia. "We were talking earlier, and Jaden pointed out that we'd never have to fight anyone else with powers. It got me thinking; that's all."

Melissa was silent for a moment.

"None of Bomani's children had powers. And we did find that curious. But we didn't possess the tech to do a genetic analysis at that time. There must have been something about Ashai's DNA—or mine or the combination that made your abilities possible."

Ashai had been an ancient Egyptian king and the father of Melissa's first set of twins. Technically, he was Malia's biological father, although she'd never given him much thought.

"And Ashai didn't have powers, did he?"

"No. And obviously, I don't, either."

"Hmm."

Malia considered this for a few minutes. Before long, she could hear her mother snoring quietly. But Malia still couldn't fall asleep.

Suddenly, she noticed the door to their quarters opening.

# Chapter Seven: Darius

Darius watched the hologram as the two anomalies did battle on the island. When the girl brought the cliff face down on top of her brother, he thought for sure he'd lost his bet.

"Hah, I win," said Sybil.

"Wait."

Darius watched with bated breath. Suddenly, the rubble pile exploded, and the boy emerged. He overwhelmed the girl, pinning her to the remains of the ridge with a tree. She fell unconscious moments later.

"*I* win," said Darius.

"Damn," Sybil replied. "I didn't think he had it in him. Well, you don't actually get anything—we never said what we were betting."

"Sore loser."

The boy flew the girl back to the beach.

"That's it, let's go," said Darius.

They dropped to the main level. Darius retrieved the box of explosives and two syringes, and they each slung a plasma cannon over one shoulder and grabbed a scanner. They had the plans for the enemy's fusion grenades, but they weren't ready for production yet. But the bombs they'd brought should be more than enough to destroy the warship.

Sybil engaged her emitter, taking on the appearance of the Martian, Venus; Darius transformed into the human, Brian Kwan. Majestic had their bio-scans on file from when they'd infiltrated Lucifer's compound. Next, they made themselves invisible. They weren't planning to interact with the enemy saucer's systems, but just in case, their underlying appearances needed to match people with security clearances for that vessel.

Darius and Sybil dropped through the airlock and hovered near the group on the ground. When they engaged the gravitational beam to board their saucer, the two of them followed close behind. They made it into the airlock and up to the main level without being detected.

Keeping utterly still and quiet and out of the other passengers' way, they waited until the saucer arrived inside the alien warship's docking port. It turned out that the aliens had not yet repaired this area, so the anomalies had to transport the non-Martians off the vessel. Darius and Sybil followed them out the airlock on their second trip, then hovered nearby as they moved the others to an open corridor. Once they'd deboarded everyone, the two of them moved into the passage themselves.

Inside the vessel's shields, their scanners had no trouble operating. Within seconds, Darius had a detailed map of the entire ship. He found a storage area on the same deck as the engine room; he sent Sybil the coordinates.

"Let's move," he said through his implants.

They made their way through the ship, careful to avoid physical contact with any of the crew. There were a couple of close calls when they barely managed to stay out of the way of passing groups. But finally, they made it to the storage room. Here they would wait until the night shift started. There would be far fewer people about, and this would give them their best chance of success.

A few hours later, they emerged from their hideout and proceeded to the engine room. Darius took care of planting an explosive while Sybil stood guard. He found an exposed bulkhead in the rear corner of the room—that would be perfect. They'd wait until they'd completed their objectives, then commandeer the enemy saucer, leave the alien warship, and detonate the bomb remotely. Putting it on a timer was too risky.

Once he'd attached the explosive, Darius crept back to Sybil's position, and they returned to the corridor. Rechecking his scanner, he found the only two sets of half-human, half-Othali life signs on the entire ship. They proceeded carefully up to the crew quarters.

They found the anomalies in adjoining rooms. Darius decided to deal with the girl first—despite her loss down on the island, she was the greater threat. Once they'd acquired her, taking the boy would be easy. The scanner showed two life signs in the girl's chamber—the other must have been her mother. Both appeared to be asleep.

Darius pulled out one syringe and tried the door. It was locked, but the mechanism was electronic. Using his scanner, he analyzed the circuitry, then emitted a signal that unlocked the door. Sybil stood guard again in the corridor. Quietly opening the door, Darius slipped inside.

# Chapter Eight: Malia

Malia's heart jumped into her throat as an adrenaline dump hit her system. She couldn't see anyone, but that door hadn't opened itself. Reaching out telepathically, she felt someone in the room with her. She penetrated the intruder's mind, sensing immediately that this was a hybrid. Forcing him to become visible, she yelped with surprise when she saw a perfect simulacrum of her uncle standing there. The man lunged, reaching for her with one hand. Malia focused with all her might on stopping him, her telekinesis overpowering his emitter's shielding. As he came to rest, she noted the syringe in his hand.

Jumping down from the top bunk, Malia forced the man to resume his usual appearance. He looked human except for his catlike eyes.

*"What are you doing here?"* she demanded telepathically.

"It's merely a social call," he said with a smirk.

Malia concentrated on surfacing his recent memories. Then, she saw him disembarking from a flying saucer hovering over the island in Fiji with a female hybrid. The two of them boarded Salvatore's saucer and entered the Othali warship with them. Then they went into hiding until the night shift. Malia watched as this hybrid planted an explosive in the engine room, and then the two of them proceeded here—the second hybrid had been waiting in the corridor, standing guard.

Suddenly Melissa woke with a scream, jumping out of her bunk.

"Mom—alert Commander Anhur that there are two intruders on board! I'm going to engineering—they planted a bomb down there!"

At that moment, Malia sensed the hybrid crushing his fake tooth and inhaling deeply. He fell to the floor, convulsing and foaming at the mouth. It took only seconds for the cyanide to kill him.

Malia stepped over the corpse and moved out into the corridor. Extending her consciousness, she tried to find the second hybrid, but there was nobody here.

"Damn," she said, hurrying off toward the engine room.

When Malia arrived, the personnel on duty gazed at her with expressions of mild surprise—nothing seemed amiss.

"Can I help you?" asked a male officer she didn't recognize.

"There are intruders on board," she told him. "One of them planted a bomb in here."

The officer gave her a blank stare for a moment as if the information had trouble sinking in. But then he became alarmed.

"Where?'

Malia looked around—she spotted an exposed bulkhead in a rear corner. She ran to that area, the officer right behind her. Examining the metal structure, she found the explosive down by the floor.

"Is it armed?" the officer asked.

"It's not on a timer," Malia told him. "We need to get Venus down here—she'll know how to take care of it."

He nodded and headed off to contact Venus. Malia searched the engine bay telepathically but didn't sense the other hybrid here. Venus arrived a couple of minutes later and examined the bomb.

"You're right—it hasn't been armed," she told them. "They must have been planning on detonating it remotely." She focused for a moment. "I've rendered it inert."

"You can access it with your implants?" Malia asked.

Venus nodded. Removing the explosive from the bulkhead, she handed it to the Othali officer.

"You should jettison this into space and then destroy it with the ship's weapons once we're at a safe distance."

The officer nodded, taking the bomb from her and hurrying off.

"So, how did that thing get here?" Venus asked.

Malia told her what had happened.

"We need to find that other hybrid—she's not in here?" Malia shook her head. "We should check the hangar bay. Chances are, she'll try to use our saucer to escape."

Malia and Venus ran to the hangar bay. They found a group of Othali soldiers stationed there, guarding the entry to the area.

"Nobody's come through here?" Venus asked them.

"Not since we arrived," one of the soldiers replied. "But we've only been here for a couple of minutes."

Malia stepped to the end of the corridor, gazing into the docking port. It was empty except for their one saucer.

"Commander Anhur ordered the entry port sealed, so nobody's getting in or out," the soldier told her.

Malia nodded. Reaching out telepathically, she searched the hangar bay but found nobody. She turned to Venus and shook her head.

"She must be on the saucer," Venus said. "Come with me."

Malia followed her into the saucer. They stopped in the airlock while Malia searched the area telepathically; there was nobody here. Moving up to the main level, Malia scanned this area but didn't find anyone here, either.

Venus pointed up toward the cockpit; Malia nodded. They moved up to the top level, and once again, Malia reached out with her mind to look for the hybrid. She found her, penetrated her mind, and forced her to become visible. The woman looked exactly like Venus; she had a plasma cannon resting on her shoulder, pointed at the two of them.

"Tell your commander to unlock the portal," she told them.

Malia used her telekinesis to form a bubble of stillness around herself and the real Venus, just in case the hybrid fired at them.

"Not a chance, honey," Venus told the woman. "You've lost. We jettisoned your bomb, and you're obviously not escaping with my young friend, here, or her brother. Now. Please alter your appearance; you don't wear *me* well."

The hybrid fired at them; the fireball froze inside Malia's bubble and dissolved.

"Nice try," said Malia.

Pushing herself into the woman's mind, she forced her to drop the weapon and return to her normal appearance.

"That's better," Venus commented. "Are there any more of you here, or was it just you and your dead companion?"

Malia could sense the woman's surprise—she'd suspected her colleague was dead but hadn't known for sure. The hybrid didn't answer Venus's question, so Malia forced her memories to the surface. What she saw confirmed what she'd learned from the other one—it was only the two of them on this mission.

"There's no one else," Malia said to Venus.

"Tell me," said Venus. "Why haven't you bitten your fake tooth yet?"

The woman only glared at her in response.

"*Well, answer her,*" said Malia. "*All the others have killed themselves as soon as we've caught them.*"

Malia could sense that this woman was different somehow. Her orders were to self-terminate if captured. But her allegiance to Majestic was weaker than the others' had been; she wanted to live. Malia relayed these insights to Venus.

"Fascinating. Well, put her under before she changes her mind."

Malia pushed the hybrid into unconsciousness; she collapsed on the floor.

"We'll take her to the Othali and let them decide what they want to do with her."

Using her telekinesis, Malia lifted the woman from the floor, moved her out of the saucer behind Venus, and deposited her on the floor in the main corridor.

"Take this one to your brig," Venus said to the officer. "I'm sure your commander will want her questioned."

The soldier nodded. He conferred with his comrades, then two of them picked the woman up from the floor and carried her off.

"Well, back to bed," Venus said with a yawn. "And thank you, young lady," she added to Malia, clasping her shoulder.

"For what?"

"You saved my life back there—the bitch was aiming at me when she fired that cannon."

Malia smiled at her. Venus headed back to her quarters, but Malia was wired. She asked the soldier for directions to the brig and then took off to find it. When she arrived, she found Commander Anhur there with the two Othali soldiers. The area looked similar to the ship's other passages, except that the walls were lined with cells that had force fields instead of doors. Malia spotted Bomani inside one of the cells; it looked like he was asleep. The hybrid's cell was farther down the passage; she was lying on her cot, still unconscious.

"Ms. Kwan," Anhur said, nodding to her. "Good work finding this one."

"Thank you," she replied; she'd never spoken to the commander much, and he intimidated her.

"Your mother's on her way. She's going to remove the fake tooth. I'd like to question this woman in the morning—could you be here to assist with that? Verify her answers?"

"Yes, of course," Malia replied.

Melissa arrived a few minutes later. She hugged Malia, and then the guard dropped the force field for her. Melissa moved inside, setting her medical bag down on the floor. She sat down on the edge of the cot and went to work. Within minutes, she'd extracted the false tooth.

"Thank you, both," Anhur said when she was done. "We should all get some sleep. I'll see you in the morning," he added to Malia.

Malia headed out with Melissa.

"You're going to see him in the morning?" Melissa asked once they'd moved out of earshot.

"Yeah, I'm going to help them question the hybrid. This is the first one we've captured that hasn't committed suicide."

They stopped by the medical bay. Melissa dropped off her kit and disposed of the tooth. Then they returned to their quarters.

Malia drifted off to sleep quickly this time, despite the night's excitement. She woke up in the morning and headed back to the brig. Anhur was already there with one of his officers.

"Ah, Ms. Kwan," he said when she walked in. He moved across the area to her, the officer right behind him. "This is Lieutenant Jamali." Malia nodded to her, shaking her hand. "She'll be conducting the interrogation this morning. I'd like you to monitor the hybrid with your powers and verify that her answers are truthful."

"No problem," Malia replied.

"We're going to be focusing primarily on the Majestic leadership—their current whereabouts, identities, and plans. There's a good chance this woman won't know very much, but see what you can glean from her thoughts—there could be some detail there that she doesn't vocalize."

Malia nodded. They walked to the cell, and the guard dropped the force field for them. Malia walked in with Jamali, and the guard re-engaged the barrier.

The hybrid was sitting in the cot, staring determinedly at the opposite wall. There were two chairs that hadn't been here the night before. Jamali moved one of them directly across from the hybrid and sat down. Malia took the other seat.

"Good morning. I'm Lieutenant Jamali. What's your name?"

The woman ignored her; Jamali nodded to Malia. Malia extended her consciousness, penetrating the hybrid's mind.

"*Your name?*"

The woman locked eyes with Malia. She could feel her trying to resist, but it was no use. The name floated into her mind.

"Her name is Sybil," Malia told Jamali.

"Here's the situation, Sybil. If you don't tell me what I want to know, my colleague here will fish the answers out of your mind anyway. So, you might as well talk."

"Go to hell," the woman said, staring at the wall again.

"Where is your base of operations, Sybil?"

Sybil said nothing. But in her mind, Malia saw images of Lucifer's old compound and Sybil flying out of it on the last saucer before the facility went up in a mushroom cloud. After that, Sybil moved to another, much larger compound. Malia saw her fellow intruder there as well.

"Sybil and her partner came from Lucifer's compound, but are based in Africa, now," said Malia.

"Dammit," Sybil muttered, rolling her eyes.

"Yeah, like I said—you might as well talk," Jamali told her with a grin. "How did your people find this warship?"

Sybil said nothing, staring down at the floor. Malia sensed the answer in the woman's mind.

"Majestic detected tiny changes in their satellites' courses—the permutations occurred with a regular period," said Malia. "They determined that something was orbiting the Earth with enough mass to disturb the surrounding objects gravitationally."

"And what was your objective in boarding this vessel?" asked Jamali.

Sybil fixed Malia with a stare, saying, "To acquire the anomalies and destroy the warship."

Malia could sense the truth of her words; this was the same information she'd already retrieved from both of the hybrids' memories the night before. She nodded to Jamali.

"Who gave the orders for this mission?"

"Base Commander Nala," said Sybil. "She's in charge of the Africa command center."

Malia nodded.

"Does the Sphinx operate out of the Africa facility?"

"No."

"Where is the Sphinx located?"

"No idea."

"Are they based at one of the other compounds? Europe? Asia, perhaps?"

"No—they're not at any of the compounds. I don't know where they are."

"Have you ever seen them?"

"No."

"When we encountered Ervin Noorani on the chariot, he was wearing an Egyptian headdress. That seems strange to me. Could the Sphinx have their own separate facility somewhere in Africa—in Egypt, perhaps?"

"Who the hell is Ervin Noorani?" Sybil asked. Malia could sense her confusion—she'd never heard that name before; Malia nodded to Jamali.

"Noorani was one of the Othali colonists who came here tens of thousands of years ago. But somehow, he became part of the Sphinx."

"Then you already know who the Sphinx is—why are you bothering me with this?"

Malia probed her thoughts. Sybil knew there had been a battle in the airspace over New York, but she hadn't been there and knew only that Majestic had lost. Malia found it hard to believe that there wouldn't have been chatter about this among the hybrids and tried to surface any memories pertaining to such events. But there was nothing.

"She doesn't know about Noorani," Malia told Jamali. "The hybrids in Africa know only that there was a battle and that Majestic lost."

"Hmm," said Jamali. "Well, we did destroy the chariot, so I guess there was nobody left to provide gossip to the troops back home."

"Noorani sent a signal right before the end," said Malia.

"Sure, but their commanders probably didn't share the info with the masses," said Jamali. "Sybil, when is Majestic going to exterminate the humans—what are they waiting for?"

"I don't know."

"How are they going to do it? A biological weapon of some kind?"

"I don't know."

Jamali glanced at Malia; she nodded.

"We know your people were conducting experiments on the humans at Lucifer's compound. Were you testing some sort of chemical or biological agent on them?"

"Maybe. We had to give them injections and then monitor changes in their condition; lots of them died. But they never told us the purpose of the experiments."

Jamali paused for a moment, taking a deep breath.

"Sybil, why didn't you use your fake tooth when we captured you? That's what all the others have done."

"I want to live," she replied.

"But you have standing orders to commit suicide if you fall into enemy hands, don't you?"

"Not all of us follow Majestic with blind allegiance."

"Oh, no?"

"We are people, just like you. Each of us is capable of independent thoughts and feelings."

THE RIDDLE OF THE SPHINX

"But your entire organization is committed to the destruction of the humans."

"Not all of us."

Malia found this difficult to believe. She probed Sybil's thoughts, trying to tease out her beliefs about Majestic's mission. But she was telling the truth. Sybil believed that the hybrids should establish their own community, separate from human civilization, and adopt a "live-and-let-live" policy. Malia explained this to Jamali.

"Oh, so you think the humans should live, but the Othali deserve to be exterminated?"

"No. Genocide is wrong—no matter the victim."

"But if that's true, why did you participate in this mission? Had you succeeded, you would have wiped out the remains of our civilization."

"I had no choice. Orders are orders."

"You disobeyed your orders regarding self-termination."

"Yes, precisely! And if I'd disobeyed the orders to carry out this mission, they would have executed me!"

"How many of your people feel the way you do?"

"I don't know," Sybil said with a sigh. "Not many. I've met only a few. It's dangerous for us to discuss these ideas. The leaders terminate anyone who openly expresses such notions."

Malia nodded to Jamali.

Jamali took a deep breath.

"How many hybrids were there in Lucifer's compound?"

"Initially around one hundred. But this one killed about half of them," said Sybil, nodding to Malia.

"And how many in Africa?"

"I don't know... more than Lucifer's. Two hundred. Maybe three hundred."

"You need to help me with some math," said Jamali. "Based on the numbers in your compounds plus your field operatives, we only know about roughly fifteen hybrids. But with all the humans your people have abducted over the years, there should be closer to ten thousand of you. So where are the rest?"

Sybil stared at her for a moment.

"What? I have no idea what you're talking about. All the hybrids work for Majestic—either at the compounds or in the field."

Malia probed her thoughts. Sybil was telling the truth; she didn't know about any other hybrids.

Jamali let out a long sigh.

"Alright, we're done here," she said to Malia as she got to her feet.

"Are you going to send me back to my people?" asked Sybil.

"That decision is way above my pay grade," Jamali told her. "But I'd tend to doubt it."

"Good. They'll kill me if I return."

"You'll be cooling your heels here for a while, at least," Anhur told her from outside the cell.

The guard dropped the force field to let Malia and Jamali out, activating it again behind them. Anhur walked them out of the brig.

"Good work, you two," he said once they'd reached the corridor.

"She provided some useful intelligence, after all."

"But she didn't know anything about the Sphinx," Malia noted with a puzzled expression.

"No. But she revealed that Majestic isn't as monolithic as we believed."

# Chapter Nine: Sydney

Sydney went to the mess hall for breakfast with Miguel, then stopped by the medical bay on her own.

"Good morning," Melissa said when she arrived.

"Hey," Sydney replied with a smile. "How's Nadia doing?"

"Very well," said Melissa. "She's itching to return to duty. And she'll probably be ready in another week or so."

"Aw, that's great. Good for her!"

"So, did you hear about our incident last night?" asked Melissa.

"No—what incident?"

"Two hybrids infiltrated the warship—they boarded the saucer with you down in Fiji. They planted a bomb and tried to abduct Malia and Jaden."

"*What?*"

Melissa told her the rest of the story.

"Unbelievable. And here's me, thinking we're safe here... But, of course, leave it to Malia to save the day. Did you have a chance to talk to them?"

"Sure did. They're not happy with me, of course. Jaden's still not talking to me, but it had to be done."

"We saw him at breakfast—he wouldn't even look at me."

Melissa sat back in her chair, letting out a long sigh.

"He's always been the difficult one. Malia's taken what we discussed to heart. I think she recognizes that they took things too far, and she wants to do better. But Jaden... he's more confrontational. He's got this anger inside of him that he keeps bottled up."

"I'm sure he'll come around in time," said Sydney. "Right now, I'd imagine he's feeling some resentment."

"About what?"

"Well, think about it... his twin sister has been showing him up ever since this craziness started. Now, for once, he outdoes her, and he's got the adults in his life coming down on him for it."

Melissa took a deep breath.

"You're right; I hadn't considered that. Let's hope I don't drive him to the very thing I'm trying to prevent."

"I don't think you will," Sydney assured her. "Jaden's a good kid—he's got a good heart."

"Well, we'd better get going, or we'll be late for Anhur's meeting," Melissa said, getting to her feet.

Sydney accompanied her up to the conference room. They took the two seats next to Miguel; the Martians were here already along with Lieutenant Buhkari and Ensign Shurani; only the commander had yet to arrive. Malia smiled and waved to Sydney and Melissa, but as before, Jaden averted his eyes. Commander Anhur walked in a minute later.

"Good morning, everyone," he said, taking his seat at the head of the table. "As I'm sure most of you have heard by now, two Majestic operatives infiltrated this vessel last night. Unfortunately, one took his own life before we could question him, but we managed to capture and interrogate the other."

He gave them a summary of the night's events and the results of the interrogation. Sydney noticed that his report seemed to upset Bastet for some reason, but she didn't say anything.

"It is imperative that we develop a means of detecting intruders using emitters to mask or hide themselves," Anhur concluded.

"We've got one," said Venus. "The trouble with the emitters is that the technology does precisely what it was designed to do: completely transform a person into someone else. It uses holographic imaging to simulate the target's visual appearance, brainwaves, and DNA. Standard scans show only what the emitter portrays, making it impossible to spot an imposter. But normal scans are *passive* in nature—they only detect signals.

"We tried using an *active* scan—in other words, transmitting an electromagnetic beam that reflects back to the scanner. This didn't yield any better results in terms of detecting an imposter, but it *did* create a visible disturbance in the emitter's output."

"Well, that's better than nothing," said Brian. "That should definitely work for our purposes."

"I'm sorry, you think you could translate all of that into English for us?" said Miguel.

"Shining the scanning beam on the test subject creates a distortion—they look blurry," Venus told him.

"So, we'd have to use this scanner on everyone boarding the ship?"

asked Sydney. "What about last night—the intruders were invisible."

"The active scan makes them visible until you turn it off," said Venus. "Ideally, we should install scanners in the saucer airlock and at the entry to the corridor leading to the hangar bay. This will alert anyone boarding the saucer to an intruder's presence, and the guards can monitor the docking port entry."

"We'll need your scanners for this?" asked Anhur.

"No—we used Othali scanners in our tests," said Venus.

"Very well," said Anhur. "I'll have our crews install the necessary equipment immediately if you can take care of the saucer?"

Venus nodded.

"We should provide hand scanners to President Mendoza," Brian suggested. "Her people could use them to root out any other imposters in the government."

"And to other world leaders, too," said Sydney. "It's not only the U.S. they've infiltrated, right?"

"Yes, definitely," Brian replied.

"That will take care of the hybrids who have used their emitters to replace existing personnel," said Hathor. "But keep in mind, there are other hybrids in those governments who are there as themselves. They're not using emitters—just contact lenses to make their eyes appear human."

"That's a good point," said Brian. "We'll have to let them know about that, too."

"Any progress with your plans to infiltrate the Majestic compound?" asked Anhur.

"Unfortunately not," said Hathor. "There's very little about their Africa facility in the data we retrieved. So I'm going to need to go down there with the saucer and do some recon. The key will be finding a hybrid who belongs there and then using an emitter to replace them. Once I'm inside, it shouldn't be too difficult to find the commander. Then I can replace that person, and it's all over."

"They do abductions from that compound, right?" asked Brian. "Could you board one of their saucers when they're transferring humans to and from the facility?"

"That's exactly what I was thinking," said Hathor. "To avoid suspicion, I'd have to complete the night's run before entering the compound."

"You mean finish their abductions for them?" asked Sydney.

Hathor nodded.

"Yes, exactly."

"Is there any chance they've started using active scanners on their personnel the way we're planning to do?" asked Anhur.

"It's possible," said Hathor. "But that wouldn't help them much—they already know their people are using emitters."

"The scanner wouldn't reveal your true identity?" asked Anhur.

"No, it wouldn't," said Venus. "It only creates a distortion; it doesn't uncover the person's underlying appearance. But if I were them, I'd initiate a protocol requiring personnel to remove their emitters before entering the compound. *Then* the scanner would catch someone trying to bypass the protocol. Of course, that would cause some trouble for Hathor."

"It's a risk, but don't forget—this is *their* tech we're talking about," said Hathor. "They know it better than we do, and it's quite likely that they've got something else in the works—some better way of detecting an imposter. But it comes back to timing. The sooner we execute this plan, the better our chances that they don't have anything in place yet."

"How soon can you go?" asked Anhur.

"I'm ready now," Hathor told him. "I can do it this evening. They run the abduction missions at night. So I'll head down before sunset, do some recon on their first couple of trips, and then move into place."

"You'll need to send your saucer back to us once you disembark," said Venus. "Otherwise, these folks won't have any way to get their soldiers down there."

Hathor nodded.

"We can always control the saucer from here, if necessary," Salvatore said.

"How many hybrids are stationed at the Africa facility?" asked Anhur.

"Roughly two hundred fifty," said Hathor.

"And how many soldiers can we fit on the saucer?"

"Fifty or so," Hathor told him.

Anhur nodded.

"Once you take control, could you send us a second saucer? It may be overkill, but I'd like to have a hundred pairs of boots on the ground in there. We're only going to get one shot at this."

"Not a problem," said Hathor. "I'll contact you the moment I take command. I'll open the blast doors and send a saucer to you right away. But it's quite likely the first team will have the situation under control by the time the second team arrives."

"Agreed," said Salvatore. "We've got the element of surprise here."

"How are y'all planning on getting fifty soldiers onto the saucer?" asked Miguel. "The way it stands right now, us non-Martians have to hitch a ride with the kids."

"Our crews are still in the early stages of repair work in the hangar bay," said Anhur. "But I'll have them erect a temporary docking platform today."

"Commander," said Bastet. "I'd like to address something you brought up earlier."

"Yes?" said Anhur.

Sydney had almost forgotten Bastet was there; she'd sat so quietly through the meeting so far.

"Salvatore, Venus, Hathor, and I are all that remain of our people in the entire universe. This hybrid prisoner reported that many of them disagree with Majestic's agenda of exterminating humanity?"

"That's what she told us."

"When we infiltrate their compound, can we make an effort to separate those who oppose Majestic? Though Lucifer was wrong about a great many things, he was correct about the hybrids representing the only viable means of continuing our species."

"I concur," said Salvatore. "We should make every attempt to isolate those who stand against Majestic's mission."

"You'll have to be careful," said Brian. "Once word gets around that you're sparing such people, I'm sure many will make false claims."

"Malia and Jaden should be able to confirm which ones genuinely oppose Majestic," Sydney suggested.

"This is your operation," said Anhur. "We will execute it as you see fit."

"Thank you," said Bastet.

"Anything else?" asked Anhur. No one brought up any other issues. "Alright. Let's proceed."

# Chapter Ten: Hathor

Hathor returned to her quarters after the meeting. Though she had several hours before she'd have to depart the warship, she needed to prepare. Mentally. She'd managed to infiltrate Majestic before, all the way to the very top of the North American hierarchy. But it was incredibly perilous; she'd lived every day in fear for her life. It had been a relief to give up that pursuit, and she hadn't counted on ever attempting it again. But she would do whatever was necessary to take that organization down.

There was a knock on her door. Answering it, she found Salvatore standing in the corridor.

"Can I come in?"

"Yes, of course."

Salvatore moved into the room.

"Please, have a seat," said Hathor, closing the door and sitting down on her bunk. Salvatore sat down in one of the two chairs.

"What's on your mind?" asked Hathor.

"I do not feel right asking you to take on today's mission," he said. "You put yourself in grave danger once already to infiltrate Majestic. Perhaps I should be the one to go this time."

"I appreciate the offer. It was a huge relief when you found me in New York—the stress I endured in that role was unimaginable."

Salvatore nodded.

"I will prepare."

"No—I said I *appreciate* your offer, but I cannot accept it. This will be much safer for me than it would be for you. I've got the familiarity with their operation."

"You could teach me everything I need to know," Salvatore suggested.

Hathor shook her head.

"No, not in the time we have. Probably not ever. I lived and worked among them for years. I've got an innate understanding of their culture and their inner workings that can only come from experience. I'll be alright."

Salvatore let out a long sigh and nodded.

"I understand. Tell me, what drove you to infiltrate their ranks the first time? I have yet to hear your story."

Hathor took a deep breath.

"I haven't discussed this with anyone before..."

She took a few moments to collect her thoughts; Salvatore waited patiently.

"I did my best to avoid any contact with the humans—for decades. And I would have been perfectly content to live out my years in peace and solitude. But I met a man one day. I was hiking in the forest near Chichen Itza, miles from civilization. I didn't expect to run into anyone, but I did. And I was about to fly away before he saw me, but... then he fell. Must have been a thirty-foot drop into the ravine. He didn't move, and I knew his injuries must have been extensive. There was no cell signal out there, and if I didn't act, he would have died.

"So... I saved him. He was unconscious and had multiple fractures in both legs and one arm. I flew him back to my compound and nursed him back to health. He had quite the surprise when he woke up and got a look at me." Hathor smiled at the memory. "I didn't tell him the truth at first. After the initial shock, he came to understand that I wasn't going to hurt him, and he accepted me."

"What did you tell him at that point? He must have asked about your appearance."

"Oh, he did. I simply refused to explain. And he remained curious, but he let it go for a while. I planned to knock him out once he'd healed and return him to a nearby town. He didn't know where we were, so that would have been the end of it.

"But we got to talking. He worked for the federal police force— basically the Mexican version of the FBI. And he'd been investigating a drug cartel that had ties to an international organized crime group. He saw some bizarre things during that investigation—things he couldn't explain."

"Like what?" asked Salvatore.

"He witnessed an abduction, for one thing. A flying saucer showed up in the middle of the night when he was on a stakeout. And soon after that, someone showed up in his apartment in the middle of the night, warned him to let the cartel go, and then vanished into thin air.

"Well, I figured Lucifer had to be behind that somehow. So I told him about us. But, you know, it didn't alarm him like I'd expected it to do. If anything, he seemed relieved that there was some rational explanation for what he'd seen.

"Of course, I didn't know about the hybrids or Majestic at that point. But once he regained his health, he promised to keep our secrets and asked me to help him with his investigation. I agreed. We worked together for months and became very close."

"You fell in love," Salvatore observed.

"Yes," said Hathor. She smiled at this but felt her eyes welling up at the same time. "I didn't know about the emitters at that time. So, I used makeup and contact lenses to mask my appearance. The work was dangerous, and there were many close calls. But the deeper we delved, the clearer it became that the organization he'd uncovered operated above any country's laws and had agents planted within every major world government. It was Majestic, though we didn't know it by name at that time.

"He'd uncovered a money-laundering scheme when Lucifer himself showed up one night and told him it was his 'final warning.' I urged him to let it go at that point. It wasn't clear how Lucifer was tied into the organization, but I tried to explain the danger he represented.

"But he wouldn't listen. And then, one night, a Majestic agent showed up in his apartment in the middle of the night and murdered him. I captured the agent before he could escape, but he crushed his fake tooth before I could interrogate him."

Hathor felt the tears streaming freely down her cheeks now. Telling this story brought back the pain she'd tried to bury for so long.

"What was his name?" asked Salvatore.

"Enrique," said Hathor. "His name was Enrique Garcia.

"After they killed him, I vowed to take Majestic down. I was going through everything we'd uncovered, trying to find a way in when they sent two more agents looking for the one I'd captured. That turned out to be my lucky break. I tracked them back to San Antonio and monitored their activities for a few weeks. In the end, I killed one of them, figured out how to use his emitter, and took on his identity. And the rest is history. I worked my way up the chain of command until I finally managed to replace their North American commander."

"I understand now why you are committed to carrying through with this," said Salvatore. "But please, be careful down there. If it becomes too dangerous, we can find another way."

"Don't worry," Hathor told him. "I know what I'm doing. And I don't have any intention of taking unnecessary risks."

Later that day, Hathor made her way to the hangar bay. The Othali had built a temporary docking platform leading to the saucer. She walked out to the end of it and floated up into the airlock. Once inside the main level, she took stock of her equipment: emitter, plasma cannon, and scanner at the ready.

"Othali warship, this is Hathor," she told the bridge using her neural implants. "I'm ready for departure."

"Message received," a female voice replied. "Good luck down there."

Hathor moved up to the cockpit. Engaging the saucer's control system, she moved the ship out of the docking port. Once she'd laid in the coordinates for the Africa compound and activated the shields, she took off. The vessel soared into the atmosphere and arrived over northern Africa minutes later.

Majestic's Africa command center was located in the mountainous region of southern Algeria—at least, that's what their radar data indicated. Hathor took the saucer into the area, staying a few miles away from the actual coordinates. Scanning the mountains, she spotted a set of giant hangar bay doors.

"That's it," she said to herself.

The sun was setting over the desert to the west. Now it was just a matter of time before their abduction ship would depart. Hathor scanned the rock formations around the hangar bay, trying to find the entrance they used for the abductees, but came up empty. This wasn't too surprising—she figured they'd have the area shielded.

The hangar bay doors opened not long after sunset, and a flying saucer took off into the night sky. Hathor waited with bated breath. When the saucer returned, it came to rest a few hundred yards away from the hangar bay. Hathor wasted no time. She made herself invisible and dropped out of her saucer. Flying across the landscape, she touched down as close to the enemy ship as she dared. Two humans were floating toward a nearby cliff face. Suddenly, a crack appeared in the rock, and she could see that there were doors. They slid open, and two more humans emerged; the two from the saucer moved into the opening, and then the doors slid closed again.

Hathor turned her attention back to the flying saucer. The airlock was open; she didn't see anyone up there, but she wasn't taking any chances. Using her portable unit, she sent a quick scanning beam through the opening. Sure enough, there was someone in the airlock. He'd pressed himself flat against one wall, using his emitter to render himself invisible—and he was using a handheld device to flood the airlock with an active scanning beam.

"Dammit," Hathor whispered to herself. There was no way she could get on board that vessel without being detected. Majestic must have realized they might try taking one of their saucers to get inside the compound; they'd taken the same precautions that her own people had.

Now what? Hathor thought about shooting the hybrid with her plasma cannon. That would eliminate their ability to detect her, but it introduced new problems. There was a good chance the hybrid could get a signal to his superiors before dying. And then she wouldn't be able to get inside their compound with this ship. Not only that, but she wasn't sure she was a good enough shot to hit him from this range.

"Othali warship, we've got a problem down here," she told the bridge through her implants. She explained the situation. "I'm returning to you. I'm going to need Malia or Jaden to come down here and knock out the hybrid for me."

"Understood," the voice responded. "We'll have one of them ready for you when you arrive."

Hathor returned to her ship. She moved away from the area first, then ascended back up to the warship. Moving into the docking bay, she spotted Malia standing on the boarding platform with Salvatore. Hathor took the saucer directly over them. Moments later, Malia floated up into the ship.

"Hey," she said, rising into the cockpit.

"Welcome aboard," said Hathor. "Thanks for helping out."

She explained the situation to her as they made their way back to Earth.

"We don't have a way to make you invisible," Hathor told her. "So, I'll take us in low—that way, you'll be able to see their airlock right here from the cockpit. You'll need to knock him unconscious quickly before he has a chance to send a signal to the compound."

"I can do that," said Malia.

"Perfect. We're going to start at the compound, but I don't want to carry this out there—they'll probably monitor the transfers. So, we'll follow them to their next stop and execute the plan there. After that, I'll send you and the saucer back up the warship, and I'll take it from there."

Malia nodded. Hathor didn't feel comfortable relying on someone so young to play such a critical role, but the girl did seem confident.

They reached the compound, and Hathor took them in low, close to the entry the abduction ship had used before. Only minutes later, the vessel arrived, hovering in the same position as last time. They watched as the saucer dropped off two humans and picked up two more. Then, the ship took off to the south, and Hathor followed; they could track the enemy's engines from this range.

The ship came to rest over an isolated dirt road outside a village in Angola. Hathor took them low, only yards from the abduction ship.

"This is it," said Hathor. "Ready?"

"Yes."

Hathor went invisible and dropped out of the ship. She touched down directly beneath the Majestic saucer.

"*Let me know when*," Malia said in her mind.

"*Go ahead*," Hathor replied as she hit the airlock with her scanning beam. The hybrid was in there with a young woman; the woman was unconscious.

The hybrid's eyes closed a moment later; he dropped his scanner and fell to the ground. Hathor didn't need her scanner to see the man hit the dirt. Using her implants, she sent the command to her saucer to return to the warship with Malia. Hurrying over to the hybrid, she got his bio-scan and then removed his emitter.

Attaching the emitter to her belt, she accessed it with her implants and inputted the bio-scan. Once she'd taken on the hybrid's appearance, she blew his head off with her plasma cannon. Then, making herself invisible, she accessed the saucer's control system with her implants and floated up to the airlock. Activating the gravitational beam, she lowered the abductee to the ground.

"Here we go," she said to herself.

# Chapter Eleven: Hathor

Closing the airlock, Hathor ran an active scan of the area just to be safe. Nobody else was here. She scanned the main level and the cockpit, but it was only her and the second abductee on board.

"Perfect," she muttered to herself.

Accessing the control system, she laid in the course for the next stop and engaged the engines. Arriving only seconds later, she moved down to the airlock and initiated the drop-off sequence. The ship's gravitational beams moved the abductee into the airlock. Hathor engaged the active scanning beam as the portal opened. The abductee moved down to the ground, and the portal closed again. No unwelcome visitors had come aboard.

Hathor checked the itinerary—all the stops tonight would be in Angola. Majestic was focusing on a group of villages in a rural section of the country. They'd taken several humans from this area who had proven to have Martian-compatible DNA, so they were harvesting as many people as they could. Sometimes, clusters of such people turned up in a concentrated geographical area.

Hathor stayed in the airlock. The system identified a woman riding a bicycle on an isolated road between two villages. Hathor initiated the abduction sequence, and the ship ran a preliminary scan of the target. The woman possessed genetic markers indicating that she was a likely candidate; they wouldn't know for sure until they harvested her eggs.

The saucer moved in low, taking a position directly above the target. The woman panicked—she tried pedaling harder but crashed her bicycle in a ditch. Hathor engaged the gravitational beam before the woman had a chance to recover.

The portal opened, and Hathor engaged her scanning beam. Next, the human woman moved into the airlock, and the system administered the initial sedatives. Then, the portal closed, and Hathor deactivated her scanner—nobody else had come aboard. Finally, the woman moved up to the main level, and the control system identified the next target.

This time, the victim was a middle-aged man sleeping outside in a hammock behind his home. He, too, possessed suitable genetic markers. Hathor ran her scan again as the man moved into the airlock; he was alone. Once the system had secured him in one of the medical pods on the main level, Hathor laid in a course back to the compound.

Hathor became nervous as they arrived for the transfer. She hadn't expected to find any Majestic agents trying to board the ship out in the field. But if they were suspicious for any reason, this was where they'd send someone to check up on the ship.

She initiated the drop-off sequence, scanning the airlock as the new abductees moved down to the ground. So far, so good. Two more humans moved up from below; nobody else came with them.

Hathor breathed a sigh of relief as she closed the portal. Once the humans were secured in their medical pods, she laid in a course for the first drop-off point and engaged the engines.

There were six more roundtrips; they were uneventful. Nobody unexpected tried to board the saucer. Majestic didn't give any indication that it knew its abduction ship had been commandeered.

Once she'd dropped off her last two abductees, Hathor moved the ship to the hangar bay. The doors opened as she approached. She took the saucer inside and moved to its docking position.

Accessing the control system, Hathor downloaded all the information she'd need to proceed. The hybrid she'd replaced was named Nathan. She found his schedule, the location of his quarters, the identities of his superiors, a map of the facility, a directory of the facility's command hierarchy, including base commander Nala, and the names and faces of the other hybrids Nathan was likely to encounter on a typical day inside the compound.

Hathor felt her anxiety rising, but she was ready. She'd done this before, and she could do it again. Hell, this would be *easy* compared to the last replacement she'd made. Taking a deep breath, she descended to the flight deck.

Heading across the hangar, Hathor ran into one of the deck crew. Hathor's implants brought up his bio, streaming it to her optic nerve.

"Hey, Doug," she said.

He nodded to her but didn't say anything.

Hathor passed through the observation area and headed into

the north wing's central corridor. She walked to the end and took the access tunnel down to level nine. Arriving at her quarters, she thought she'd made it home free. But when she went inside, she found a woman lying in bed wearing only skimpy lingerie.

"Hey, babe," the woman said with a seductive voice.

Hathor knew she was in trouble. Her implants brought up the woman's bio—this was Misty, who worked in abductee processing. But according to the data, she lived on level eight and didn't share any duty assignments with Nathan. Moreover, Nathan was supposed to be living alone. So clearly, the information contained in the database wasn't as thorough as she would have liked.

"Hey," said Hathor, flashing the woman a smile that she hoped looked genuine. Her mind was racing to find a way out of this situation. But Misty got up from the bed, embraced her, and plunged her tongue into Hathor's mouth. "Mm—listen," she said, pulling away, "I'm pretty tired from tonight's run. I could use some rack time..."

"Exactly what I had in mind," Misty replied, kissing her again.

"No, seriously—I need to sleep."

Finally, the message seemed to sink in. Misty backed away, staring at her with hurt in her eyes.

"I'm sorry, I didn't want to upset you," said Hathor. "Maybe tomorrow night..."

Misty climbed back into the bed.

"I don't understand. You've never rejected me before."

"I know... it's just... it was a long night, you know?"

"Hmph."

Misty lay on her side, turning her back on Hathor. She showed no signs of leaving the quarters.

"So, uh... I'll see you tomorrow, then..."

Misty turned to face her again.

"You want me to *leave?*"

"I... um... you normally sleep here? Right, of course. But I mean, you do have your own quarters... right?"

Misty stared at her for a moment, showing confusion and disbelief. But when Hathor didn't say anything further, she got out of bed and started getting dressed.

"I don't get you, Nathan," she said, striding toward the door. She stopped, turned to give Hathor one last questioning gaze, and then left.

"Shit," Hathor muttered.

Hopefully, Misty would simply suspect "Nathan" of being unfaithful and not realize he'd been replaced. But if she reported the odd behavior to anyone else, it could spell disaster. Hathor needed to hurry. She waited a few moments to make sure Misty had had time to exit the corridor. Then, using her emitter to go invisible, she stepped through the door. The shift would be changing soon, and the passages would become crowded for a time, but her corridor was clear for now.

Hathor brought up a map of the facility and plotted her route to the command center. The compound had two separate wings—she needed to get to the third level on the south wing. So she moved into the access tunnel at the end of the corridor and flew up six levels, careful to avoid passersby.

Emerging into the corridor, Hathor headed down the tunnel to the south wing. The commander probably wouldn't arrive until the new shift began, but at least Hathor could get inside the room before the commotion of personnel coming and going. She found the command center and slipped inside. Then, moving to the far corner of the room, as far away from people as possible, she waited.

Sure enough, the night crew started filing out minutes later. Hathor brought up Commander Nala's bio and studied her photo. But she didn't see her among the new arrivals. She gave it twenty more minutes, but there was no sign of the commander.

Hathor figured she must have gone directly to her office instead. That was better—Hathor would need the woman to be alone before she could replace her. Moving back out the door, she found the commander's office directly across the corridor.

Going inside would be more dangerous this time—the door would shimmer briefly as she passed through. In addition, the room was much smaller than the command center, and the commander was likely to be alone, making it far more difficult to slip through unnoticed.

Hathor would have to wait until someone else entered or exited—then she could use their passage to mask her own. But only moments later, she spotted the commander walking up the corridor in her direction, talking to another hybrid. Hathor stayed out of their way as they passed into the commander's office, then followed them in.

"I don't understand," Nala said as she took a seat behind her desk. "What does the Sphinx need with another order this large? Command modules, gravitational arrays, saucer-grade laser blasters—what are they doing with all of this?"

"I'm not sure, ma'am," the other hybrid replied, standing across the desk from her. "They didn't include an explanation with the order."

"No—of course not."

"Perhaps they plan on replacing the chariot we lost in New York."

"We already sent them the components for the second chariot. They must be planning a third. Oh, well, it's not for us to question the Sphinx. Go ahead and transmit the request to fabrication. We'll have to put the weapons on hold."

"Yes, ma'am."

The hybrid turned to leave—this was Hathor's chance. But before the man could exit, a woman walked in.

"Ma'am, abductee processing is reporting a problem with one of the humans they brought in last night. They're requesting your presence."

"Thank you, Bridgette," said the commander, getting to her feet. She followed the other two out of her office.

"Damn," Hathor thought to herself.

She moved back into the corridor. There was no reason to follow the commander to the lower levels—she'd be surrounded by people down there. So Hathor decided to wait here until she returned. But when the commander came back twenty minutes later, she went directly into the command center. Hathor followed her in and headed back to her quiet corner.

Commander Nala ended up spending her entire shift in the command center. Apparently, it was a bad day for the Africa compound. They ended up having three abductees who didn't react normally to the standard sedative, an engine failure on one saucer, and a breakdown in the gravitational array system on another. On top of that, the fabrication team balked at the Sphinx's order, claiming they needed to harvest additional raw materials to accommodate it. And the armory complained about having their weapons production delayed. But finally, the shift came to an end, and Nala headed out of the command center.

Hathor's situation was growing more dangerous. Nathan was scheduled for another abduction run tonight. If he failed to show up, they would discover that he was missing, and that would raise the alarm. Hathor could head down to the hangar bay and work the shift, then make another attempt to replace Nala the next day.

But the longer she kept this up, the more likely it became that she'd be caught. It might be better to follow Nala home and replace her there. Hathor checked the file again—Nala lived alone.

To hell with it. She was going for broke. Hathor followed the commander to her quarters in the north wing, level nine—at the opposite end of the corridor from Nathan's. Nala moved through the door, and Hathor followed close behind.

The commander's quarters were quite a bit larger and more luxurious than Nathan's. There were several rooms here, including a kitchen and living room. The commander walked into the kitchen. Hathor pulled out her scanner, but at that moment, a voice called out from the bedroom—Nala was not alone.

"Hey, honey—is that you?"

The voice was male. Hathor rechecked the file—there was nothing to indicate that anyone else lived here. She followed the commander into the bedroom.

"What are you doing here—I thought you were working tonight?"

"I got the night off," the man said, embracing Nala and kissing her passionately.

Hathor checked his face against the directory. This was Stuart, another saucer commander. Sure enough, he'd been scheduled for an abduction run tonight but had traded shifts with Nathan.

But a moment later, Stuart pulled away from Nala.

"Stuart here," he said. Someone must have contacted him through his implants—only he could hear what was being said. "Are you kidding me? Alright. I'll be right there."

"What is it?" asked Nala.

"Nathan hasn't shown up for his shift, and he's not answering their messages. So I've gotta go out tonight after all."

This was alarming—Hathor should have been receiving any communications being sent to Nathan. Her emitter must have been out of sync with the network. The bio-scan would have included the transponder codes for Nathan's neural implants, and that should have allowed her to replace him in their system. But if the emitter was out of sync, it might not have updated—she didn't have time to worry about that now.

"I'll alert security," said Nala.

"I wouldn't worry about it," Stuart said with a grin. "He's probably... uh, busy."

"Doing what?"

"Not what—whom." Nala gave him a blank stare. "Misty."

"From abductee processing?"

"Yeah, they've been shacking up together for the last few weeks. He probably turned off his transmitter."

"I'm going to send security to his quarters just to make sure," said Nala. "The Sphinx has warned all the command centers that the enemy might try replacing our personnel to infiltrate one of our compounds. They could have taken Nathan during his run last night."

"Ah, I heard about that," Stuart said with a nod. "Well, better safe than sorry, I guess. I'd better get going."

"Fly safe," Nala told him, kissing him once more before he left.

The moment Stuart was out the door, Hathor ran her bio-scan on the commander.

"Security, this is Commander Nala," the woman said.

Remaining invisible, Hathor hoisted her plasma cannon onto her shoulder shot the commander in the head at point-blank range. Her headless corpse collapsed on the floor. Hathor went visible and loaded the woman's bio-scan into her emitter. She felt herself transforming. Tapping into the network with the new transponder codes, she synced her emitter. Sure enough, she heard a voice addressing her as the commander.

"Ma'am? Are you there?" the woman said.

"Sorry—there was some sort of glitch in my implants."

"Is everything alright?"

"Yes—everything's fine. I was just testing the com link. Sorry for the interruption."

"No problem, ma'am. Have a good night."

Hathor breathed a sigh of relief. That had been close. Accessing the network, she went to work. First, she assigned herself, Salvatore, Venus, and Bastet command-level access. Next, she dropped Nala and her top officers to low-level positions in the hierarchy. She could remove them altogether, but eliminating too many people at once would raise red flags with security. To top it off, she applied a passcode with gigabit encryption to ensure the enemy couldn't do the same thing she was doing, even if they managed to replace one of the Martians.

After that, she locked down the communication grid, denying access to anyone lacking command status. This would ensure nobody could alert the Sphinx or any other bases to what was going on here.

Finally, she went to work on the saucer fleet. She reneged the credentials of every pilot, assigning command of each ship to herself or one of her fellow usurpers. And just to cover all the bases, she revoked flight deck control to everyone but command-level personnel. This would make it impossible for any hybrids to stop them from coming and going from the hangar bay as they pleased.

Letting out a long sigh, Hathor initiated a long-range communications transmission.

"Othali warship, this is Hathor. Mission accomplished. I repeat, mission accomplished. Everything here is ready for phase two."

"Understood, Hathor," the familiar voice replied. "Commander Anhur confirms receipt of your message and says we are on our way. Congratulations, ma'am."

# Chapter Twelve: Malia

Malia returned to her quarters and told Jaden and their mother how she'd helped Hathor. She had trouble getting to sleep that night; she knew Hathor would be running abductions all night, and she wondered how that was going. And she felt anxious about playing her role in the operation the following day.

She woke early and got ready, then headed down to the mess hall with Melissa and Jaden. The area was packed with Othali soldiers. Melissa had heard from Nadia that the mess hall was the only place on the ship where they could fit so many people. They used to hold gatherings like this on the docking platform, but that had been destroyed in the battle.

Malia and Jaden saw Salvatore standing with Bastet and Venus on the other side of the room and headed over to them. As they reached them, Commander Anhur arrived and stepped up to the podium on the small platform they'd erected at one end of the room.

"Good morning. Our operative should be in position inside the enemy compound at this time. She will be using her emitter to replace their commander and take control of the facility, but we don't know how long that will take. So we'll need to maintain mission readiness until we receive her signal.

"Alpha Team, once that happens, you will be using our existing saucer to enter the base and establish control of the hangar bay. We'll have taken over their systems and locked them out of their saucers, but the enemy forces will still be armed. So you'll be rounding them up and disarming them—we're looking to minimize casualties. Once the hangar bay is secure, you'll be clearing the facility's south wing, one level at a time. In particular, you'll need to secure the command center and fabrication facility—the hybrids will likely make a stand at one or both of those locations.

"Our operative will send us a second saucer for the Bravo Team. You will be responsible for securing the north wing. The labs, medical bay, and maternity ward are all located there, and those may prove to be trouble spots if the hybrids try to use the noncombatants in those areas as living shields.

"Venus will be leading the Alpha Team, while Salvatore takes control of the Bravo Team with assistance from Bastet. Malia Kwan will accompany Venus, and Jaden Kwan will join the Bravo Team. There is a good chance those two will be able to overpower the enemy forces, but you will need to be on the lookout for stragglers.

"With any luck, we will have the element of surprise. However, we believe the hybrids are expecting us to attempt a takeover of one of their compounds. So you can expect a strong and well-organized resistance."

Anhur paused for a moment, gazing around at everyone.

"Good luck. We will alert you as soon as we receive our operative's signal."

And that was it. The room grew noisy with conversation as Anhur left the podium.

"Are you two ready?" Salvatore asked Malia and Jaden as they headed out of the room.

"I think so," said Malia.

"Hell yes," Jaden told him.

"You'll need to tap into the Earth's magnetic field to ensure you can overpower the hybrids' shielding," Salvatore reminded them. "And don't forget to shield yourselves from weapons fire. If you two can—"

"Yeah, yeah, relax," Jaden said with a grin. "We've got this. Don't worry."

Salvatore regarded them for a moment longer, then nodded.

"I know you do. I'll see you later."

Malia and Jaden went back to their quarters. Though she knew it might take most of the day for Hathor to accomplish her mission, Malia couldn't help feeling impatient. She thought the suspense might kill her. At any moment, they could receive Hathor's signal, and they'd have to swoop into action.

But they still hadn't heard anything by lunchtime. Malia and Jaden met Sydney and Miguel in the mess hall to eat.

"I can't believe you're not going," said Jaden when Sydney told them she'd be hanging back on the warship.

"Well, fighting and killing aren't my thing," she said with a frown. "But I'll come along once you've secured the place."

"How about you, Miguel?" Malia asked.

"Oh, don't you worry—I'll be there," he said with a grin. "I ain't got a problem with the fighting thing."

"Yeah, but you can't use the plasma cannon this time," Jaden reminded him. "They want to take as many hybrids alive as they can this time."

"That's alright," said Miguel. "I'm just as happy to shoot 'em with a laser blaster."

Malia stopped by the medical bay after lunch. She found her mother in one of the rooms with Nadia.

"Hey, there," Nadia said with a smile when she saw Malia. "I was just telling your mom that I was hoping to talk to you." She was sitting up in her bed, eating lunch. Malia couldn't believe how much stronger she looked already.

"What about?"

"Well, I never had a chance to thank you for bringing me out of the coma. I'm not sure if I ever would have woken up if it weren't for you."

"It was no problem," said Malia. "I'm just glad you survived—Jaden and I thought Bomani had... well, that you were gone."

"I keep requesting authorization to pay him a visit in the brig, but Anhur won't allow it for some reason."

"Maybe once you've fully recovered," Melissa suggested. "That much stress wouldn't be good for you right now."

"I'm fine, Doc. And I should be joining this little raiding party today, but Anhur won't allow that, either."

"At *my* recommendation," Melissa said with a stern look. "You should be able to visit Bomani soon, but you've got a while longer before I can clear you for active duty."

"She's killing me here," Nadia said to Malia.

"I'll come back and give you the play-by-play once we're done, I promise," Malia told her.

Malia went back to her quarters. The hours slipped by, but there was still no word. By the time she headed back to the mess hall for dinner with Jaden, she was starting to worry. What if they'd caught Hathor? Would she have been able to send them a signal? Probably not—the compound must have been shielded. Malia could contact her telepathically. But she thought she'd better check with Salvatore first.

"Not yet," he said when she went to see him in his quarters after dinner. "Give her a little more time. There could have been difficulties—she might have to do another abduction run and wait till tomorrow."

"*Tomorrow*? But what if something went wrong—they might have captured her. I could just check in—"

"It could do more harm than good. If she's in the middle of a sensitive situation, it could distract her. Wait a few more hours. By then, she'll be on her run and out of harm's way."

But Malia had nothing to worry about. Just then, there was an announcement over the intercom system.

"Attention all crew members. Alpha Team, report to the hangar bay. I repeat, Alpha Team, report to the hangar bay. Bravo Team, please stand by."

"There we go," said Salvatore. "I'll walk you down there."

Malia followed him down to the docking port, her heart beating a mile a minute with anticipation. They ran into Venus on their way there. Some of the Othali soldiers had already arrived, forming a line in the corridor.

"Good luck, both of you," said Salvatore. "I'll see you down there."

Malia went with Venus to the front of the line and boarded the saucer, and then Venus activated the gravitational beam to bring the soldiers onboard. Malia headed up to the cockpit with her.

Once everyone was aboard, Venus took them out of the hangar bay. The ship shot through the atmosphere, coming to rest near the compound. As Venus took them in closer, Malia spotted the hangar bay doors opening. Venus took them into the area fast. A group of hybrids was waiting for them; they opened fire with their plasma cannons.

"Multiple direct hits," said Venus. "Shields are down to ten percent, and engines are offline."

Venus fired the ship's laser blasters into the group, felling several of them.

Malia and Venus dropped to the main level.

"Give us ten seconds, then follow us down," Venus told the soldiers. "Ready, kid?" she added to Malia.

Malia focused on kicking her adrenal glands into gear. Once she felt the extra power flowing through her, she formed a bubble of stillness around herself.

"I'm ready," she told Venus.

Venus held her laser pistol at the ready, and the two of them dropped down to the flight deck. Malia reached out with her mind, disarming the remaining hybrids—she could feel the resistance their emitters provided, but she had no problem overpowering them.

Malia held the hybrids still as the Othali soldiers dropped to the flight deck. Then, she started penetrating their minds, one at a time, to knock them unconscious. But the soldiers began shooting them with their laser rifles, knocking out the rest by the time Malia had taken care of only three.

"I'm sending one of their saucers up to the warship," said Venus.

Malia watched as one of the vessels left the hangar bay and shot into the sky.

"Red squad, you'll remain here and secure the hangar bay," Venus said to the soldiers. "Blue and green squads, follow me."

But as they set out across the cavernous space, a plasma shot came out of nowhere. They'd been aiming at Malia, but the fireball came to rest inches from her chest. A couple of the soldiers stared at her in surprise while the rest scanned the area for the shooter. Another shot hit Malia's bubble; one of the Othali returned fire. Malia spotted his target—there was an equipment locker in the side wall, and the hybrid was hiding in there. The soldier hit him with her second shot, and the hybrid fell to the hangar bay floor.

Venus led them out through the viewing area and into the corridor. A few more hybrids were rushing toward them; Malia used her powers to disarm them, and the soldiers shot them. They fell to the floor unconscious.

"This way," said Venus, hurrying off toward one end of the hall. They reached a passage to the south wing and ran down that. At the end, they arrived at the central corridor—there was nobody here.

"This level is all storage—we'll have to clear it one room at a time," Venus told the soldiers. "Make sure to check any closets or lockers—and use your scanners; they could be invisible. Let's do it."

Malia stuck with Venus; they moved into the first room on the right. There were several rows of crates inside, piled high. Venus used her scanner to check each row, but the area was empty, so they returned to the corridor. Within minutes, they'd cleared the level without finding a single hybrid.

They moved to the access tunnel at the end of the corridor, and Venus stuck her head through the wall. "It's clear," she reported.

One of the soldiers produced a rope ladder and unfurled it into the pit.

"We'll go one level at a time," Venus told the soldiers. "We'll see you on level two—that's all administrative offices. You're with me," she added to Malia.

They flew down one level and moved into the corridor. Once the soldiers had arrived, they started checking the rooms. They found a few hybrids hiding under their desks or in closets, but none were armed. Malia knocked them out, and they returned to the access tunnel.

Venus and Malia dropped into the tunnel, flying down to the third level. They emerged from the tunnel to find a dozen hybrids waiting for them. Malia grabbed Venus and stepped in front of her just as the hybrids fired their plasma cannons. A dozen fireballs came to rest in her bubble. Malia reached out with her mind and disarmed the hybrids as the plasma shots dissolved. Then, she started knocking them out one by one, as Venus went to work with her laser pistol. By the time the Othali soldiers had arrived, the hybrids were all unconscious on the floor.

Malia moved into the command center with Venus while the soldiers checked the rest of the rooms. They checked every desk, cubicle, and closet, but there was nobody here.

"Hathor locked them out of the system, so they probably fled the moment they heard that we were here," said Venus. "Let's go."

They regrouped with the soldiers out in the corridor and headed down to the next level. One floor at a time, they cleared the wing but found only a handful of hybrids trying to hide. There were two floors dedicated to abductee processing. They found the human victims unconscious on their lab tables, abandoned by their captors; Venus ordered the soldiers to leave them alone for the time being. Finally, they were ready to drop to level eleven—the second from the bottom.

"The fabrication facility is located down there," Venus told the soldiers. "We haven't found too many hybrids so far, and chances are, that's because most of them are preparing to defend fabrication. This represents an incredibly valuable asset for Majestic and not one they'll give up easily. So be ready for a fight. Malia and I will go first again and take care of anyone waiting to ambush us."

Malia followed Venus into the access tunnel. They dropped to level eleven, and this time, Malia moved into the corridor first, her bubble of stillness ready for the onslaught. Sure enough, the moment she emerged from the wall, at least twenty fireballs slammed into her cocoon.

Reaching out with her mind, Malia disarmed the hybrids. Venus stepped out from behind her and began firing on them as Malia used her telepathy to knock them out. The soldiers arrived, and they headed down the corridor.

Venus explained that the production facility consisted of two separate areas. The north side was smaller—that was dedicated to small equipment, like weapons and system components. The other side was much larger and included its own hangar bay on the mountain's south side. This was where they assembled the saucers. They could take them out for test flights from here and then dock them in the primary hangar bay once they were certified.

Malia moved into the south side, Venus right behind her. This area was enormous—Malia could see a dozen saucers at various stages of construction. But she didn't see any hybrids.

"It's going to be tough scanning an area this large," said Venus. "But there could be a hundred hybrids in here, all using their emitters to go invisible."

"I'll take care of it," said Malia. Reaching out with her mind, she searched the cavernous space for any sentient beings but found none. "It's empty."

"The bay doors are open," said Venus. "I wonder if any of them escaped that way."

Malia followed her across the bay. They stood at the edge of the opening, looking out across the landscape. There was a sheer drop of at least forty feet here, but the hybrids could have flown down to the desert floor.

"I don't see anyone," Venus observed. "But they could be long gone by now. Let's head back."

Venus accessed the control system to close the bay doors as they made their way back to the corridor. They regrouped with the soldiers, and then Malia moved into the north side. The moment she stepped through the door, a plasma shot hit her bubble—but this one was four times larger than a normal one. Malia could feel its energy crackling against her skin.

Reaching out with her mind, she found the hybrid who'd fired it hiding behind a lab table. Malia penetrated his mind and forced him into unconsciousness. Then, searching the rest of the room telepathically, she found six more hybrids and knocked them all out. Venus and the soldiers entered the room and fanned out to search the rest of the area.

Malia told Venus about the unusual plasma shot. Then, they headed over to the shooter to investigate.

"I'll be damned," said Venus, examining the plasma cannon with her scanner.

"What is it?" asked Malia.

"They've found a way to increase the energy output almost tenfold. Can you wake this one up?"

Malia nodded. Reaching out telepathically, she penetrated his mind again and rekindled his mind. The man opened his eyes, staring up at them fearfully, but didn't try to get up.

"Are these in the field yet?" Venus asked him.

The man shook his head.

"It's an advanced prototype. They were supposed to go into production today, but there was a delay."

"I need to know what this does," said Venus. "You wouldn't happen to be a member of the resistance, would you?"

"Uh—resistance... Yes, as a matter of fact, I am."

Venus nodded to Malia, giving her a skeptical look. Malia focused on the hybrid.

*"You're not really part of the resistance, are you?"*

"Wha—how are you doing that?"

*"Answer the question."*

*"I am... I swear I am. I hate Majestic!"*

Malia could sense the lie. This man was utterly loyal to the organization.

"Liar," she said out loud.

"I figured," said Venus. "Get up," she added to the hybrid.

"Alright, but please don't shoot me," he said, getting to his feet.

"Tell me what this would do if I shot you with it."

"It um... well, it would vaporize me."

Venus hoisted the cannon onto her shoulder and shot him at point-blank range. The hybrid screamed, but sure enough, the fireball hit him and incinerated his entire body.

"There's still one more level to clear," said Venus. "But first, we need to warn the others about this."

# Chapter Thirteen: Jaden

Jaden returned to his quarters after dinner. He lay down on his bunk and let out a long sigh. Malia had gone off to see Salvatore—she was worried about Hathor. That girl needed to chill out. Hathor was an expert in this kind of operation—hell, she'd infiltrated Majestic's North American command center and replaced its commander. Jaden was pretty sure she would be fine.

Minutes later, he heard the announcement summoning Alpha Team to the hangar bay. He got up and stretched, then headed that way himself. By the time he arrived, the corridor was crowded with the Othali soldiers waiting to board the saucer.

Someone put their hand on his shoulder. Jaden turned to see that it was Salvatore.

"You're early."

"Yeah, I had nothing better to do."

The Othali boarded the saucer, leaving only Salvatore and Jaden in the corridor. Moments later, there was an announcement on the overhead speakers summoning the Bravo Team to the hangar bay. Othali soldiers began lining up in the passage again. Brian showed up with Miguel, and Bastet arrived right behind them. A minute later, a saucer showed up in the docking port.

"That's us," said Salvatore.

Jaden, Brian, Miguel, and Bastet followed Salvatore out to the docking platform and boarded the ship. The Othali soldiers came aboard, and then Jaden moved up to the cockpit with Salvatore. He took them out of the hangar bay, and they flew down to the surface.

They arrived at the compound to find the hangar bay doors open. Salvatore took them inside, and they disembarked. One of the Othali soldiers reported to Salvatore, giving him a status update.

"Very well," said Salvatore. "Hold your position here, and we'll clear the rest of the north wing."

Salvatore led the new arrivals out to the main corridor. They headed to the far end, and he summoned a giant freight elevator. He addressed the group once everyone was aboard.

"This wing houses the living quarters and research labs—we'll need to clear those levels one room at a time. We may encounter individual hybrids hiding in those areas. But we may also encounter groups of fighters waiting to ambush us. Have your weapons ready. And remember—use your scanners. No room is clear until you've scanned it for invisible hybrids."

Jaden focused on stimulating his adrenal glands. Moments later, he felt the Earth's magnetic field augmenting his powers. He reached out with his mind and formed a cocoon of stillness around himself.

They moved down to the next level. Jaden stood close to the elevator doors so he could shield the others from whatever awaited them. But as they opened, he found Hathor waiting there for them, her plasma cannon in hand and several hybrids lying on the floor with holes through their torsos.

"Fancy meeting you here," she said with a grin, lowering her weapon.

Jaden moved out of the elevator; the others followed. Salvatore handed Hathor an extra laser pistol.

"We'll try to keep the rest alive," he told her.

"If you insist."

The group headed down the corridor, scanners in hand. Jaden followed Salvatore into the first room on the left. This looked like some sort of lab. They checked the whole room, including three storage closets, but there was nobody here. They regrouped with the others back in the corridor. Hathor approached Salvatore.

"You need to see something."

She led Salvatore to a room halfway down the passage. Brian had overheard, too—he and Jaden followed them. Once inside, Hathor led them to a cold storage area at one end of the room. It reminded Jaden of a walk-in freezer in a restaurant. Inside, cabinets with glass doors lined the walls. Through the glass, Jaden could see rows and rows of glass vials.

"What are we looking at here?" asked Brian.

"According to their records, these are live virus samples," said Hathor. "They've been running experiments here similar to the ones Lucifer was conducting."

"Fascinating," said Salvatore. "We'll need to study this, but it's going to have to wait. For now, let's leave one squad here to guard this area."

They returned to the corridor. Salvatore spoke to the soldiers and ordered one group to remain on this level. They stationed guards by the elevator, at the entries to the lab, and by the entrance to the access tunnel at the opposite end of the corridor.

One of the other soldiers spoke to Salvatore for a moment and led him and Hathor into the room beyond the lab; once again, Brian and Jaden followed. Inside, there were several glass chambers. They reminded Jaden of prison cells, each with a cot, a sink, and a toilet.

"Quarantine chambers," said Hathor. "They injected the test subject with a virus and then confined them to one of these cells to ensure they couldn't infect the rest of the community."

"I think we're finally going to get some answers here," said Brian.

They moved down to the next level. The medical bay and more laboratories were here, but they didn't encounter any hybrids. The next several floors housed the living quarters; they cleared one room at a time. Jaden stuck with Salvatore. In one room, they found a woman hiding in her bathroom. Jaden used his telepathy to knock her out. Most of the soldiers also encountered individual hybrids trying to hide, but they used their laser rifles to render them unconscious.

Finally, they boarded the elevator again.

"We're moving down to level ten," Salvatore told them. "This is where they house the nursery and maternity ward. I don't expect to find much resistance here, but there are still about fifty hybrids unaccounted for—so be ready for anything."

They moved down to the next level, and Salvatore opened the

elevator doors. Jaden stood by the opening, shielding the others with his cocoon of stillness. The moment the doors opened, fireballs flew like rain. Jaden noticed that some of them were much larger and stronger than the others—this was something they hadn't encountered before.

The corridor was full of hybrids. Jaden reached out with his mind, disarming all the ones he could see. Then he got out of the way, and the Othali soldiers moved into the passage, using their laser rifles to stun the hybrids unconscious.

But more poured out of the first couple of rooms, firing plasma cannons at the soldiers. One of the stronger ones hit a nearby soldier, vaporizing him before Jaden's eyes. Jaden disarmed the newcomers, and the Othali fired on them, knocking them out.

Suddenly, Jaden spotted a band of armed hybrids moving a group of women and children into the access tunnel at the far end of the corridor. He pointed this out to Salvatore and reached out telekinetically to stop them, but it was too late—the last of them disappeared through the wall.

Three more waves of hybrids emerged from the rooms, many of them wielding the stronger plasma cannons. They managed to kill ten more Othali soldiers before Jaden was able to disarm them. But finally, the corridor grew still. Dozens of hybrids lay unconscious on the floor.

"I've warned the other teams to be on the alert for the rogue hybrids," Salvatore told the others. "Venus reports that they've encountered the more powerful plasma cannons in the south wing as well."

"What rogue hybrids?" asked Hathor.

"The group that left through the access tunnel a minute ago?" asked Brian.

"Yes—it appears they are attempting to remove the mothers and children," said Salvatore. "We've left guards posted at the elevator entry on every level, so they'll try to escape through either the north or south hangar bay."

"They concentrated an awful lot of firepower against us here to cover their escape," said Bastet. "Why?"

"Unknown," said Salvatore. "Let's finish clearing this wing, and then we can regroup with the other teams."

They cleared the rooms on this level but found no more hybrids. Level eleven housed a large dining hall and recreational facilities; these were empty. Finally, they moved down to level twelve. They found a room housing two massive power generators.

"It looks like they're using one for each wing," said Salvatore, scanning the equipment. "And there's a service tunnel running parallel to the shafts for the heat pumps."

"Like the one we used to escape Lucifer's compound?" asked Jaden, eyeing the manhole cover in the floor.

"Precisely," said Salvatore. "We'd better check it—the hybrids might have used it to escape."

Bastet and Brian stayed with the soldiers to clear the rest of the level. Jaden used his powers to lift the cover out of the floor—it turned out to be a metal cylinder. Casting that aside, he headed into the service tunnel with Salvatore. Jaden went first, shielding them with his protective cocoon. They flew deep into the ground before the tunnel leveled out. They followed it for a while longer, finally emerging into a small chamber. Directly overhead, Jaden found another shaft; it appeared to go straight up toward the surface, but he could see only darkness.

Jaden led the way again. As they rose higher, he could make out pinpricks of light far above. They arrived at the top to find a metal grate covering the opening. Jaden tried pushing it open, but it wouldn't budge. He reached out with his mind, blasting the grate out of the way.

The two of them flew out of the shaft and landed on solid ground. Scanning the landscape, Jaden could see only desert and mountains.

"It does not appear that anyone came this way," Salvatore observed. "But we'll need to station guards in the generator room until we can seal off this passage."

They flew back into the compound and regrouped with the others. Salvatore told Brian and Bastet what they'd found, and they stationed two soldiers to guard the entry to the service tunnel.

"There's something you'd better see," Brian told him; he and Bastet led them through a door at the far end of the corridor.

Jaden gasped—this was an enormous morgue, larger even than the one in Lucifer's compound. The chamber extended as far as the eye could see and rose at least twice as high as the rooms on the upper levels. Row upon row of hatches lined both walls. They'd opened a few of the hatches and pulled out tables with corpses lying on them.

"Human?" asked Salvatore.

"Yes," Hathor confirmed.

"They must have been testing their viruses on the abductees and keeping the victims in cold storage here," Brian suggested. "We'll have to have Melissa perform autopsies on a few of them to confirm that, though."

"Uh... could we catch a virus from one of these bodies?" asked Jaden, backing away from them.

"That would be extremely unlikely," said Salvatore. "They aren't breathing, so there would be no way for them to transmit a virus through the air. Perhaps one could spread through physical contact, but I doubt that as well—viruses can't survive very long once the host body has died."

"Our scans did not show any live viruses," Bastet told them.

They pushed the tables back into the wall and closed the hatches.

"Venus reports that they've captured the rogue hybrids attempting to escape through the south hangar bay," Salvatore told the others as they returned to the corridor. "They've disarmed the escorts, but the mothers and children are being difficult. She's requesting assistance."

They left soldiers to guard the entries to the elevator and access tunnel, then headed off to help Venus. There was no passage connecting the two wings on this level, so they had to move up to level eleven first and then move across. They found Venus, Malia, and several soldiers herding the captives away from the hangar bay doors. Several of the women were screaming and swearing at them. Jaden could tell that Malia was using her powers to keep them from running off.

"My first instinct was to shoot them," Venus told Salvatore, "but Malia insists that would be overly traumatic for the children."

"Can the two of you use your powers to render them unconscious?" Salvatore asked Malia and Jaden.

"You got it," said Jaden.

Malia looked like she was going to object but nodded instead. Together, the two of them used their telepathy to knock them out.

"Now, we need to get them back to the residential area and confine them there," said Venus.

There were nearly thirty of them, so it took a few trips, but together, Malia and Jaden used their telekinesis to move all of the captives back to the north wing. They met up with Salvatore, Hathor, and Brian again when they were done.

"Excellent, thank you," Salvatore said. "Next, we're going to need to move all the unconscious hybrids to their residential levels in the north wing."

"But there are like dozens of them all over the compound," Jaden complained. "This is going to take hours."

"Yes," Hathor agreed. "I'll be assisting you. We're going to confine them to the residential levels, but they won't be able to move between floors. So, we'll have to identify them and get them to the right level. We can drop them in the corridors, and they can find their rooms when they wake up—that'll save a little time, at least."

"Great, thanks," said Jaden, rolling his eyes. This was still going to take all night.

"While they're doing that, we should bring Melissa down and have her get started on some autopsies," Brian said to Salvatore. "Figure out exactly how these viruses operate."

"Agreed—I'll go pick her up now," he said.

"There's extensive data in their system regarding the virus samples we found," Hathor told him. "You should have access to everything."

"Very well," Salvatore said with a nod. "I will coordinate with Melissa and see what we can learn. Venus is organizing the soldiers to make sure we keep all areas secure."

"Sounds good," said Brian. "It's going to be a long night—we'd better get to work."

# Chapter Fourteen: Malia

Malia and Jaden spent several hours working with Hathor to return the hybrids to the appropriate levels. By the time they were done, Salvatore and Melissa were finishing up for the night as well. Malia was exhausted, and the others looked as tired as she felt. Salvatore took all the humans and Martians back up to the warship on one of the saucers. The Othali soldiers stayed behind to guard all the key access points and keep the compound secure, and Bastet remained to supervise their efforts. But the others slept in their quarters on the Othali vessel that night.

In the morning, Malia and Jaden joined Melissa and Brian and headed up to Anhur's conference room. The commander was already there with Bukhari and Shurani, Sydney, Miguel, Venus, Salvatore, and Hathor.

"Good morning, everyone," Anhur said as the newcomers took their seats. "I'd like to review our progress and decide our next moves. I understand the operation has been quite the success so far?"

"Yes, it has," Salvatore confirmed. "We have secured the compound with only light casualties. It does seem that Majestic suspected that we would attempt this, but they were not ready for this specific attack. Hathor's success in replacing one of their saucer pilots undetected afforded us the element of surprise. She had already taken control before any of the hybrids realized what was happening.

"Venus, Hathor, Bastet, and I have command-level access to the systems, and Hathor has revoked the hybrids' access. They can no longer use the elevator, control the hangar bay doors, or operate any saucers. We have guards stationed at all entry points to the access tunnel, and the hybrids are restricted to their own residential levels in the north wing. There are also guards monitoring the entry to the service tunnel by the power generators."

"For the time being, we must keep up the manual scans of all personnel entering the warship or the compound from the saucers," said Hathor. "We'll need to continue working on an alternative. At this point, our best option would be to automate the existing process—we can program the scanners to recognize the visual perturbations to the emitter holograms."

"We did discover that they were developing an enhanced version of my plasma cannons," said Venus. "They have ten times the energy output of the previous generation. We encountered them in battle— they vaporize their targets."

"Should we expect to see these units elsewhere?" asked Anhur.

"I don't think so," said Hathor. "The units we encountered were prototypes. They were scheduled to go into production the day I arrived, but an order came in from the Sphinx, and that superseded the weapons."

"An order for what?" asked Salvatore.

"Components that could be used for another chariot," Hathor said with a long sigh.

"Another chariot?" said Anhur.

"The base commander said that they'd already sent the Sphinx components for a second chariot—I was able to confirm that in their records. But she speculated that they might be constructing a *third*."

"Where would they be building them?" asked Brian. "The Africa compound is their largest, and a ship that size wouldn't fit inside its hangar bays."

"Most likely, they'd assemble them in space," said Salvatore. "We've scanned the area around the planet and couldn't detect anything. They could have cloaked them, but their mass would be sufficiently large to perturb the orbits of the Majestic satellites."

"That's how they found us," Anhur pointed out.

"Yes, but there's nothing else up there disrupting the satellites' orbits that way," said Salvatore.

"Well, it's a big solar system," said Hathor. "They could be building them anywhere."

"Should we expect Majestic to retaliate?" asked Anhur. "We've struck a major blow—I don't imagine they're going to take it lying down."

"I don't think so, either," said Salvatore. "But at this point, there may not be much they can do. We must be diligent in preventing them from employing the same means we used to retake the compound. But without the abduction operation, we have far less exposure to such tactics than they did."

"Not only that, but we now control the majority of their saucer fleet, not to mention their sole production facility. Between the saucers and this warship, we would outgun them by a wide margin even were they to attack with their entire remaining force."

"And their saucers don't have my advanced weaponry," Venus told them, "so they cannot get through the hangar bay doors. They've got the plans for the saucer-grade plasma cannons but were concentrating on developing the handheld units."

"Well, the only problem is that only your people can operate the saucers," Anhur pointed out.

"Yes, however, we can operate them remotely, so we can each control multiple saucers at once," said Venus. "Nevertheless, we should begin training your people on them as soon as possible."

"How long will it take to equip some of them with your neural implants?"

"The procedure itself is simple," said Venus. "We can take care of that today if you'd like—the operation takes only a few minutes. The hard part is adapting to the technology and learning how to use it. So, the sooner we get started, the better."

"Yes, we could start that immediately. I'd like to have all of our pilots participate—there are fourteen of them."

"Perfect. We can transport them down to the compound once we're done here," said Venus. "The medical bay in the compound has the necessary equipment."

"I'm very much looking forward to this," Ensign Shurani said with a grin. "I've studied the specs on those saucers; they're very impressive."

Malia had forgotten that Shurani was a pilot.

"Do you think me and Malia could get those implants, too?" Jaden asked. "I'm not gonna lie; I'd love to have my own flying saucer..."

"Jaden!" said Melissa. "The answer is no! This is important business—not to enable you to go for joyrides!"

"Actually," said Anhur, "it would make good tactical sense for the twins to possess this capability. They've proven to be our most valuable assets in battle—providing them independent mobility would be wise. If you approve, of course, Melissa."

"I agree," Salvatore added. "Not only that, but it would increase their chances of escaping should Majestic capture them again. We could outfit them with emitters as well, and it would give them the ability to replace any hybrid and commandeer their vessel."

Malia had to admit that she loved this idea. Being able to go anywhere at any time would be amazing—no more relying on others for transport. And having an emitter would be incredibly useful, too. Escaping Lucifer's compound would have been much easier if she'd had one then.

Melissa regarded her children and let out a long sigh.

"You know, I was dreading the day these two would start driving, and now you're talking about giving them *flying saucers*. I don't know about this."

"Mom, *come on*," said Jaden. "We're always in the middle of every battle—having our own ships would help us!"

"The vessels are much safer than your automobiles," Salvatore told her. "Most of the operation is automated, so they couldn't crash them even if they wanted to do so."

"Alright, go ahead," Melissa told them, shaking her head. "But they are to use the saucers only when necessary! No joyrides!"

"Sure, Mom," Jaden said with a grin. "No joyrides."

"I hate to rain on the parade," said Hathor, "but before these two start training with their implants, we're going to need them to identify the resistance members among the hybrids. We'll need to separate them according to allegiance as they do that—otherwise, there's a good chance those loyal to Majestic will assassinate the traitors."

"How many hybrids remain in the compound?" asked Anhur.

"Just over two hundred," said Hathor. "We killed about twenty during the operation. Another thirty or so escaped through the southern hangar bay before we could get to them."

"So it's a good bet Majestic knows what we've done by now," said Salvatore.

"I'm sure of it," Hathor replied. "I severed communications with the rest of their people the moment I replaced the commander, so there's no way any of them could have notified the other compounds or the Sphinx using the com system. But the ones who escaped could have reached one of the other compounds by now."

"Where's the closest one to ours?" asked Brian.

"The European command center is located in the Swiss Alps, according to the radar data. That's the closest, by far."

"It's still a long way to fly," Malia pointed out. "When Jaden and I were running from Bomani, we could only fly a few miles at a time before we tired out."

"It's different for us," Salvatore told her. "The nanoparticles we use alter the gravitational field around us, so we are not constantly using our energy to fight gravity the way you are. The hybrids would not have much trouble flying all the way to Switzerland."

"Oh," said Malia. "I had no idea."

"Have any of the captives used their fake tooth?" asked Brian.

"Not yet," said Hathor. "At least, not that we know of so far. If they think we're going to interrogate them, I'm sure we'll see some take that way out to avoid questioning."

"What are you going to do with the hybrids who remain loyal to Majestic?" asked Sydney.

"Death by firing squad?" Venus suggested.

"That's not right," said Sydney. "They're prisoners of war, essentially. You can't do that."

"Darling, we had no qualms blowing the hybrids in Lucifer's compound to kingdom come," Venus pointed out. "This is no different."

"We did have some qualms," Brian retorted, "and this *is* different. We killed Lucifer's hybrids in battle. But Sydney's correct—the ones we've captured here are prisoners. It's unethical to kill them now that the battle's over."

"What do you propose?" asked Venus. "Set them free to rejoin Majestic so you can face them in battle again another day?"

"We may be able to deradicalize them," Sydney suggested. "Majestic has brainwashed them since childhood to believe that humans are evil and should be destroyed. There are ways to reverse that."

"We should keep them prisoner for the time being," Salvatore suggested. "We can revisit this at a later date. We should focus on our next steps."

"Agreed," said Anhur. "We've taken their most valuable base. What remains is to destroy the rest of the compounds, find and eliminate the Sphinx, and stop them from exterminating humanity."

"Are you and your people helping with all of that?" asked Brian. "You've fulfilled your end of the deal by assisting with the sacking of the compound. Once your people are trained to use the implants, you could take your saucers and be on your way."

"I've discussed the matter with my staff, and we'd like to continue this alliance until we achieve the remaining objectives—if you'll have us. It wouldn't sit well with us to abandon the mission before it's completed."

"We would be happy to have you," said Salvatore. "And I believe we should destroy the other compounds as soon as possible. Doing so would effectively cripple Majestic's organization—it would eliminate their ability to abduct the humans and create more hybrids. But we also need to search our current compound's systems for any information pertaining to the identity or location of the Sphinx.

"And we will need to infiltrate the other compounds before destroying them—to search for information about the Sphinx, but also to rescue the mothers and children and any resistance members we may find."

"It would be so much easier to nuke the places and be done with it," said Venus. "That's going to be a lot of additional bodies we have to cram into our new home. And it's unlikely the smaller compounds would possess anything about the Sphinx that we don't have in Africa."

"We need to be sure," Salvatore insisted.

"She has a point, though," said Hathor. "We're going to have to figure out the housing situation. We'll need to clear out one level for our own people, and we can devote another to members of the resistance. The rest of the residential floors can house the prisoners, but it's going to get pretty crowded down there once we add the people from the other compounds."

"What about the autopsies?" asked Brian. "And the viruses— what were you able to learn?"

"Quite a bit," said Melissa, "and it's extremely disturbing. According to the data Salvatore found in their system, Majestic has been developing their virus for decades, making each generation more lethal and more infectious. We're talking about a disease that is as deadly as rabies and spreads as virulently as... well, more than anything Earth has ever seen. It's more contagious than the measles, for example."

"But untreated rabies has a one hundred percent mortality rate," said Brian.

"Yes, and that's the point to which they've developed this. Every person they infect dies—well, except the ones who have immunity. And I haven't been able to determine yet who's immune or why."

"And how could they determine its infectiousness?" asked Sydney. "Normally, they measure R naught in open populations, but they haven't released this virus into the world, yet."

"True," said Melissa. "But they have conducted experiments that involved putting multiple humans into the same enclosure and measuring the rate of transfer of the virus. They've developed a pretty sophisticated algorithm to calculate what the effective R naught would be in the wild. And the number is somewhere north of forty."

"*Forty?*" asked Brian. "That's astounding—the measles spread like wildfire, and they typically assign that disease an R naught of twelve to eighteen."

"I'm sorry, what is R naught?" asked Anhur.

"It's the number of people an infected person is likely to infect. And they've designed this virus to be exceptionally contagious. It can be transferred through physical contact, and it's airborne. The simple act of exhaling sheds the virus into the atmosphere. And it can survive indefinitely on most surfaces. The other problem is that it can take up to a week for symptoms to manifest, but the person is contagious that whole time."

"So, an infected person would be spreading the virus to others before they even know they're sick themselves," said Brian.

"Yes, exactly," Melissa confirmed. "The virus acts on the central nervous system. It causes confusion, partial paralysis, and hallucinations in its early phases. But within days, it causes swelling of the brain and death.

"If Majestic releases this virus, it will spread worldwide in a matter of weeks. And if there is no vaccine, it will only take a few months for it to kill every human being on the planet."

"It would happen much more rapidly if they release it from multiple sites at once," said Salvatore.

"But we've established that Majestic plans to spare those people whose DNA is compatible with our people," said Venus. "How would they accomplish that?"

"I don't know," Melissa said with a shrug.

"That data is not contained in the system," Salvatore added. "One would think they must have developed a vaccine in conjunction with the virus itself. It would make sense for them to give the vaccine to those abductees found to have DNA compatible with ours before returning them to their homes. But again, there is no record of their doing this."

"And there's no vaccine present in the lab where we found the virus samples," Melissa added. "So if they do have a vaccine, they must be storing it somewhere else."

"Well, I was abducted," said Sydney. "Could you tell from a blood sample if I have the virus—and the vaccine?"

"Yes," said Melissa. "We can do that as soon as we're done here."

"Very well," said Anhur. "Our people will begin planning our strike against Majestic's European headquarters."

"In the meantime, we can transport your pilots down to the

compound," said Salvatore. "Once Venus has equipped them with the neural implants, we will begin their saucer training."

"And the twins and I can get to work processing the hybrids and separating the resistance members," said Hathor. "There's one more thing I want to report, though. I've detected some sort of rogue program running on the compound's systems."

"What does it do?" asked Brian.

"Well, that's the strange thing—it doesn't seem to do *anything*. But every time I terminate the process, it just relaunches itself. I can't get rid of it."

"Can you delete the program itself?" asked Brian.

"No—I've tried. I don't have sufficient permissions."

"But that makes no sense—you used the previous commander's credentials to give yourself command-level access, didn't you?"

"Sure did. But as far as I can tell, she wouldn't have been able to wipe this program, either."

"That's very strange," said Brian. "Can you let me take a look when we get back down there?"

"We'll have to create a holographic interface for you—the hybrids all access the system through their implants. But, sure—we can do that."

"We've got a lot to do," said Anhur, getting to his feet. "Let's get to work."

# Chapter Fifteen: Jaden

After the meeting, Salvatore transported the humans and
Martians back down to the compound. One of the Othali
scanned them as they disembarked from the saucer, but there
were no imposters. Jaden and Malia followed Hathor to the
second level in the south wing. They set up one of the larger
offices for their interrogations. There were four Othali soldiers
here, and Jaden noted that they were wielding plasma cannons
today.

"Soldiers will be bringing the hybrids here two at a time,"
Hathor told them. "We've taken away their emitters, so you two
won't have any trouble overpowering them if they try anything. But
just in case, the soldiers have orders to shoot to kill in the event of
an attack. And I'll be here with you the whole time, too.

"You can ask each captive if they support Majestic or not, but
chances are that many will lie and say that they do not. So, you'll
have to use your powers to determine the truth. Are you ready?"

"Yes," said Malia; Jaden nodded.

A few minutes later, Othali soldiers brought the first two
hybrids into the room. One sat down across from Malia, the other
in front of Jaden.

"Hey," said Jaden. The woman stared at him with contempt in her eyes. "So, do you agree with Majestic's plan to kill all the humans?"

"Go to hell, little boy."

"Alright, we'll do this the hard way."

Jaden reached out telepathically, quickly penetrating her mind. He immediately sensed her overwhelming hatred for him and all humans. This woman was wholly invested in Majestic's vision.

"She's Majestic, all the way," Jaden said to Hathor.

Hathor nodded to the soldiers. One of them approached Jaden's hybrid.

"Let's go."

The woman got up and left the room with him. A few minutes later, a different soldier arrived with a male hybrid. The man looked extremely nervous and kept eyeing the soldiers.

"I've got just one question," Jaden told him as the man sat down. "Do you support Majestic's plan to exterminate all the humans?"

The man said nothing. He looked Jaden in the eye for a moment before averting his gaze, but Jaden could sense his fear.

"Majestic's not here anymore, I promise you. If you oppose them, we'll protect you."

"You can't protect me; nobody can."

"So, you oppose Majestic?"

The man went silent; Jaden penetrated his mind. Again, he felt his fear, bordering on panic. This man believed he was going to be killed, and probably soon.

*"Tell me how you feel about Majestic's plan."*

The man's eyes snapped to Jaden's in surprise. He didn't reply verbally, but Jaden could sense that he felt trapped. There was no way to leave Majestic alive—they assassinated anyone who tried it. But he wanted no part of their grand plan.

"This one's resistance," Jaden said to Hathor.

"You're sure?"

"Absolutely."

Hathor nodded to the soldier.

"We'll be moving you to new quarters," she told the hybrid. "Only those who oppose Majestic will be on your floor. You'll be safe here; you have my word."

"I wish I could believe that," the man replied as the soldier escorted him out of the room.

A different soldier brought a younger man into the room a few minutes later. He seemed nervous but not terrified like the last one. The man sat down, and Jaden asked him if he supported Majestic's extermination plan.

"Oh, no, not at all," he said, shaking his head. "I've supported the resistance for ages, but, you know, they terminate anyone who openly opposes them. I've had to keep quiet until now."

Jaden didn't believe him. Reaching out telepathically, he delved into his mind.

*"The truth. Do you want to see Majestic kill every human?"*

*"No—that's genocide. I cannot agree to that."*

But the man's emotions gave him away. Jaden could sense the same loathing for humanity that the first woman felt. He was eager for the hybrids to replace humans as the dominant life form on the planet.

"Majestic," Jaden said to Hathor.

"No—what? I swear I'm not loyal to them! I'm *not*! Why don't you believe me?"

"You're certain?" Hathor asked Jaden.

Jaden nodded.

The soldier grasped the man by his upper arm, pulling him to his feet. But as he rose, the hybrid grabbed the soldier's plasma cannon. The soldier struggled to regain control of it. Jaden used his powers to slam the hybrid against the wall.

"You're all going to die!" the man shouted, spitting at Jaden; he dodged in the nick of time. "And I hope I'm there to watch it!"

A second soldier came over to assist the first. Jaden returned the hybrid to the floor, and the pair removed him from the room.

Jaden interrogated one hybrid after another and quickly grew tired of the process. He was surprised by how many there were who truly disagreed with Majestic's mission. But the majority were loyal to Majestic. None of the others became violent, but Hathor reported that several had used their fake tooth to self-terminate before reaching the interrogation room.

"That's the end of it," said Hathor once they'd finished with the last two hybrids. "Thank you both for doing that—I know it was a lot of work."

"No... no problem," Jaden said through a yawn.

"What's going to happen to them all now?' asked Malia.

"Well, I'm going to head over now and help the soldiers rearrange people. The resistance members will have a little more freedom now, but we'll still keep them confined to the residential areas. But the others are officially prisoners until we decide what to do with them.

"But if you feel up to it, Venus is ready for you two."

"For what—the implants?" asked Jaden. Hathor nodded. "Oh, hell yes—let's do this!"

Hathor walked them over to the medical bay, where they found their mother waiting for them with Venus.

"Mom!" said Malia. "What are you doing here?"

"It's the *medical bay*," Melissa said with a smirk. "What do you think I'm doing here?"

"Oh, right..."

"But I wanted to be here for you both regardless," said Melissa. "My babies are having their very first surgical procedure."

"Surgery?" said Jaden. "Uh... you mean you have to like drill holes into our skulls or something? I didn't think about that..."

"Nothing so dramatic," said Venus. "I'll be injecting nanobots into your brain stems, and they'll navigate to the appropriate structures inside your brains."

"Nanobots?" asked Jaden. "What are those?"

"They're microscopic machines that can carry out tasks inside your body," Venus explained.

"So, kind of like the nanoparticles your people use to defy gravity?" asked Malia.

"They're a little more complex than that, but yes. The

gravitational nanoparticles act almost like tiny mirrors, deflecting the gravitational force to whatever degree we specify through our implants. But the implants themselves—the nanobots have to provide quite a bit more functionality. They're essentially miniature computers. Some of them will interface with your brainstem and the areas of your cerebral cortex responsible for consciousness. They will interpret your commands. Others will reside in the optic and acoustic nerves to process and simulate visual and auditory data."

"This sounds complicated," said Jaden.

"Don't worry," Venus replied with a grin. "The procedure is quick and painless. We performed it on all of the Othali pilots earlier today and had no issues with any of them."

"Have they trained on the saucers already?" asked Malia.

"Yes, they have," Venus confirmed. "They've got a lot more work to do, but they did complete the preliminary training."

Venus instructed them each to take a seat on an exam table. She retrieved a device that looked like a syringe from the counter and moved to Jaden first.

"This will feel just like getting a shot," she told him. "A little prick in the back of the neck. Ready?"

Jaden took a deep breath. He was feeling more anxious about this now than he'd anticipated.

"Yeah, I'm ready."

He barely felt the prick below the base of his skull.

"Now, in the next few minutes, you may experience some minor dizziness or lightheadedness—these are normal side effects and nothing to worry about. They'll fade within a couple of minutes."

Venus moved to Malia's table. Sure enough, Jaden did feel a little lightheaded a few moments later.

"I feel weird," said Malia. "Not dizzy or anything, but my face and arms are tingling."

"Yeah, now that you mention it, I feel some tingling, too," said Jaden.

"That's normal," Venus assured them. "Now, these implants will provide you with access to any nearby computer systems—well, Martian ones, anyway. So for your first training exercise, I want you to think about accessing the network here in the compound."

"How do we do that?" asked Malia.

"It's hard to explain," Venus said with a frown. "Well, from what I understand about your powers, it won't be much different from penetrating someone's mind. Try to sense the carrier signal the way you would hear someone's thoughts."

Suddenly, Jaden saw a holographic image appear before him. There were odd symbols and shapes glowing red around the edges of his vision as if he were wearing a set of augmented reality goggles.

"Hey, I've got something here," he told Venus. "But it's like some other language or something."

"Give it a moment—the implants will learn from the language center of your brain," said Venus.

She was right—moments later, the symbols changed. Now the word "COM" appeared below a symbol that looked like an antenna. Other symbols resembled a belt and a flying saucer with the words

"EMT" and "SCR" beneath them—these were grayed out.

"Yeah, I can see it now," said Jaden.

"Good. Focus on the antenna, and say Salvatore's name in your head," Venus instructed him.

"Uh... okay."

Jaden focused on the symbol and called out Salvatore's name in his mind.

"This is Salvatore," a voice answered—it sounded as if he were standing in the room with them.

"Whoa! Hey, this is Jaden," he said out loud.

"Hello, Jaden," Salvatore replied. "I take it your implants are functioning?"

"Yeah, this is crazy!"

Malia gave him a dirty look.

"You're talking to Salvatore?" Jaden nodded. "Well, we could already do that with our telepathy."

"You don't see anything, do you?" said Jaden. "You're jealous because I can do this, and you can't!"

"I am *not* jealous—it just seems a little redundant, don't you think?"

"Enough bickering, you two," said Melissa.

"Jaden, do you see a symbol that looks like a box with a dot in the center?" asked Venus.

"Yeah."

"I want you to focus on that while you're looking at your mother."

"Okay..."

Jaden stared at his mom and focused on the symbol. Suddenly, information appeared around Melissa's head, including her name, her status as a doctor, and her present location inside the compound.

"This is awesome," Jaden said with a grin.

Malia frowned at him.

"Why isn't this working for me?" asked Malia.

"Give it time, dear. It will."

"So... can I go try a flying saucer, now?" said Jaden.

"Sure," Venus said with a grin. "Let's go."

"Good luck, you two," said Melissa.

"You're not going with us?" asked Jaden.

"Ah, no—this would give me way too much anxiety. I've got more work to do here, anyway."

Jaden and Malia followed Venus up to the hangar bay. The Othali soldiers were standing guard, but nobody else was here.

"Pick one," said Venus, holding one arm out toward the saucer fleet.

"They're all the same, right?" asked Jaden.

"Identical."

"Doesn't matter then. This one," he said, pointing to the nearest one.

"Look at it and focus on the saucer symbol in your display."

Jaden did as she said. Suddenly, a red outline formed around the edges of the vessel. The word "Link?" appeared over the saucer.

"Should I link it?"

"Yes."

Jaden focused on the word and thought, "Yes."

A new set of symbols appeared around the edges of his vision.

"Whoa—I think I've got it," he said.

"Great," said Venus. "Now, look at your sister and me in turn, and focus on the symbol that looks like a person."

"Okay..." Jaden stared at Malia and focused on the symbol. It looked like a stick figure person. Then, he did the same with Venus. "I did it."

"Let's go aboard," Venus suggested. They moved beneath the vessel, but nothing happened. "You'll need to engage the gravity beam."

"How do I do that?"

"Do you see a symbol that looks like a triangle underneath a saucer? Focus on that."

Suddenly, the beam engaged, and they moved up to the airlock.

"Perfect," said Venus. "Let's go for a ride."

They moved up to the cockpit, each taking a seat.

"So, if I hadn't used the little stick figure with you two, you wouldn't have been able to get on board?" asked Jaden.

"That's correct," Venus confirmed. "Well, I have command access, so I could have overridden the system and come aboard anyway. But only the rest of the Martians and I can do that."

"Awesome. Alright, how do I fly this thing?"

"First, you're going to need to open the bay doors," said Venus. "Focus on the control symbol again, and imagine them opening."

Jaden stared at the doors, visualizing them opening, and focused on the symbol. It worked; they opened, and he could see the desert and sky beyond.

"Now, focus on the saucer symbol again, and nothing else."

"Got it."

"You should have a symbol that looks like a map."

"Yep."

"Focus on it, and choose a destination."

Jaden focused on the icon, and suddenly a map appeared in his vision—it was transparent, so he could still see everything else beyond it. So... where did he want to go? Maybe Paris... The map shifted to show him France, with a circle around the capital city in the north. Jaden focused on the circle, and it changed from white to red.

"Okay, I think I did it."

"Go back to the saucer image, and now select the green circle."

"Alright."

Jaden did it, and suddenly the saucer moved out of the hangar bay. The moment it had cleared the doors, they shot into the sky, and before long, were flying over the Mediterranean.

"Holy shit," said Jaden, failing to suppress a huge grin.

"This is *so* unfair," Malia complained.

"Shut it," said Jaden. "You got every single thing before me since we first realized we had powers. Let me enjoy this moment, would you?"

Jaden couldn't believe the freedom he felt. He now possessed the ability to go anywhere he wanted. This was the coolest feeling ever. They arrived over the city minutes later, and Jaden could see the Eiffel Tower all lit up below them.

"I can't believe how easy that was," said Jaden. "Just pick a place and say 'go.' But what if I want to like slow down, or go faster or something?"

"Lay in a course back to the compound, and I'll show you," said Venus.

Jaden brought up the map again and found their compound back in Algeria. He selected it and engaged the engines. The saucer shot off into the sky.

"You should have a slider icon," Venus told him. "Select that, and then you can control our velocity. But be careful—don't exceed the red line."

"Why, what's that?"

"If you accelerate beyond that threshold, Majestic will be able to detect your engine output."

"We don't want that," Jaden muttered.

He focused on increasing their speed but couldn't tell the difference. Of course—the ships always prevented them from feeling any acceleration. Instead, he concentrated on lowering their velocity to zero. The saucer came to rest.

"How do I take us lower?"

"There's another slider icon that controls altitude."

Jaden found it and focused on it. The symbol enlarged, and he could use the control to take them all the way down near the ground. They were hovering over a dirt road out in the middle of some vineyards. A man was riding toward them on a bicycle.

"Now, he can't see us, right?"

"Correct—we've got the saucers set to engage shields upon leaving the compound."

"How do I lower them?"

"Focus on the icon with the glowing saucer."

Jaden concentrated on that and then lowered their shields. The man on the bicycle spotted them, fell off, then got back on and pedaled furiously in the opposite direction.

"Jaden!" said Malia. "That's not nice!"

"Hah—but it sure is funny! So how do we abduct him?"

"Jaden, no!"

"Use the crosshairs icon," Venus told him. "You can use that to move us incrementally forwards, backward, or sideways. Or you can look at the man while you do it, and the ship will move us directly over him and track his movement."

Jaden stared at the man while focusing on the icon. The saucer moved directly over him.

"Now engage the gravitational beam."

"This is not a good idea," said Malia.

"Oh, live a little," said Venus. "We won't harm him. Well, assuming he doesn't have a heart attack…"

Jaden chuckled, then engaged the gravitational beam.

"Now, how can I tell if it worked?"

"Use the icon that looks like a pair of glasses. That will give you access to the optical sensors, then select the airlock."

Jaden followed her directions, and suddenly a video image appeared in his vision, showing the man and his bicycle inside the airlock. He had fallen to his knees and appeared to be praying.

"This is the coolest thing ever," said Jaden.

"That's enough," Malia insisted. "Put him back!"

"Alright, alright," said Jaden.

He navigated the icons to engage the gravity beam again and lower the man back to the ground.

"What about weapons?"

"See that old barn over there?" asked Venus.

Jaden gazed out the cockpit windows and spotted the derelict structure.

"Yeah."

"You should have two icons—blasters or cannon. But we haven't installed the cannons yet so that one will be grayed out."

Jaden chose the blaster. Staring at the barn, he focused on the red circle that had appeared. A laser blast slammed into the structure, sending it up in flames.

"Well done," said Venus. "But I think that's enough for tonight. Take us back to the compound."

Jaden found the icon to resume their course and engaged the engines. They shot into the sky again. Once they'd arrived, he opened the hangar bay doors and took them back inside.

"You learned quickly," Venus told him as the three of them moved down to the flight deck. "The pilots had a harder time picking this up."

"It must be from all the video games he used to play," said Malia.

"Yeah, you're probably right," Jaden replied. "I bet you wish you played them more, now."

"Don't worry," said Malia. "I'm gonna get this."

"Hey, what about the emitters?" Jaden asked Venus. "Can I get one of them, too?"

Venus took them over to a storage locker in the far wall. She grabbed an emitter and a scanner from inside and handed them to Jaden. He wasn't wearing a belt, so he had to clip the emitter to the pocket of his jeans. Venus gave Malia a set of devices, too.

Jaden spent the next several minutes learning how to use the equipment. Through his implants, he used the scanner to get Malia's bio-scan. Next, he fed the data into his emitter and engaged the holographic system.

"I hate you," said Malia, staring at him with her eyes wide but grinning in spite of herself.

Jaden gazed down at his hands—his nails were longer and painted different colors. He was wearing Malia's clothes, and his body had changed—or at least, its appearance had. Everything still felt the same from the inside, but moving his hands up and down this simulated form, it was different to the touch.

"Oh, my God," said Malia, rolling her eyes. "I can't believe I'm seeing this right now."

"This is unbelievable!" said Jaden, and his voice even sounded like Malia's.

"Can you stop, please?" Malia demanded. "And promise you'll *never* take my appearance again!"

"I can't promise that," he told her but disengaged the hologram. "So many possibilities spring to mind!"

Just then, Jaden spotted Melissa and Salvatore walking into the hangar bay, Brian, Sydney, Miguel, Hathor, and Bastet close behind them.

"You are absolutely *the worst*," Malia said to Jaden, walking off toward the newcomers.

"I'm impressed," Venus told him. "You picked everything up very quickly."

"Yeah, well, I'd better enjoy it while I can. Malia's going to mess with me big time once she learns how to do this stuff."

"Oh, yes, she is," Venus said with a grin. "Come on."

They joined the others.

"We're heading back up to the warship," Hathor told Venus and Jaden. "Ready to go?"

"Yes," said Venus. "How soon can we take up residence here?"

"We should be ready tomorrow," Hathor replied. "We've got the hybrids sorted out, and we've cleared out one whole level for our use."

Bastet stayed behind again as the others boarded the saucer and headed back to the warship for the night.

# Chapter Sixteen: Brian

Brian headed up to the conference room first thing the next morning. He sat down next to Melissa as the others filed in. Once everyone had arrived, Anhur started the meeting.

"I'd like to go over the plan for taking out Majestic's compound in Europe this morning, but let's get a status update first. Hathor, where are we at with the prisoners?"

Hathor told everyone about the interrogations.

"All told, we've got a little over thirty hybrids who are against Majestic's extermination plan. We've moved them to their own level, and we've given them duty assignments—cleaning and maintenance and what not. They won't have access to any secure areas, but this morning, they'll be taking care of housekeeping on the quarters we'll be using, so we should be able to move in later today.

"Ten others self-terminated using their fake tooth—Melissa will be removing the rest of those today. The rest are restricted to the other residential levels."

"Perfect," said Anhur.

"Commander, I've taken inventory of the weapons," said Venus. "We aren't missing anything, so I don't think the hybrids who escaped took any of the advanced plasma cannons. But I did find records indicating that they shipped out prototypes to the other compounds for testing. So we may encounter those weapons in battle."

"Understood," Anhur replied. "That's not ideal, but at least we know to expect it."

"They'd collected the necessary components for the fusion grenades but hadn't moved those into production yet. I've assembled enough to take out the other compounds, but that's all we have so far. Also, we should begin retrofitting the saucers with my plasma cannons," Venus suggested. "We've got the schematics now and the production facility. I'd like to contact the team from my old compound—I could pick them up from our waystation in New Zealand and bring them here. With their help, we could have the entire fleet upgraded in ten days or so."

"Agreed," said Anhur. "Any developments with the virus?"

"Yes," said Melissa, letting out a long sigh. "Sydney and Miguel have both been infected—but don't worry, they're *not* contagious."

"How is that possible?" asked Anhur. "I thought the virus was extremely infectious and always fatal?"

"Yes, that's true," said Melissa. "And I'm afraid I don't have an explanation yet. The virus is present in their systems, but it's completely dormant. I can tell you that their DNA is compatible with the Martians'. So somehow, they found a way to stop the virus from affecting a host with the right set of genetic markers."

"And you didn't find any vaccine in their systems?" asked Brian.

"No, I didn't. I've got some ideas, though—I have a lot more work to do."

"Keep us posted," said Anhur. "Anything else to report?" he asked the others.

"We've lost access to the Majestic satellites," said Salvatore. "The Sphinx must have locked us out—we were able to transmit and receive data with them yesterday morning but lost the connection by evening."

"What impact will this have?" asked Anhur.

"Minimal," said Salvatore. "We still have access to the satellite network we put into orbit when my people first arrived on this planet. I've connected them to the compound's control systems."

Anhur nodded.

"Any progress with the rogue computer process?"

"None," said Hathor. "We still have no idea what it does, nor have we been able to remove it from the system."

"It worries me," said Brian. "Each Martian has top-level clearance in the system, so any one of them should be able to erase the program. But they can't."

"Is it possible Majestic could use this program to regain control of their system somehow?" asked Anhur.

"Theoretically, that shouldn't be possible now that we've locked them out of the system," said Brian. "But we can't access the program code, so there's no way to tell what it might do. So far, it hasn't done a damn thing. It's just there. It's made no attempt to access any other part of the system."

"Let's continue monitoring it," said Anhur. "And let us know if anything changes. How are we doing with pilot training?"

"So far, so good," said Venus. "We successfully equipped all fourteen of them with the neural implants, and they each linked to a saucer. They've completed the basic operational functions, and today we'll be taking care of flight training."

"How long before they can operate the vessels in combat situations?" asked Anhur.

"It's hard to say," said Venus. "Some may need a few weeks; others may need only another session or two. We'll have a better idea today.

"Jaden Kwan has already completed a test flight and seems to be a natural. He flew us to Paris last night and blew up a small building."

"Indeed?" Anhur said with a grin, gazing at Jaden. "Well done, son."

"Thank you," said Jaden, returning the smile.

Brian noted that Malia looked upset and was staring down at the table. Had Jaden finally managed to outdo her at something? Good for him. He could use the confidence boost.

"Once we've got at least one pilot through basic flight training, I'd like to station one of the saucers here for shuttle services," said Anhur. "But we'll keep it out of combat situations until the pilots are ready."

"That won't be a problem," Venus replied.

"We've analyzed the tactical situation with the European compound," Anhur told them. "At the moment, only this warship possesses the firepower to penetrate their hangar bay. So we will fly into the combat zone and destroy the blast doors. We can take out any vessels docked there, as well, and then you'll be able to move inside with three or four saucers. Your ships can provide cover fire as our soldiers disembark. Once we've taken the hangar bay, we can move into the rest of the complex.

"We'll need to download their data, and we should remove any children with their mothers. How do we want to screen the rest of the hybrids to identify resistance members?"

"There are roughly one hundred hybrids stationed there," said Hathor. "We could have the twins interrogate them there and take any separatists with us."

"That will take time," said Salvatore. "Unless we incapacitate *all* the hybrids as we did in Africa, the loyalists will use every minute we give them to strike back."

"Forget that," Venus said with a shake of her head. "One of us will have to replace the commander to access the network anyway, so when we do that, we can announce that we'll provide safe harbor to any separatist who wants to join us. Let them surrender to us in the hangar bay, and then we'll interrogate them at our compound. We can retrieve their data, rescue the mothers and children, plant the nukes, and get the hell out of there."

"And if any of the other hybrids spot them going to the hangar bay, they'll shoot on sight," said Sydney. "Why not stun every one of them unconscious and take the time to interrogate them individually like you did in Africa? That's the only way you can be sure to provide refuge to every separatist."

"Our objective here is to destroy the compound, not sack it," Salvatore pointed out. "The operation in Africa was extremely risky—but it was worth it to take the facility. We won't have the element of surprise this time. After what we did to them, they're going to be ready for us at the other compounds. They could have planted explosives, and I have no doubt they'd be willing to sacrifice the facility to take us out. I agree with Venus—we need to be in and out as quickly as possible. If we make an announcement, any separatists who may be there can use their emitters to make their way to the hangar bay without being seen."

"I agree," said Hathor.

"Bastet has expressed a desire to stay behind," Venus told them. "And it would be wise for one of us to remain at our compound. The Othali pilots aren't ready for combat missions with the saucers yet, but if the three of us each pilot one ship, that should be plenty."

"Yes," Hathor agreed. "Europe has only two saucers. Even if they're both out when we arrive, the warship can monitor and defend against them if they return during the operation."

"What sort of weapons should we expect to face?" asked Brian. "We know they might have at least one advanced prototype, but what about regular plasma cannons?"

"Be ready for anything," Hathor suggested. "They probably prioritized the chariot and the Africa compound for the weapons they extracted from Venus's compound. You may encounter them at the other compounds as well, but I suspect they'll primarily be using laser blasters."

"Malia and Jaden will be able to shield the troops from cannon fire, but their defenses will not be effective against energy weapons," Salvatore reminded everyone.

"But we can overpower their emitters with our telekinesis, now," said Malia. "So, we should be able to disarm them regardless of what type of weapon they're using."

"All the same, we'll need to back you up with covering fire," Salvatore insisted.

"And I'm afraid the humans will need to stay behind," said Anhur. "We'll send in the three Martians, the twins, and our soldiers."

"You can't be serious," said Miguel. "I reckon I've gotten pretty good using that cannon—I want to help."

"Don't take this the wrong way, but you're superfluous," said Anhur. "The Martians are the brains of the operation, the twins provide unique tactical advantages, and our people are combat trained. It'll only hinder them if they have to stop to protect you."

Miguel opened his mouth to argue, but Brian spoke first.

"He's right. I'd like to go, too, but we should stay out of the way and let the experts do their job. It was all-hands-on-deck in Africa, but our presence won't be necessary at these other compounds."

Miguel let out a sigh and shrugged.

"Alright, then."

"Very well," said Anhur. "We can execute the mission today. If you can be here at fifteen hundred hours with the saucers, we'll have our troops ready to board."

"Perfect," said Venus. "That will give me time to pick up my team in New Zealand and transport them to the compound."

The meeting broke up, and Brian headed back to the hangar bay with Sydney, Miguel, Melissa, and the Martians.

# Chapter Seventeen: Malia

Malia and Jaden had nothing more to do down on the surface, so they waited on the warship.

"You get your implants to work yet?" Jaden asked when they arrived at the mess hall.

"No, I wish," Malia said with a sigh. "How do you access yours? Like what do you actually *do*?"

"I just think about them," he replied with a shrug. "It's kind of like reading someone's mind. Except it's inside your own head."

They got in line for the buffet. Once they'd filled their plates, they found a couple of empty seats at a table in the back of the room. Malia kept trying to engage her implants while they ate, but it was no use. No matter what she did, she couldn't get them to activate.

Back in their quarters, Jaden used his emitter to take on Malia's appearance again. Malia punched him on the arm.

"Come *on*, Jaden—knock it off!"

"Ow, that hurt!" he said, rubbing his triceps.

Although Malia found it fascinating that the emitter could so perfectly replicate her appearance and even her voice, it also infuriated her that Jaden could do this, and she could not. She had her emitter clipped to her jeans and had pocketed the scanner, just in case she suddenly gained control of her implants—she was eager to get her revenge against her brother. But in the meantime, she'd have to try ignoring him.

Melissa showed up a little while later, explaining that their new quarters were ready down on the surface. She collected what few belongings they had.

"So, did you change your mind?" asked Malia. "Are we staying on Earth, after all?"

"Ah, no," said Melissa. "But it's going to take a while to finish our business with Majestic, and in the meantime, I'll be doing most of my work in the compound. So, for now, it makes sense to relocate there with the others."

"The Martians, you mean?" asked Jaden.

"Yes, and Brian, and Sydney and Miguel. They're all moving their things down now, too."

Melissa gave them each a hug, wishing them luck, and then headed out again. Malia continued trying to access her implants but had still had no glimmer of success by the time the saucers arrived again. There was an announcement over the intercom summoning the soldiers to the hangar bay, so Malia and Jaden headed down there, too.

They found Salvatore on the docking platform, ushering a group of soldiers onto his ship. The Othali workers were still rebuilding the docking port, and for now, it was only possible to load or unload one saucer at a time. Malia suspected the other two were waiting outside.

"You're with me," Salvatore said to Malia. "You'll be going with Venus," he added to Jaden. "She'll be here next."

Jaden nodded, and Malia boarded the saucer with Salvatore. She made her way up to the cockpit with him and took a seat. Salvatore handed her a plasma cannon.

"I brought this for you. We're shooting to kill, this time."

Malia nodded.

Salvatore moved them out of the docking port but then brought them to rest far above the Earth.

"We'll wait here until the others are finished boarding," he explained.

Malia gazed out the window but couldn't see any of the other ships.

"When we rode on the Othali shuttles, they were able to see each other, even though they were invisible to everyone else. Is there a way to do that with the saucers?"

Salvatore nodded. Suddenly, Malia could see red outlines around the Othali warship and the other two saucers.

"Whoa! So, the windows are displays?"

"No—if you can see the ships, now, then your implants are projecting their images into your optic nerve."

"Seriously? So they're working after all?"

"You haven't been able to access them yet?" Malia shook her head. "Do you see anything else besides the ships?"

"No... wait, yeah—now, I do. There are symbols around the edge of my vision—just like Jaden said he had!"

"Sometimes, it takes a little nudge to get them going. We don't have time now, but once we're done with this operation, I'll teach you how to use them."

"Perfect. Thank you, Salvatore."

Malia couldn't help grinning ear to ear. She couldn't wait to use her emitter to give Jaden a taste of his own medicine.

Once the other two saucers had finished boarding their soldiers, they moved out of the docking port, and the three vessels shot down toward the surface. They came to rest near the Swiss Alps. Malia couldn't see the Majestic compound anywhere until Salvatore pointed out the hangar bay doors. The three saucers took positions several hundred yards away. Minutes later, Malia spotted the Othali warship moving into view. It took several laser blasts, but it finally managed to blow a massive hole in the doors. Malia could see only one saucer inside; the warship fired on it, too. Moments later, Salvatore moved them into the hanger bay, the other two saucers flanking them.

"Let's go," said Salvatore.

Malia dropped down to the main level with him and then moved into the airlock. The soldiers were waiting for Salvatore's signal before disembarking—they had microphones and earpieces. Malia tapped into the Earth's magnetic field, surrounded herself with a bubble of stillness, and descended to the flight deck.

On her way down, she spotted a group of hybrids waiting for them across the hangar bay. The saucers hit them with several laser blasts, but one of them still managed to shoot a fireball at Malia; it froze when it hit her defenses.

Reaching out with her mind, she disarmed the remaining hybrids. Salvatore landed next to her and signaled the soldiers. They began dropping through the airlock.

"This is Hathor. Disembarking from saucer two now."

Malia looked around in confusion for a moment before realizing she'd heard her voice only in her head. The transmission must have come through her implants.

"Saucer three on our way down," said Venus's voice.

The soldiers from Salvatore's ship rushed the hybrids, firing on them as they went. Within moments, Hathor's soldiers joined them, and then Venus's. Malia brought up the rear with Jaden and the three Martians.

They moved into the main corridor, but the soldiers had cleared the area. About a dozen hybrids were lying on the floor, all of them either dead or unconscious. Malia and Jaden followed the other three to the end of the corridor.

"I'll take care of the command center," said Hathor. "You two take the lower levels. Malia, you're with me."

They moved into the access tunnel; Malia dropped to the next level with Hathor, while Jaden kept going with Salvatore and Venus. Emerging through the wall, Malia could see a group of Othali engaged in a firefight with several hybrids at the other end of the passage.

"The command center is this way," Hathor told her, leading them into the first room on the right.

The soldiers had already secured the area—they had the hybrids lying face down on the floor. Hathor went around and checked their faces, scanning each one to make sure they hadn't engaged their emitter.

"Damn," she said, returning to Malia's side. "The commander's not here. Let's check his office."

Malia followed her back into the corridor, and they stepped into the room directly across from the command center. It was empty; Hathor scanned the area to be sure.

"Shit," she muttered.

Malia heard her through her emitters next.

"This is Hathor. The commander's not here—limit the soldiers to stunning only."

"Too late—he's dead," Venus replied through the implants. "The soldiers found him in the armory going for one of the cannon prototypes."

"Now what?" Malia asked Hathor.

"We'll have to find his deputy—control will have passed to her upon the commander's death. She wasn't in the command center, either."

"Any sign of Theresa?" Hathor asked through the implants.

"Negative," Venus replied.

"We'll have to go room-to-room," Hathor said out loud. "Let's go."

They returned to the corridor, but at that moment, a voice in Malia's head said, "Hathor, this is Indra in the hangar bay. We have a problem up here—a Majestic saucer just showed up with fifty more hybrids. We're taking heavy fire and require assistance."

"On my way," Hathor replied through her implants before

shouting, "Damn!" out loud. She rounded up several soldiers and led them back toward the hangar bay.

Malia entered the area right behind Hathor. They found Sergeant Indra taking cover in the observation area with several other soldiers. There were a dozen more Othali lying out on the flight deck—Malia suspected they were all dead. A large group of hybrids was advancing on their position, wielding plasma cannons.

"How the hell did they get that saucer past the warship?" Hathor demanded.

"It showed up out of nowhere and started firing on us," Indra explained. "The ship was invisible—they must have kept their shields up until they were inside the hangar."

"We've got active scans running at the entry points, don't we?" Hathor demanded.

"Yes, ma'am, and the ship interrupted the beams, but that gave us about a one-second warning."

"Dammit," said Hathor. "Malia, can you disarm them?"

Malia nodded. She made sure her protective bubble was in place, then moved into the hangar bay. The hybrids fired on her immediately, several plasma shots freezing around her. Malia reached out with her mind, ripping the weapons out of their hands.

Hathor, Indra, and the other soldiers moved in from behind her, firing their weapons at the hybrids. Malia used her plasma cannon to take out several of them. But suddenly, one more hybrid dropped out of the saucer's airlock. He shot Malia in the chest with his laser blaster.

# Chapter Eighteen: Hathor

Hathor spotted a hybrid dropping out of the saucer, but before she could fire, he hit Malia with a laser blast. The girl hit the deck, but she was only stunned. Hathor shot the hybrid with her plasma cannon, blowing a hole through his abdomen. He fell down and didn't move. Hathor rushed over to Malia as she struggled to her feet. But suddenly, she disappeared.

"Malia!" Hathor shouted.

Where had she gone? Either she'd figured out how to use her emitter, or an invisible hybrid had grabbed her. Hathor was about to check the area with her scanner when Malia suddenly reappeared, fighting to escape a hybrid's grasp. She must have used her powers to force the hybrid to become visible. Hathor aimed her plasma cannon but didn't have a clear shot—she was more likely to hit Malia than the hybrid. But a moment later, Malia escaped his grasp; Hathor shot him, and he dropped to the flight deck.

"Are you alright?" Hathor asked Malia.

But before she could answer, a massive plasma shot hit her, incinerating her entire body.

"*MALIA!*"

Hathor stood there in shock for a moment before spotting the hybrid who'd just dropped out of the saucer's airlock. He fired another shot, and Hathor hit the deck in the nick of time—he was wielding one of the advanced prototypes. Hathor returned fire, ripping a hole through the man's chest. He collapsed, dropping the weapon.

A dozen more Othali soldiers hurried into the hangar bay, Salvatore in the lead. For the next few minutes, they exchanged heavy fire with the hybrids. Finally, the enemy retreated to their saucer. Hathor fired her plasma cannon just as the vessel went invisible; Salvatore followed up with a shot of his own. The saucer became visible again as it moved out of the hangar bay; they must have damaged its shields. The Othali warship hit it with several laser blasts, and it went up in a giant inferno, its remains crashing to the desert far below.

"Where is Malia?" Salvatore asked Hathor.

Hathor stared at him for a moment, then shook her head. She couldn't get the words out, but Salvatore took her meaning.

"Oh, no..."

"We can mourn later," said Hathor, though the words tore her heart out. "We still have a job to do."

Salvatore nodded, and they headed back out to the corridor. Hathor felt rage bubbling up inside of her—nearly as powerful as it had been when the hybrids had assassinated Enrique. Though she'd barely known Malia, she understood how much she'd meant to those who opposed Majestic.

Hathor rounded up a group of soldiers as Salvatore headed back down the access tunnel. She split up her group into pairs, and they proceeded with a room-to-room search for Theresa, the new Majestic commander. Hathor shot every hybrid dead once confirming they weren't her.

Once they'd cleared the floor, Hathor assigned two soldiers to stand guard and moved down to the next level with the others. But as they began their search, Venus contacted her.

"We found Theresa. She wasn't very cooperative, but we stunned her before she could use her fake tooth. Transmitting the bio-scan to you now."

"Perfect—well done."

Hathor received the scan and headed back up to the command center. Once inside, she fed the bio-scan into her emitter and took on Theresa's appearance. Accessing the central system, she assigned herself command-level access, then deactivated her emitter. Next, she revoked all the hybrids' privileges. Using her saucer's com system, she created a link to the control system back in the Africa compound and initiated a data transfer. Finally, she interfaced with this compound's internal intercom.

"Attention all hybrids," her voice blared over the speakers. "This is the Martian, Hathor. We have taken over this facility and are preparing to destroy it. However, we are willing to provide safe harbor to any member of the resistance movement. If you want to leave Majestic, report to the hangar bay and prepare for immediate departure. You have two minutes."

In reality, it was going to take longer than that to finish the data transfer, and she had no idea how the others were progressing on the lower levels. But it was better to light a fire under their asses; they would not be waiting for stragglers once they were ready to leave.

Hathor headed back to the hangar bay. Her work here was done; now, it was only a matter of waiting for the others to finish theirs. The Othali soldiers were standing guard around the area, maintaining active scans of all entry points. No hybrid imposters would be getting to their saucers.

As a group of soldiers escorted the human abductees to one of the saucers, visions of Malia's death played over and over again in Hathor's mind. She couldn't believe the girl was gone, just like that. But then a thought occurred to her. Accessing the network, she checked the optical sensor logs for the hangar bay. Sure enough, there was footage there of the event. The invisible hybrid had grabbed Malia, making her invisible, too. But that lasted only a few seconds before she reappeared, only feet away from where she'd started.

The hybrid appeared, too—that had to be Malia's doing. And then, almost the moment she escaped his grasp, the other one shot her with the prototype cannon. This loss was difficult to process, but it had unfolded precisely as she remembered; the data revealed nothing suspicious.

And yet...

Why had they tried to abduct her, only to incinerate her moments later? *That* didn't add up. Hathor reviewed the data again.

She couldn't spot any evidence that they'd somehow replaced Malia with a hybrid before shooting her.

Unless... Could they have removed her from the compound, somehow?

Hathor watched the same sequence again from a wider angle and kept watching in fast motion right up to real-time. The soldiers had maintained active scans of the entry points the entire time, and there had been no visual perturbations. Nobody invisible had left the hangar bay.

So, what if they were still here?

Hathor accessed her saucer and flooded the room with active scanning beams. An invisible hybrid would have been exposed now, but she searched the entire area, and there were none here. Keeping the saucer's beams engaged, she checked every storage area with her handheld scanner but still found nothing.

There was only one other possibility. Hathor moved to the edge of the docking port entry and gazed down at the wreckage of the enemy saucer on the desert floor below. It was still smoldering. She scanned it, but there were no remains. Any living tissue on board that ship had been blown to dust in the warship's blaster fire. If they'd somehow managed to replace Malia and get her on board that saucer, she was gone, now. Whether they'd abducted her or not, her body had been incinerated.

Hathor could think of no other way this could have gone down.

Over the next few minutes, a handful of hybrids showed up, hands in the air, claiming to oppose Majestic. It wasn't Hathor's job to determine the veracity of their claims; she checked them for weapons and confiscated their emitters, then sent them up to her saucer with several Othali soldiers to stand guard over them.

Venus arrived next with a large group of Othali soldiers escorting the hybrid children and their mothers. They sent them up to Venus's saucer. Several more hybrids came seeking asylum. Finally, Salvatore and Jaden showed up with the remaining soldiers.

"We've planted the grenades," Salvatore told them. "It's time to go."

"Hey—where's Malia?" asked Jaden.

Salvatore gave Hathor a look, then let out a long sigh.

"I'm sorry, Jaden. Malia is gone."

Jaden fixed him with a blank stare for a moment, as if the words hadn't registered. But then his face contorted in pain, and his eyes welled up.

"*What*? What do you mean she's *gone*?"

"We need to go—let's get up to the saucer, and I'll explain—"

"Hell, no! We're not going away *anywhere* without Malia!"

Jaden backed away, giving him a mutinous look.

"Jaden, she's dead," Hathor told him. "I'm so sorry—"

"Yeah? Then where the hell is her body?" he demanded, looking around the flight deck. "We gotta take her back!"

"Another Majestic saucer showed up while you were gone," Hathor explained. She felt her chest constricting, and she had to fight down bile. "They had one of the prototype cannons... There is no body. They vaporized her."

"That's impossible! Malia can't be dead—you're wrong!"

"I saw it with my own eyes," Hathor told him.

Jaden stared at her in disbelief. He opened his mouth as if to speak, but no words came out. Salvatore pulled him into a hug.

"I'm so sorry, Jaden."

Jaden sobbed uncontrollably, collapsing against him. Salvatore managed to get him aboard his saucer. Venus gave Hathor a look, sorrow in her eyes, before boarding her own ship. Hathor made sure the rest of the Othali soldiers made it up to the vessels and then ascended into her airlock. She moved up to the cockpit and took her saucer out of the docking port behind the other two. Once they'd achieved the minimum safe distance, Salvatore sent the command to detonate the fusion grenades. The European compound went up in a gigantic mushroom cloud. The warship headed back up to its orbit while the three saucers took off for the Africa compound.

"Salvatore, this is Hathor," she said through her implants.

"Go ahead."

"I'm sending you some data from the compound's internal optical sensors. Can you check this for me and see if you spot anything suspicious?"

Hathor sent him the data.

"You think they might have replaced Malia—and then incinerated her simulacrum to trick us into thinking she's dead?"

"Sounds like something they'd do, doesn't it?"

Salvatore made no reply for a minute.

"Did you scan the hangar bay before we left? They could have still been there."

"I did. They weren't."

"What about the wreckage of the enemy saucer?"

"No remains."

"So, one way or another, she was incinerated."

"That's what it looks like," Hathor agreed. "But I've got a nagging feeling we might have missed something."

"I don't think so. We've checked every possible escape route. I don't see any way they could have removed Malia from that hangar bay without our notice. As much as I don't want to accept it, I do believe this happened the way we saw it. An invisible hybrid grabbed Malia; she used her powers to force him to go visible, and then they shot her."

"Right. So, why would they try to abduct her, only to incinerate her seconds later?"

Salvatore took a moment to reply.

"That is curious. I have no answer."

They arrived at the compound. The hangar bay doors opened, and they moved the saucers inside; Othali soldiers ran active scanning beams across the threshold as they passed. Each saucer positioned a soldier armed with a scanner in its airlock before unloading its passengers.

"Venus and Hathor, this is Salvatore," he said through the implants. "Please wait aboard your saucers for a moment."

"What the hell for?" Venus demanded.

"Stand by."

Everyone else disembarked, and Hathor watched through the cockpit windows as the soldiers escorted the new hybrid arrivals off to the residential areas.

"That's it; everyone's off," said Venus. "Now, what is this about?"

"I'd like us to each conduct an active scan of our ships' interior before departing," Salvatore told her.

"You think we've got a stowaway?" asked Venus.

"I don't believe so, but let's be certain."

Hathor scanned the cockpit but found no one. She moved down to the main level and checked that area, but it, too, was empty. There was nobody in the airlock but the soldier. She dropped to the flight deck with him and met Venus and Salvatore. She spotted Indra accompanying Jaden out of the hangar bay.

"Do you mind telling me what that was all about?" asked Venus.

"It was nothing," he said, giving Hathor a look. "I need to go speak to Melissa Kwan."

"I'll go with you," said Hathor.

As she left the hangar bay with Salvatore, she vowed again that she would take Majestic down if it were the last thing she did.

## Chapter Nineteen: Sydney

Sydney and Miguel had only just finished setting up their new quarters at the Africa compound when Melissa contacted her, asking her to come to the medical bay. So, Sydney headed down on the elevator to see what was up.

"Hey, lady," she said with a smile when she walked in.

"Hi, Syd, thanks for coming," Melissa replied.

There was a hologram of what appeared to be a virus floating in midair in front of Melissa. Sydney noted that she had a keyboard and trackpad at her workstation—something she hadn't seen inside a Majestic compound before. She asked Melissa about it.

"Oh, yeah—well, I don't have the Martian implants, so Hathor was able to tie the Othali input devices into their system for me. This holographic display is pretty neat, though."

"Sure is," Sydney agreed. "So, what's going on?"

"Well, even though we didn't detect a vaccine for the Majestic virus in your system, I wanted to check for antibodies."

"You think my body might have fought off the virus *naturally*?"

"Maybe. But it's also possible that they treated you with the antibodies themselves instead of administering a vaccine. Or that they *did* use a vaccine, but we just can't detect that for some reason."

"But you'd still be able to find the antibodies it triggered."

"Yes, precisely," Melissa confirmed.

"Okay, sure. You need to draw blood?"

"Not anymore. Venus took some time to acquaint me with these systems today—I have to say, the tech is quite impressive. If you lie down on the table here, it can scan your system for the antibodies without the need to remove any blood."

"Oh, wow," said Sydney, getting onto the table. "I wish we'd had this back at the hospital!"

"No kidding."

Sydney lay still for a few moments while Melissa performed the scan.

"I'll be damned," she muttered.

"What is it?" asked Sydney.

"You don't have any antibodies, either."

"Then, I don't get it. Why didn't the virus kill me?

Melissa shook her head.

"I have *no* idea."

"Maybe the antibodies don't last very long after they neutralize the virus," Sydney suggested. "That's what happens with the cold virus, right? Our bodies don't ever produce very many antibodies in the first place, so they wane pretty quickly."

"Well, that's possible," Melissa skeptically. "But in large part, that's because our bodies don't see the cold virus as a serious threat. That type of pathogen never moves past the upper respiratory tract. But this Majestic virus invades the central nervous system. That would generate a much stronger immune response."

"And that means the antibodies should last longer," Sydney concluded.

"Right—yet you have none. And *something* neutralized the virus in your body."

"Medical miracle?" Sydney suggested with a grin.

"Hah," Melissa replied. "Well, it's back to the drawing board for me."

"Hey, have you heard anything about the Europe mission yet?"

"Not a word—and I'm trying not to think about it. I get so worried when Malia and Jaden get involved with these operations."

"They're crazy powerful, now," said Sydney. "I'm sure they're fine."

"I know, but still. Anything could happen, and I can't help imagining the worst. That's why I always work when they're gone— helps keep my mind off of it."

"Yeah, that makes sense. Have they buried the hatchet yet after their spat the other day?"

Melissa let out a long sigh.

"You know, it's hard to tell with those two. I mean, it seems like they have—they're talking to each other, at least. But they both tend to hold grudges—especially Jaden. So, I don't know."

Just then, Salvatore and Hathor walked in, their expressions grim.

"Melissa, Sydney," said Salvatore, nodding to them. Sydney noticed that Hathor was diverting her gaze from them and began to worry. They may not be human, but their body language was not conveying anything good.

"I'm afraid I have bad news," said Salvatore. "It's Malia..."

"What is it?" asked Melissa, a quaver in her voice. "Is she alright? What happened?"

Salvatore shook his head.

"I'm so sorry."

Melissa stared at him in shock for a moment.

"No—no! It can't be! Tell me where she is!"

"They hit her with one of the prototype weapons," Salvatore told her. "It would have been painless—she died instantly."

"*NO!*" Melissa screamed. "No, no, no!" She broke down sobbing.

Sydney gathered her into a hug, tears streaming down her cheeks. Melissa pulled away after a minute.

"How? Tell me how it happened!"

Salvatore told her the whole story.

"No. There must be some mistake," Melissa insisted. "They replaced her—when she went invisible. It must have been a hybrid masquerading as her with one of those emitters. My Malia has to still be alive—they want us to believe that she's gone, but they took her..."

"I saw the whole thing with my own eyes," Hathor told her, looking at Melissa for the first time. "And I checked the optical sensor data over and over again. There's—"

"You have video of it?" Melissa demanded. "I want to see it."

"Melissa, this is not a good idea," said Salvatore. "Seeing your—"

"*SHOW ME!*" she screamed, spittle flying from her mouth.

Salvatore nodded. Moments later, the holographic image of the virus that had been floating in midair since Sydney's arrival disappeared. The scene in the European hangar bay replaced it.

Sydney watched as a hybrid descended from the Majestic saucer and hit Malia with a laser blast. She fell to the floor, then struggled to her feet only to vanish into thin air. She reappeared seconds later in the arms of a lone hybrid. The moment she escaped his grasp, another one fired his plasma cannon, blowing her into oblivion.

Sydney gasped, covering her mouth with one hand. She couldn't stop herself from sobbing. It was impossible to imagine Melissa's pain right now.

"But they replaced her—don't you see it?" Melissa demanded. "When she disappeared. She came back, but that couldn't have been her. They must have taken her—"

"We had active scans running continuously at every point of entry," Hathor told her. "I scanned the entire hangar bay, including every storage area, and there was nobody invisible."

"We scanned inside the saucers, as well," Salvatore added. "I'm sorry, Melissa. She's gone."

Melissa started sobbing again. Sydney held her, but Melissa slid down to the floor, shaking with grief. Sydney was crying freely, too. She hugged Melissa, gently rubbing her back. Melissa's sobs subsided after a couple of minutes.

"I need to see Jaden," Melissa said through her sniffles. "Where is my son?"

"Indra from the warship escorted him to your quarters," Salvatore told her.

Sydney helped Melissa to her feet. They left the medical bay; Salvatore and Hathor bade them farewell in the corridor. Sydney guided Melissa to the elevator, and they made their way up to the second level. They ran into Brian in the passage.

"What's wrong?" he asked. "Has something happened?"

Melissa broke down sobbing again, pulling Brian into a hug. He gave Sydney a questioning look over Melissa's shoulder. Sydney mouthed the word "Malia." Brian started crying, closing his eyes tight.

"I'm sorry, Melissa. I'm so, so sorry…"

Sydney accompanied them as far as the door to Melissa's quarters, then decided to let them be alone together as a family. She returned to her quarters. The moment she saw Miguel, she burst into fresh tears.

"Hey! What's wrong?" he asked, getting his feet and embracing her.

"Malia," was all Sydney could say through her sobs.

"Oh, no…"

Miguel guided her to their bed. Sydney lay next to him, crying into his chest for several minutes. Finally, she calmed down enough to tell him what had happened.

Miguel took a deep breath.

"Majestic is gonna pay for this. I promise you."

# Chapter Twenty: Jaden

Jaden lay in his bed with the lights off, staring up at the ceiling. Indra had shown him to their new quarters and insisted on staying with him until Melissa arrived. But Jaden wanted to be alone, so she waited in the living room.

Right now, Jaden felt numb. He'd cried like a baby on the way back from Europe and sobbed uncontrollably when he'd first arrived in his quarters. But now, he couldn't feel anything. Nothing seemed real.

Suddenly, he heard his mother's voice.

"Thank you for taking care of Jaden."

"No problem. I'm so sorry for your loss."

It was silent for a few moments.

"Jaden?"

He didn't respond. Melissa walked into his room, Brian right behind her, and turned on the lights. Jaden sat up, and at the sight of his mother, burst into tears again. Melissa sat down next to him in the bed and hugged him. Brian sat on his other side, hugging them both. They sat like that for a few minutes; Jaden cried the whole time and felt his mother shaking with sobs.

Finally, they pulled apart.

"I'm sorry, Mom," he said. "I should've been there. With her in the hangar bay, I mean. Maybe I could've saved her..."

"Oh, Jaden," she said, sobbing again. "It wasn't your fault—don't you think that. If you were there, they might have taken you both from me."

Jaden opened his mouth to reply, but there was nothing else to say.

"Jaden, listen to me," said Melissa. "From now on, that's it. No more combat missions for you. You'll stay here in the compound where you're safe—"

"*What?* Mom, no! Not a chance! I'm gonna help them take out the rest of the compounds—I have to! I'm going to make them *pay!*

"Jaden, your mother's right," said Brian. "It's too dangerous."

"I won't lose you *both*," Melissa told him. "I can't go through this again. Every time you two went out there, I was a nervous wreck—no more!"

"That's not fair! They killed Malia! I want *justice!*"

"We're going to blow those compounds to high heaven, Jaden," said Brian. "There will be justice. But it was wrong of us to send you two into danger like this. Let the—"

"Why the hell are you two ganging up on me like this?" Jaden demanded. "I am *going* on those missions, and neither one of you can stop me!"

Jaden got up and stormed out of the room.

"Jaden, no—come back here!" Melissa yelled. "Where are you going?"

Jaden ignored her, hurrying out of their quarters and running down the corridor. He had to get away from them—from everyone. At the end of the passage, he moved into the access tunnel and flew up to the top level. He ran into the hangar bay and used his implants to access his saucer. Once inside the airlock, he moved up to the cockpit. Taking a seat, he sent the command to open the hangar bay doors. Moving the saucer out of the hangar, he shot into the night without bothering to enter a destination. He set it to go straight, rising high into the sky.

"Jaden, this is Salvatore," he said through his implants. "Return to the compound immediately."

"No," Jaden replied. "No way."

"If you don't, I'll override your command and bring the saucer back remotely."

"Go ahead. I'll leave through the airlock and fly on my own."

There was no reply for a moment.

"Where are you going?"

"I don't know, man. Who cares. I just need to be alone, alright?"

Salvatore didn't respond, and Jaden thought he was done with him. But then, he said, "Promise me three things."

"What, goddammit?"

"Keep your velocity below the detection threshold. Do not lower your shields for any reason. And stay away from the Majestic compounds."

"Yeah, yeah. Alright."

"You promise?"

"Yeah. Sure."

"The others are going to want to come after you. I'll buy you as much time as I can."

Jaden let out a long sigh.

"Thanks, Salvatore."

Checking his location with the implants, Jaden realized he was flying over Egypt. He called up the map and set a course for the ancient pyramids. Moments later he arrived, setting the saucer to hover high above the Giza complex.

"Back where it all started," he muttered to himself. Jaden still found their history—his and Malia's—difficult to believe sometimes. To think that they were created from genetic material left in a secret chamber below the Great Pyramid for millennia... It still seemed crazy.

There was no solace for Jaden here. He took the saucer high into the atmosphere, careful to keep his velocity below the detection threshold. As he moved into the blackness of space, he spotted the Moon just above the horizon. For a moment, he considered flying there—getting away from the entirety of humanity for a little while seemed appealing. But the thought of going so far away completely alone frightened him; he decided against it.

His implants prompted him to insert the saucer into a low-Earth orbit, which he did. Floating high above the planet, he had a thought. Malia was dead, but...

*"Malia, can you hear me? It's me, Jaden..."*

Of course, there was no reply. Jaden tapped into the Earth's magnetic field and tried again.

*"Hey, Malia—are you out there? Somewhere?"*

Still, she did not respond. Jaden wasn't sure if he believed in an afterlife, but it had been worth a shot. Maybe if her soul or whatever were still floating around out there...

No, this was stupid; Malia was gone. Tears streamed down his face again, and moments later, he was sobbing. Looking back on his life, it struck him for the first time how close he and Malia had always been. They'd argued and fought almost constantly, but as twins, they'd been each other's shadow their entire lives.

And when the police killed their father, and they became fugitives, Malia was the only person in the entire world who understood. Sydney had helped them, and they'd known they could trust her, but she hadn't just watched officers shoot her parents. Only Malia had shared that experience.

Suddenly, Jaden knew where he wanted to go. He flew the saucer back into the atmosphere, calling up the map with his implants. What the hell was the name of that town, again? It was in New Mexico; he knew that for sure. Not too far from the Texas line. Scanning the map, he found the highway they'd taken with Sydney. There it was—Tucumcari. He laid in the course, and the saucer sped across the sky.

Before long, he crossed over into daylight and flew over North America. Only minutes later, he reached the southwest United States. The ship came to rest high above the town. Now, what was the name of that campground? The map showed him every site in and around Tucumcari.

"That was it—Lone Star Campground," Jaden said to himself.

The saucer moved to the area, and he took it in lower. Finally, he dropped to the airlock and went down to the ground. But as he walked up to Savannah's house, it became apparent that the place was vacant. Several windows were boarded up, and the glass was broken in the others. The front door had a padlock on it.

"What the hell?" Jaden muttered.

Looking in through one window, it was clear nobody lived here anymore. Jaden had been hoping to see Savannah again. Maybe visiting someone uninvolved with all the insanity in his life would provide some comfort. But she was gone.

Jaden set out across the campground. The whole place had been abandoned, not only the house, and the grass had grown knee-deep in all the campsites. Jaden walked into the woods and made his way to the lake where they'd swam last time he was here. He found the beach and moved around to the ridge where they'd dived into the water. Sitting down with his legs dangling over the edge, he lay back and stared into the sky.

"I miss you, Malia," he said out loud, fresh tears forming.

He couldn't believe this had happened. His sister had been a constant presence his entire life, and just like that, she was gone. First his dad, and now Malia. Jaden thought back to what life had been like before her powers had manifested. He'd had a normal life—they all had. Their dad worked at the lab, and their mom took care of them and the house and everything. Malia and Jaden went to school and hung out with their friends. He remembered Seth trying to ask her out to homecoming and had to laugh.

Jaden wanted that life back. He wanted to go home and walk into the house and smell whatever his mom was cooking, argue with Malia about some stupid thing, and hang out with his dad in the living room. But that entire existence was gone. Only he and his mom remained, and they were in the middle of some crazy shit fighting half-alien hybrids who were trying to destroy the world.

It wasn't fair. Why did it have to be him and Malia? Why did Malia have to die for this? Jaden didn't know if he believed in God or not, but if such a being did exist, he hated him for taking Malia away.

Jaden sat up, screaming at the top of his lungs. He hung his head low, sobbing anew. But suddenly, he heard footsteps approaching. Turning, he spotted Hathor emerging from the trees.

"Hey, kid," she said, sitting down next to him. "This place is nice."

"How the hell did you find me?" Jaden demanded. "I kept my shields up the whole time."

"We can track our own saucers."

"Oh," he said with a sigh. "Well, I kinda wanted to be alone right now."

"I'm sorry about Malia," she replied.

Jaden wanted to thank her, but suddenly, his throat was burning, and he couldn't get any words out.

"Majestic took someone I loved, too. That's the reason I'm in this fight. I mean, yeah, preventing planetary genocide is pretty important. But that's not what gets me out of bed in the morning. It's Enrique; I miss him so much… My people aren't usually too emotional. But losing him broke my heart; I never knew anything could hurt this bad."

"I'm sorry," said Jaden. "How long ago was that?"

"Almost five years now. I still cry over him every day."

"I didn't know Martians have tear ducts," Jaden said with a grin.

"Oh, we do," Hathor replied with a chuckle.

"Damn, though… five years, and it's still that painful?"

"Yeah. Part of it… I won't *allow myself* to get over it. I feel like if I let go of my grief, then I lose him completely, you know? The grief is all I have left."

Jaden considered this for a moment. Would he continue bearing the burden of this loss for the rest of his life?

"But what about the memories? You'd still have those, right? It's gotta be better to remember the good times than to keep feeling sad all the time."

"I don't know. Maybe. But I'm not ready to find out. Once we've taken down Majestic… I'm going to help destroy them. For Enrique. Then I'll think about letting go of the grief."

Jaden had to wonder if beating Majestic would provide any relief. It wouldn't bring Malia back; he knew that for sure. But all the same, he wanted to take them down, too.

"My mom's not gonna let me go on missions anymore. I want to help destroy them, too, but I can't anymore."

Hathor nodded.

"She doesn't want to lose you, too. Be thankful you still have someone."

"But you still have people, too. Salvatore and Venus and Bastet. Right?"

Hathor took a deep breath.

"Yeah. I guess you're right. Well, I'll tell you what. I'll take down Majestic for Enrique *and* Malia. On your behalf."

"Better than nothing," Jaden said with a sigh.

The two of them sat there for several more minutes, staring out at the lake, without saying anything more. Finally, they returned to their saucers and headed back to the Africa compound.

Jaden docked the ship and returned to his quarters. Despite the late hour, he found his mom sitting up with a glass of wine. He expected her to yell at him, but she didn't.

"Am I in trouble, now?" he asked, sitting down next to her.

Melissa regarded him for a moment, took a sip of wine, and set her glass down on the table.

"No. Salvatore told me you were safe. But I'm not backing down on the combat missions."

"I know."

They sat quietly for a moment, then Jaden broke down again. Melissa hugged him tight, rocking him back and forth.

# Chapter Twenty-one: Abram

Abram guided the saucer into position. He dropped to the main level, where he and his team gathered their weapons. The Sphinx was sending a strike force of five to complete this mission. He looked around at his teammates and nodded: they were ready.

Abram led the way down through the airlock. They floated to the ground, then hiked the short distance across the mountainside to the hidden entrance. The Sphinx had feared the enemy might try taking over the Africa compound. And just in case they succeeded, the Sphinx had ordered this secret tunnel constructed. It didn't show up on the plans for the complex, and there were no sensors inside. The enemy would never know they were coming.

They'd used the ship's gravity beam to remove the boulder covering the entrance. The tunnel bored into the rock at a steep angle. Abram dropped into the opening, sliding into the darkness. Before long, the passage leveled out, and he flew the rest of the way.

Finally, he reached the end. Pushing the hatch out of the way, he emerged inside the morgue, his teammates right behind him. They'd used one of the mortuary chambers for this end of the tunnel. Unless the enemy had taken the time to scan every single cell in the entire morgue, there was no way they could have found it.

They used their emitters to go invisible, then Abram led them across the massive room and out into the corridor. They found two soldiers guarding the access tunnel. Abram hoisted his cannon onto his shoulder and shot one of them. The second guard pointed his weapon, but Abram's teammate shot him before he could fire.

Abram led the way into the access tunnel. They flew up two levels, killing the guards the moment they stepped into the corridor. Halfway down the hall, they found the maternity ward. Abram ordered two of his teammates to stand guard in the passage, then went inside with the other two. They found the two women they were looking for; Abram went visible, then woke them.

"The Sphinx sent us to rescue you," he told them quietly. "Come with us."

"What about the others?" one of the women asked.

Abram shook his head.

"Only the two of you. Put these on," he said, as his teammate handed them each an emitter. "Make yourselves invisible, and then follow me."

Once they'd disappeared, Abram went invisible again himself. Their implants would allow them to see him. He led them back into the corridor, collected their two guards, and led the way toward the access tunnel.

But at that moment, some unseen force ripped the plasma cannon out of Abram's hands. It clattered to the floor, and he found himself flattened against the ceiling along with his teammates and the two women.

Suddenly, someone appeared in the corridor in front of them.

# Chapter Twenty-two: Jaden

Jaden had great difficulty falling asleep. He dozed off a couple of times only to start awake again a few minutes later. The third time this happened, he sat up in bed, with a nagging feeling that something was wrong—as if someone were in their quarters with them who didn't belong.

Jaden's heart was beating a mile a minute, and he could feel the adrenaline dump hitting his system. Reaching out with his mind, he searched his room telepathically, but there was nobody else here. He got out of bed and moved into the living room but found no intruders here, either. Melissa was sound asleep in her bedroom, alone.

Stepping into the corridor, Jaden extended his thoughts in both directions but found nobody out here but the soldiers standing guard by the access tunnel. He couldn't shake the sense that something was wrong, though, and for some reason that he couldn't quite pinpoint, felt like it was somewhere on the lower levels. Jaden walked to the access tunnel.

"Everything alright?" one of the soldiers asked him.

Jaden almost told him what he was sensing but then thought better of it. He'd feel foolish for raising the alarm if this turned out to be nothing.

"Yeah, just going for a walk. Can't sleep."

The soldier nodded, and Jaden stepped through the wall. He flew down to the bottom level and moved into the corridor. Jaden gasped when he spotted both guards for this level lying on the floor, holes through their chests. There were definitely intruders in the compound.

"Salvatore, this is Jaden," he said through his implants. It took a minute for Salvatore to reply.

"Yes, Jaden. What is it?"

He explained what he'd found.

"Stay where you are—I'll be right there."

Jaden used his emitter to go invisible. Reaching out telepathically, he searched the rest of this level but found nobody who didn't belong. But he didn't want to wait for Salvatore. Flying up one floor, he emerged into the corridor and searched again, but nothing was amiss here. When he moved up to level ten, he found the guards lying dead on the floor. Scanning the level with his mind, he found people who didn't belong—five of them, halfway down the corridor, with two more from the compound. He could sense them in the passage but couldn't see anyone—they must have been invisible.

These had to be hybrids, and they were probably armed. Jaden imagined he could see them holding plasma cannons. Using his powers, he tore the weapons out of their hands and hurled the people into the ceiling. Next, he penetrated the leader's mind, forcing him to become visible. The man stared at Jaden with hatred in his eyes.

Jaden started extinguishing his consciousness, but the man bit down on his fake tooth and took a deep breath.

"*No!*" Jaden shouted in his mind, but it was too late. The man died.

Jaden hurriedly penetrated another of the intruder's minds, but she, too, killed herself before he could stop her. He tried again and again, but the intruders all committed suicide before Jaden could knock them out.

"Salvatore, this is Jaden. I found the intruders on level ten. They're dead."

"I told you to stay put!"

Jaden didn't respond. But a moment later, Salvatore emerged from the access tunnel, a dozen Othali soldiers behind him. Jaden lowered the corpses to the floor, then forced their two captives to become visible, setting them down as well.

"It's the two pregnant women," Salvatore observed.

"The intruders were trying to get them out of the compound," Jaden told him.

"That is curious," said Salvatore.

Jaden followed him over to the two women.

"What happened here?" Salvatore asked them. "Were you in communication with these people prior to their arrival?"

"No," one of the women told him. "We were sleeping, and they woke us up. The leader told us that the Sphinx sent them to rescue us. He gave us emitters and told us to go invisible and follow him, so we did."

"And they wanted only the two of you—none of the others?"

The woman nodded.

"Do you have any idea why they singled you out?"

"No," the woman said with a shrug.

"Jaden?" said Salvatore.

Jaden nodded. He penetrated each of their minds in turn, verifying the story.

"She's telling the truth," he said.

"Why them, I wonder," Salvatore said quietly. "I'm going to ask Melissa to do a full medical workup on them. Take them to the medical bay and keep them under guard," he added to one of the soldiers.

"Yes, sir," the soldier replied. He and two of the others escorted the women toward the elevator.

Salvatore looked far away for a moment.

"I've contacted your mother," he said to Jaden. "Now, we need to figure out how they got inside the compound."

"I found two more dead guards on the bottom level," Jaden told him. "Maybe they found a way in down there."

"Let's go," said Salvatore.

Jaden went with Salvatore and the rest of the soldiers down to the bottom level. Salvatore had the soldiers start searching while he took Jaden down to the generator room. The cover to the maintenance tunnel was gone, and the shaft had been filled with concrete.

"I'm pretty sure they didn't get in this way," Jaden commented.

"No," Salvatore agreed. "We sealed off the tunnel from both ends, but I wanted to be sure."

One of the soldiers approached them as they returned to the corridor.

"We found something in the morgue."

Salvatore and Jaden followed him into the massive room. In the far corner, they found a mortuary chamber that had been left open. Peering inside, Jaden could see that there was a tunnel delving far into the earth.

"Fascinating," said Salvatore. "Majestic must have dug this out well in advance of our arrival. I'll assign a crew to fill this in, but we'll need to scan the rest of the area to make sure there aren't any others."

Salvatore started at one end of the morgue, Jaden at the other. Using their scanners, they undertook the tedious process of checking every chamber for escape tunnels. But by the time they met in the middle, neither one had found anything that shouldn't have been there.

"Let's go check in with your mother," said Salvatore.

Jaden followed him up to the medical bay. They found Melissa with the two women, the three Othali soldiers standing guard.

"Your timing is impeccable," said Melissa. "I've just finished their exams. They're both in perfect health, as are the fetuses."

"The Sphinx sent a strike team here to abduct these two women and nobody else," said Salvatore. "And when we first infiltrated the compound, they fought very hard to protect them along with the rest of the mothers and children. What makes these two special?"

Melissa considered this for a moment.

"Let me check one more thing," she said, moving to her console.

"I'm going to run a full DNA scan." A minute passed, and then she added, "Well, that's strange. They're both half-Martian hybrid women, but their DNA has been altered."

"In what way?" asked Salvatore.

"I'll have to run more tests, but it seems like someone swapped out a handful of their chromosomes for human ones."

"What about the fetuses?" asked Salvatore.

Melissa went back to her console.

"I'll be damned," she said.

"What is it?" asked Jaden.

"The babies are hybrids, alright. But not Martian ones. They're half-Othali and half-human."

"*What?*" said Jaden.

"That must be why they altered their DNA," said Melissa. "Normally, Martian hybrids wouldn't be able to carry these babies. Hold on; I want to check one more thing."

A minute later, a pair of holographic double helixes appeared next to each exam table.

"I don't believe it..." said Melissa, staring at the holograms with a look of shock on her face.

"What is all of this?" asked Salvatore.

"These are identical, right?" asked Melissa, pointing to the images next to the first woman.

"Yes," Salvatore confirmed. "They appear to be."

"And these?" Melissa asked, indicating the holograms next to the second woman.

Salvatore nodded.

"These women are carrying clones of my children."

Jaden stared at her in shock for a moment.

"You've got to be kidding..."

"I wish I were," said Melissa. "But there's no doubt. This woman is carrying a baby who is genetically identical to Malia. And the other baby has DNA that is indistinguishable from yours."

"They must have brought your DNA samples here from Lucifer's compound before we destroyed it," said Salvatore. "Now we know why they tried so hard to reacquire these women."

"And why they were willing to kill Malia," Jaden added, his throat burning. "They won't need *us* anymore once they've got our clones."

Salvatore took a deep breath.

"We should all try to get some sleep. Return these two to their quarters—and increase the guard," he added to one of the soldiers. "Station two additional soldiers at each end of the corridor and two more outside these women's rooms."

Jaden and Melissa returned to their quarters. Jaden went back to bed but got no sleep that night.

# Chapter Twenty-three: Melissa

Melissa had been asleep when Salvatore contacted her, but he'd woken her from a nightmare. Now, lying in bed, the dream came back to her. She had to know if it had any basis in reality.

Getting out of bed, she got dressed again and ran back to the medical bay. She'd watched the holographic imagery of Malia's death a hundred times already, but she needed to review it again to see if what she'd dreamed was real.

She accessed the system through her console and played the footage. There was nothing resembling her nightmare, but she zoomed in on the hangar bay entry and played it again. This time, she spotted a minor glitch right in the middle of the opening. Zooming in further, she replayed it in slow motion, pausing at the moment of the anomaly.

Melissa gasped, covering her mouth with one hand.

She returned to her quarters and went back to bed but was unable to fall back to sleep. There was a meeting first thing in the morning; once that was finished, she'd pull Salvatore aside and show him what she'd found.

A few hours later, she headed to the south wing with Jaden. There was a conference room in the administrative area. Brian, Sydney, and

Miguel were present, as were Bastet, Venus, Salvatore, and Hathor. Holograms of Commander Anhur, Lieutenant Bukhari, and Ensign Shurani were seated at the head of the table, their images beamed here from the Othali warship. Anhur called the meeting to order, and Salvatore gave his report about the previous night's events.

Brian sat back in his chair, heaving a deep sigh.

"They cloned Malia and Jaden... This explains quite a bit."

"You'll need to increase security and scan for other hidden entries," said Anhur.

"We already have," Salvatore replied. "We found no other secret tunnels. And we've doubled the guard on every level."

"Majestic will not give up on this," said Bastet. "They'll do whatever it takes to reacquire those two women."

"No doubt," Venus replied. "Which is yet another reason we need to resume our mission right away."

"We're ready to take care of the Majestic compounds in Asia, Australia, and South America today," Anhur told them.

"So are we," said Salvatore. "We can commence with Asia as soon as we're done here."

"What about Antarctica?" asked Venus. "Do we know if they have a compound there?"

"There are no radar facilities, so we were unable to implement the method we used to find the other compounds," said Salvatore. "However, I have moved one of our satellites over the continent. It will take a couple more days to complete the scans, but so far, we have found no evidence of a facility there."

"You probably won't if they've shielded the place," said Brian. "The data we retrieved from Europe contained no more information about the identity or whereabouts of the Sphinx than what we had here. And I doubt we'll find anything more at the remaining compounds. Antarctica may very well be where they've holed up."

"Once we've taken out the other compounds, we can move the warship over the continent and conduct active scans," Anhur told them. "We should be able to find them that way."

"Maybe they ain't on land at all," Miguel suggested. "Any reason they couldn't've built a place under the ocean somewhere?"

"That's possible," said Salvatore. "Our ships have no trouble operating underwater."

"We still have to find their new chariots, too," said Venus.

"Antarctica will be a dead end," Bastet told them. "And so will the ocean floor. Find the chariots, and you'll find the Sphinx—that's what I think. And they're almost certain to be in orbit somewhere."

"I agree," said Hathor. "But in orbit of *what*—that's the question. It may not be the Earth. If I wanted to hide a construction project like that, I'd put it somewhere else in the solar system. Around one of Jupiter's moons, maybe. Keep the chariots and the Sphinx completely hidden from us."

"But we know they were building components for the chariots here," said Sydney. "How long would it take to keep hauling parts out that far?"

"Not long at all with our engine tech," Venus reminded her. "I think Hathor's probably right. But we should still rule out

Antarctica, at least. The ice covering the vast majority of the land is thousands of feet thick, so I doubt you'll find anything there. But they could have constructed a compound in the same area where I built mine—the ice is the thinnest there."

"Well, let's revisit this once we've got the results of the scans," Brian suggested. "For now, we need to focus on our assaults of the remaining compounds."

"Agreed," said Anhur. "We should proceed with the same plan we implemented in Europe. The only difference is that we won't have the twins with us, so it will be critical for the saucers to provide covering fire as the soldiers disembark."

"I want to go with you," Jaden said. "Please, let me do this."

"Jaden, no!" Melissa said, turning toward him.

"I can't just sit here knowing everyone else is out there fighting. Give me a chance to avenge Malia's death."

"I'm sorry, son," Anhur said, giving him a sympathetic look. "You're too valuable. We can't risk you in the field like this anymore. Don't worry—we'll exact justice for your sister."

Jaden sat back in his chair, shaking his head. Brian could tell he'd been hoping Anhur might overrule Melissa, but at the same time, he didn't seem to have been counting on it.

"Now that that's settled, let's get this show on the road," said Venus.

"Yes," Anhur agreed. "Our soldiers are ready to board as soon as you get here with the saucers."

They finished the meeting. The holograms of Anhur and his

people disappeared, and the others rose from the table. Brian shook hands with Salvatore, Venus, and Hathor.

"Good luck out there," he told them.

As the others filed out of the room, Melissa grabbed Salvatore by one elbow.

"I need to show you something—can you come down to the medical bay?" she whispered.

"Yes, of course."

They walked together in silence. Once they'd arrived, Melissa played the footage for him, pointing out the glitch, then zooming in and pausing the hologram.

"There," she said, pointing to the anomaly. "Tell me that's not a foot."

Salvatore leaned in to get a closer look.

"I think Malia's still alive," Melissa told him. "One of the hybrids replaced her when she went invisible, and *that's* who they incinerated. Whoever grabbed her flew out of the hangar bay with her and took her to the Sphinx."

Salvatore took control of the playback, scrubbing it back and forth one frame at a time. But finally, he let out a deep sigh.

"Melissa, this is nothing more than random noise in the data stream."

"But that's a foot! Someone flew through the scanning beam!"

Salvatore shook his head.

"I'm sorry. I understand how difficult it can be to accept a loved one's death. But while I concede that the shape you see here does resemble someone's foot, it is just an error in the footage. The brain wants to find patterns even where there are none."

Melissa felt crestfallen. She'd latched onto this "evidence" and convinced herself that Malia could still be alive. But staring at the glitch now, she could see that Salvatore was probably right.

Once Salvatore had left, she sat down and sobbed, covering her face with both hands. Malia was gone.

# Chapter Twenty-four: Nephthys

Malia struggled to open her eyes; she felt so groggy. She didn't know where she was or how long she'd been unconscious.

Memories came flooding back... The hybrid had hit her with a laser blast inside Majestic's European compound. Malia had dropped to the floor, struggling to remain conscious. She knew she'd lost her bubble; she'd tried to reform it, but her vision was going black. It had taken every ounce of concentration to stop herself from passing out. Finally, she'd felt her strength returning. Malia had managed to get back to her feet. But at that moment, someone had grabbed her from behind. Before she could do anything else, she'd felt a prick in the side of her neck—they'd injected her with something. Malia had felt the chemical coursing through her veins; this was the same sedative Lucifer had used on her. She'd focused with all her might on eliminating it from her system, but the dose had been massive. Everything had gone black.

Malia could still feel the last of the sedative in her body. Focusing with the little strength she possessed, she managed to remove the chemical from her bloodstream. She had a pounding headache, but finally, she was able to open her eyes all the way.

She was lying flat on her back in a room only a little larger than her quarters on the Othali warship. Three of the walls were made of gray stone; the fourth was glass or some other transparent material. Malia sat up, taking in more of her surroundings.

Beyond the glass was a viewing area with a stone bench. She could see into a passageway at the rear of that area, but nothing was visible beyond that.

There was a doorway on one side of her chamber, up near the glass. It appeared to be filled with metal, like the doors in the Majestic compounds. Slowly, Malia rose to her feet; she felt weak. Shuffling over to the door, she tried passing her hand through the metal, but it was solid. The edges of her vision started going black, and she had to sit down again.

"Hello?" Malia called out.

There was no reply. She reached out with her mind but discovered that she could not penetrate these walls with her powers. Focusing on the door, she tried blowing the metal out of the frame, but this had no effect. They must have built this chamber with the same material they'd used for the testing facility in Area 51.

Malia focused inside of herself, creating an adrenal dump. She felt her heart beating faster and knew the hormone was coursing through her veins, but it made no difference—there was no surge of power like she usually experienced. What the hell? Had they somehow shielded this chamber from the Earth's magnetic field, too? It wouldn't surprise her.

She was about to try figuring out how to use her implants; if she could do that, then maybe she could contact someone that way. But at that moment, a tall Indian woman walked into the observation room.

"Who are you?" Malia demanded.

The woman gazed at her with a serene smile. She wore a red sari and a golden headdress—it looked exactly like the one Ervin Noorani had worn on the chariot, except that the figure above her forehead was a cat instead of a cobra.

"You may call me Durga," the woman told her. She had a slight Indian accent. "I am the Sphinx."

Malia had figured she would say that.

"I thought Ervin was the Sphinx."

"He was. Until you killed him."

Malia glared at her, but the woman continued to smile.

"Let me out of here," she demanded.

"I don't think I will."

"My people will come looking for me. They'll kill you and rescue me."

The woman giggled; she sounded like a little girl.

"Do you know where you are right now?"

"I have no idea," said Malia. "But they'll figure it out."

"I doubt it. But in point of fact, they have no reason to search for you."

"Of course they do—"

"I'm afraid they believe you to be dead."

"*What?*" said Malia. "Why would they think that?"

"Let me show you..."

A holographic image appeared in the observation area, filling most of the room and making it appear that Durga was standing inside the hologram. Malia recognized the setting immediately—it was the hangar bay in Majestic's European compound.

Malia watched herself move into the area. The hybrids fired their weapons, and the plasma shots froze inside her protective bubble. Suddenly, the hybrids' cannons flew out of their hands. Hathor ran into the room with a bunch of soldiers, all firing on the hybrids. Malia shot several of them with her plasma cannon.

But a moment later, a lone hybrid dropped out of the saucer and hit her with a laser blast. Malia watched herself fall to the floor, then slowly regain her feet. But then she disappeared.

"What? I don't remember that..."

"Keep watching," Durga told her.

Only seconds later, Malia watched herself reappear and escape the grasp of a hybrid who'd also been invisible. But as Hathor approached her, another hybrid dropped from the saucer, fired his plasma cannon, and incinerated Malia.

"That didn't happen!" Malia screamed.

"Oh, but it did!"

"I'm still alive!"

"Yes, but my faithful servant is not, and he had taken on your appearance when he died. So, as you can see, your people believe we killed you."

Malia felt her heart sink. Her mom, Jaden, Uncle Brian—they all believed she was dead. What must they have been going through, thinking they'd lost her? Tears came to Malia's eyes, imagining her mother's grief...

"You're a monster..."

Durga only smiled at her.

"But they would have thought of a hybrid using an emitter to replace me. Salvatore and Hathor—they were scanning every point of entry. They must have realized that you faked my death..."

"No, I'm afraid not. Your captor flew you right out the hangar bay doors so fast that your passage would have registered only as random noise. They have already analyzed the data from their optical sensors and concluded that you are truly dead."

Malia felt this information slowly sinking into her brain. Right now, her family would be grieving for her the same way she had when they'd killed her father and when she thought her mother had died. And Durga was right: they wouldn't be looking for her.

Tears slipped down Malia's cheeks. Reaching out with her mind, she tried to contact Jaden, but it was no use. She could not penetrate these walls.

Malia screamed at the top of her lungs.

"Good," the woman said, her smile growing. "You're accepting the truth of your situation."

"But it's *not* the truth—you've engineered a massive lie!"

"I've been watching your progress from afar, and I'm impressed. Your powers have grown stronger and faster than we ever dared to imagine. And now, you've killed a member of the Sphinx. You could fill that vacancy. Join me, and together, we shall usher in a new world order."

"Never. You are evil, and I will never cooperate with you."

Durga regarded her for a few moments.

"You will in time. But you need a new name—'Malia' is so... plain. From now on, we shall call you Nephthys."

"*What*? No—my name is Malia!"

"I will leave you now. Take some time to consider your situation."

Durga turned and strode out of the room.

"*LET ME OUT OF HERE!*"

The woman ignored her. Malia lay on the floor, crying freely. What was she supposed to do now? Everyone thought she was dead, so there would be nobody coming to the rescue. It was up to her to find a way out of here...

She remembered her implants again. The icons were there, around the edge of her vision. Too bad she'd never learned how to use them. But she had to try—it was the only chance she had.

One of the symbols looked like an antenna and had the letters "COM" beneath it. That had to be the communication system. Now, how did she access it?

Malia focused on the antenna and imagined pressing it like an icon on a touchscreen. The words "Choose contact" appeared along the top edge of her vision.

"Salvatore," she said in her mind.

But then the words "Access denied" appeared.

"Damn!" Malia said out loud.

The flying saucer icon was grayed out—of course. She'd never linked herself to one of the vessels like Jaden had. The belt icon was grayed out, too; that had to be for her emitter—Malia checked her pockets, but the device was gone. Either Durga or one of the hybrids must have confiscated it on the way here. And she didn't have a scanner, either, so the scanner icon didn't work.

Malia tried the antenna again with the same result. There was another icon that looked like a box with a dot in the middle. Malia focused on that. The words "Enter passcode" appeared across the top of her vision. This must have been the portal to the local computer system, but Malia had no idea what the passcode might be.

Curling up in fetal position on the floor, Malia tried to think of some way out of this. But she had no idea where she was, her powers didn't work here, and she had no way to contact anyone to let them know she was alive. Malia was profoundly alone. She cried again, eventually drifting off to sleep.

# Chapter Twenty-five: Salvatore

Salvatore went to the hangar bay. Hathor and Venus were already aboard their saucers. Salvatore boarded his, then contacted Hathor once he'd reached the cockpit. Despite what he'd told Melissa, the glitch she found had aroused his suspicions. He asked Hathor to review it.

"I saw this, too," she told him. "At the time, I passed it off as noise, but I'll take a closer look once we're done today."

"If someone did manage to fly through the scanning beam undetected, then our safeguards are not nearly as secure as we thought."

"Well, I don't know about that," Hathor replied. "I still think it's noise. But if a person *was* flying out the entry, they had to have built up an awful lot of speed to show up in only one frame like this. That would have been possible only because we'd blown off the blast doors. There's no way for someone to move that fast through the saucer airlocks. And we're flooding the entire hangar bay with active scanning beams whenever we open *our* blast doors, so there's no way anyone could escape our notice like that."

"Those are valid points."

"And think about it—the hybrids who showed up to abduct the pregnant women chose to enter through their secret tunnel. It would

207

have been easier to fly in through the hangar bay if they thought they could do so undetected."

Her logic was sound, but Salvatore couldn't help harboring some doubt.

"You're probably right," was all he said, though.

"Don't worry; I'll run a deeper analysis on the footage," Hathor assured him.

Salvatore sent the command to open the hangar bay doors. Sure enough, active scanning beams flooded the entire area. They flew out of the compound and took off into the sky. Minutes later, they reached the Othali warship. Salvatore docked first and loaded his group of soldiers. Once the other two had done the same, they headed back down to the surface.

Majestic's Asia compound was located deep in Nepal's Himalayas, carved into a mountainside. The saucers moved into position and awaited the warship. Once the Othali had arrived, they repeatedly fired on the compound's blast doors, blowing them apart. The saucers flew into the hangar bay and opened fire on the hybrids rushing to the defense.

Moments later, the Othali soldiers disembarked and secured the area. Salvatore dropped down through the airlock and met Venus and Hathor on the flight deck. Hoisting his plasma cannon onto his shoulder, he followed them out to the corridor. Hathor's soldiers were already at work securing this level.

Hathor went off to find the commander while Venus and Salvatore headed to the access tunnel at the end of the corridor with their soldiers. They moved through the wall and began their descent; once the soldiers had secured their rappelling lines, they followed them down. Venus headed to abductee processing while Salvatore continued to the bottom level.

He helped the soldiers clear the floor, but there weren't many hybrids down here. Once that was done, he went into the morgue and planted a fusion grenade on the bulkhead in the far corner. Returning to the corridor, he placed the second grenade at the far end by the elevator.

"This is Hathor," a voice said through his implants. "I've replaced the commander. You should have access to the system now."

Salvatore connected to the network and tapped into the internal com system.

"Attention, Majestic personnel," he said through his implants, his voice booming through the corridor, "this is Salvatore. We will be destroying this compound. Anyone wishing to leave the organization and seek asylum with our people must report to the hangar bay and surrender themselves to the soldiers. You have two minutes."

Salvatore moved up to the next level with the soldiers, but moments later, Venus contacted him.

"Salvatore, I'm on level six. I found something in the brig. You'd better come to see this."

"On my way."

He moved back into the access tunnel and flew up to the sixth level. Hurrying down the corridor, he found Venus in the brig, standing outside one of the cells. Looking inside, he saw a man wearing only a loincloth, suspended from the ceiling by both arms. He had lashes and burn marks on his chest and legs.

"Who is this?" asked Salvatore.

"No idea. He doesn't know, either."

"What?"

"He claims to have lost his memory. The first thing he remembers is waking up in this cell."

Salvatore found himself wishing Jaden were here with them.

"Have your soldiers take him up to the saucers. We'll secure him with the asylum seekers and interrogate him back at the compound."

Venus nodded.

Salvatore rejoined his soldiers. They'd cleared the level where he'd left them, so he moved up to the next floor with them.

Unlike the hybrids at the European compound, the ones here were all armed. Majestic must have issued guidance for all personnel to bear arms at all times in anticipation of their arrival. But the Othali soldiers overwhelmed them by sheer force of numbers.

Once they'd cleared the remaining levels, Salvatore returned to the hangar bay with his soldiers. Venus had rounded up the children and their mothers, the human abductees, and the asylum seekers and had them under heavy guard on her saucer. Hathor had downloaded the data from their network. They were ready to go.

The three of them boarded their saucers with the soldiers and moved out of the compound. Once they'd reached minimum safe distance, Salvatore issued the command to detonate the nukes. The mountainside went up in a gigantic mushroom cloud.

This operation had seemed almost easy. Majestic had been unable to adjust their tactics in any meaningful way to repel their assault. But it was the Othali warship that had made all the difference. Majestic had designed their compounds to withstand any known weapons technology. But the Othali had built their warship to battle the Malor, who possessed armaments far beyond anything Majestic had ever imagined. And they were not about to give Majestic enough time to devise a stronger defense.

Salvatore set a course back to their compound, and the three saucers shot into the sky. They disembarked inside their hangar bay. Venus and Hathor supervised the soldiers transporting the captives down to the lower levels for processing. But Salvatore and three of the Othali took the amnesiac prisoner down to the medical bay.

Melissa gasped and did a double-take when she saw the prisoner. "Who is this?" she asked.

"We don't know," said Salvatore. "They were holding him prisoner. You recognize him?"

"He uh... reminds me of someone, that's all. He's been tortured," she said, looking him over with an expression of concern. "Can you lie down on the exam table?"

The prisoner nodded. Once he was in position, Melissa ran a quick scan.

"I don't see any internal damage. These burns and lacerations need attention, but he should be fine—physically, at least."

"He doesn't show up in the Majestic database here or at the Asia compound," Salvatore told her.

"How odd," Melissa said with a frown. "He has neural implants, so he must have been involved with Majestic in some capacity, I would think."

"Interesting," Salvatore replied. "He shouldn't be able to access our systems, but just to be safe, I'm going to block his transponder."

"Is there any way you can tell us where he's from?"

"I'll run a DNA scan—hang on." She worked at her console for a moment, then said, "This is very strange."

"What is it?"

"This man is half-Othali and half-human."

"Strange, indeed," Salvatore agreed.

"There's more. His human genetic markers are consistent with someone from ancient Egypt. Which explains why he looked familiar."

"Meaning what?"

"Salvatore, he looks almost exactly like my first husband."

"King Ashai from ancient Egypt?"

Melissa nodded.

"But this man is roughly forty years old. I'll need to run more tests to figure out why his DNA seems to be so much older."

Salvatore stared at her in silence for a moment.

"We need to head out to the next Majestic compound. Could you have Jaden interrogate this man telepathically? See if he can help restore his memory?"

Melissa nodded.

"Yes, of course."

"And I think once you've finished your tests, we should move him to the brig. Jaden can work with him there."

Salvatore headed back up to the hangar bay. But he alerted Bastet to the prisoner's presence and assigned four more soldiers to stand guard in the medical bay. This prisoner gave him an uneasy feeling. They would have to consider any information Jaden could glean with extreme skepticism; there was a distinct possibility that Majestic had planted this person as some sort of Trojan horse. But if that were true, then his purpose here remained to be seen.

# Chapter Twenty-six: Nephthys

Malia woke with a start. Scrambling to her feet, she frantically looked around the chamber, trying to remember where she was—until she recalled that she had no idea. That woman—Durga was keeping her prisoner here. Her mother and brother and everyone else back in the Africa compound thought she was dead.

Her heart sinking, Malia sat down again. Though she could feel this new shot of adrenaline hitting her system, it still did not affect her powers. She reached out with her mind but was no more able to penetrate the walls of her cell than she had been before.

Just then, Durga walked into the observation area.

"You're awake," she said with that serene smile. "Have you considered my offer?"

"Go to hell. I don't need to consider it. I'll never join you."

"More's the pity, Ms. Kwan," she drawled.

Malia fixed her with a suspicious stare. Not only had she used her real name, but her voice was different—it sounded male, and her accent was gone. As Malia watched, the woman transformed. A man was now standing there—a man wearing a black suit and tie and sunglasses: Lucifer.

"No," Malia said, her voice barely more than a whisper, as she got to her feet, backing away from him. "We killed you—I knocked you out, and Salvatore blew your head off. I watched you die!"

"You are, happily, mistaken, Ms. Kwan."

"This is impossible. You're still Durga, but you're using your emitter to *look* like Lucifer..."

"Or perhaps the man you killed that day was a hybrid using an emitter to look like *me*," he drawled.

Malia thought back to that day. She'd penetrated his mind and extinguished his consciousness before he could send a signal. But she'd had to do it so quickly that there was no time to examine his thoughts and confirm that it was him... Malia gasped.

Lucifer fixed her with a smile.

"You see your mistake, now? I never followed you when you left New York. I remained safely aboard my saucer the whole time. And *I* am the Sphinx."

Malia didn't know what to believe anymore. She *hadn't* verified Lucifer's identity before they killed him. But she knew that whoever this person was, they could use their emitter to appear as anyone.

"Now," Lucifer continued, "I would like to provide you with a little extra motivation to reconsider our offer. We have an agent embedded in the Africa compound. And while it is not their *primary* objective, when the time is right, they will be assassinating your beloved mother and brother."

"*What*? No—you're lying. You can't have anyone there—they secured the entire compound..."

"Oh, I assure you, our agent is there. But there is a little time left before they initiate their mission. If you agree to join me as a member of the Sphinx, we will rescind the order to assassinate your family. But you must decide soon—the clock is ticking."

Malia shook her head. He was lying; he had to be.

Then again, Lucifer *had* always coerced them to cooperate by threatening violence to others. And he'd never failed to carry out his threats.

But Malia wasn't convinced that this was Lucifer—nor that they had anyone inside the Africa compound. The whole thing just seemed so unlikely.

"I will give you one hour to make your decision, Ms. Kwan," he said, then turned on his heel and strode out of the observation area.

Malia sat on the floor, letting out a long sigh. Now what?

## Chapter Twenty-seven: Jaden

Jaden was lying in his bed, staring up at the ceiling. He still felt angry about being left behind; he desperately wanted to participate in the missions and help take out the remaining Majestic compounds.

And he missed Malia. Random thoughts or memories of her kept coming up out of nowhere, driving him to tears. He tried again to reach out to her telepathically—maybe if there were some sort of afterlife, she'd be able to communicate with him. But then he felt stupid; he didn't think he believed in heaven or anything like that.

Suddenly, he heard footsteps out in the living room, distracting him from his reverie.

"Hello?" he called out, sitting up in bed.

"Hey," Melissa said with a smile as she walked into his room.

"Oh, it's only you," he replied, collapsing on his back again.

"You're such a charmer. How are you doing?"

Jaden sighed.

"This sucks. I should be out there with Salvatore and the rest of them. And... I miss Malia."

Jaden fought back the tears as he uttered his sister's name.

"I know," Melissa replied. "I miss her, too. But I've got a special project for you—one particularly suited to your skills."

"Mom, I just want to be left alone. Please."

"Alright, if you're sure that's what you want. I'll have to find someone else to interrogate the prisoner, I guess."

"What prisoner?"

"Someone they found in the compound in Asia. He claims to have total memory loss—he can't even remember his name. But he's half-Othali, and his human DNA seems to come from ancient Egypt. But don't worry—I'll see if Bastet is available."

Melissa started walking out of the room. But there was no way Jaden would pass this up—it was a chance to do *something* helpful, at least.

"Hang on," he said, getting up from the bed. "I'm coming."

Melissa shot him a sly grin as they walked out of their quarters.

When they arrived at the brig, Melissa stopped him in the corridor.

"We'd like you to try to help him remember anything—where he came from, or who he is, and why they imprisoned him. He doesn't show up in any Majestic database, but he does have neural implants, so we believe he must have been involved with them in some capacity."

"I got it, Mom."

"Also, he was wearing only a loincloth when they found him. He's fully clothed now, so you won't see it, but it looks like they tortured him—he's got burns and lacerations on his torso and legs. See if you can find out why they did that to him."

Jaden nodded.

Inside, he spotted four Othali soldiers guarding one of the cells and had no doubt that was where they were keeping the mystery prisoner. Like on the warship, the front of each cell was protected by a force field. There were two chairs positioned between the soldiers; Melissa and Jaden each sat in one.

"This is my son, Jaden," Melissa said to the prisoner. "He's going to try to help you restore your memories."

The prisoner was sitting on the edge of the cot; he looked at them and shrugged but said nothing. Jaden thought he looked bored and that his expression was smug or arrogant.

"Hey," he said. "So, you don't remember *anything*?"

"My first memory is waking up in the cell at the other place. I can recall nothing before that."

"You don't know how long you were there or why they put you in prison?"

The man shook his head.

Jaden reached out telepathically, penetrating his mind.

"*Show me the first thing you remember.*"

The man shot him a startled look, but his memory of waking up that day rose to the surface. He was suspended from the ceiling of his cell by both arms; his back and shoulders ached terribly. His injuries burned. He didn't feel like he'd slept well.

Jaden tried to probe his memories, but it was like wading through a dark sea. There was no light here at all. Malia had told him once that when Lucifer suppressed someone's memory, it was dark like this. Jaden imagined shining a searchlight, but this darkness was thick, like a black fog.

Suddenly, he caught a glimpse of something in the distance; it was like a pinprick of light. Jaden approached it, and it seemed like an island in the ocean—a lone memory in the vast emptiness. The prisoner was sitting in a room that looked like someone's bedroom. His mind felt younger somehow; Jaden guessed that he was probably about the same age that Jaden was now.

A man was sitting across from him. He looked worried about something.

"Abrax, the time has come for me to tell you where we come from."

The prisoner's name was Abrax. Jaden could sense the eager anxiety he felt at these words—as if he'd been waiting a long time for this information.

"I am not human," the man said. "And I did not come from Earth. My people are from a planet called Othal that orbits a distant sun. A long time ago, we sent a ship here to establish a colony on Earth. That colony is remembered among the humans only in legend. It was called Atlantis."

"*How* long ago was that?" Abrax asked; Jaden could feel his anticipation. It seemed like Abrax had always suspected something like this.

"More than 40,000 years ago," the man told him.

"But... how can you still be alive?"

"My people learned how to alter their genome to eliminate aging. We live forever—and so will you. The other colonists and I lived in Atlantis for millennia, including my wife."

"My mother?"

"Ah... no," his father said, looking uncomfortable with the question. "One of the colonists, a woman named Tessa Gosher, was part of a team that spent a lot of time with the rulers of ancient Egypt. The Egyptians were hungry for knowledge, and our people helped educate them in mathematics and science. Using that knowledge, they developed the skills necessary to build the pyramids.

"But Tessa became intimate with their king, a man named Ashai. Such relationships were forbidden, but she fell in love and broke the rules. Tessa bore Ashai two children. They aged very rapidly and lived less than ten years. But they developed powers..."

"Like what?" Abrax asked.

"They could communicate telepathically with each other and with my people. And they were able to move physical objects with their minds.

"After their deaths, Tessa worked with one of our geneticists, Bomani. She'd preserved genetic samples of her children, and though it took decades, they finally found a way to alter their DNA to eliminate the rapid aging.

"By that time, Ashai was an old man. And the Athenians had grown aggressive. They demanded that we supply them with our technology. Of course, we refused—they were warlike and not ready to wield such power. So, they attacked. We tried to defend our colony, but they sent a force of ten thousand men, overwhelming us by sheer force of numbers.

"Tessa fled the colony with Bomani to take the genetic material somewhere else for safekeeping. And in the end, the rest of us decided to destroy Atlantis and sink the island into the sea to prevent the Athenians from acquiring our technology.

"The Athenians went berserk, killing everyone they could find. The carnage was unimaginable. My wife died that day, as did our two adult children, along with all the other colonists. I alone survived."

"How?" asked Abrax.

"Luck. Pure luck. I clung to some debris—wood from the shattered hull of one of the Athenian ships. I stayed low in the water and submerged my head whenever they came close, searching for survivors. Eventually, they gave up and headed for home.

"I don't know how long I floated adrift at sea. But by the time I'd washed up on land, somewhere in modern-day Spain, I was emaciated and dehydrated. I would have died were it not for the villagers who found me and nursed me back to health.

"For a long time, I tried to find Tessa and Bomani. I went to Egypt, but they took me prisoner. By the time they released me, I could find no sign of my fellow colonists. I never was able to find them.

"For millennia, I roamed the Earth, living among various societies and taking on different identities. I was an engineer, so typically I worked as a builder. And I took quite a few lovers who bore many children. But they all aged quickly and died young."

"Did any of them have powers, like Tessa's children?"

"No. Not one. There must have been something unique about Tessa's DNA or Ashai's that produced their abilities. But one day, only a few decades ago, I found a woman who changed my life." The man chuckled. "It would be more accurate to say that *she* found me. I'd kept my true identity a secret for all those millennia, but this woman was special. She knew there was something different about me, and I told her the truth.

"The story of Tessa's children fascinated her. She believed that she could give me a child who would have similar powers and live forever, like my people."

"Was *she* my mother?"

"No. Abrax, the truth is that you have no mother."

"*What?*"

"Well, not in the sense that other people do. This woman speculated that King Ashai's royal heritage had supplied the unique DNA that gave Tessa's children their powers. So, she found his burial site and exhumed his mummified remains. She was able to extract enough viable genetic material to produce a child.

"The woman used advanced gene-editing techniques to combine Ashai's DNA with mine. She then found a suitable human surrogate and injected one of her eggs with the genetic sample she had created. The fertilized egg was then implanted in her uterus, and she carried the baby to term."

"Are you telling me that *I* was that baby?"

The man smiled at him.

"Yes, Abrax."

"But... I don't have powers."

"True. Yet you are still special. You are descended from an ancient line of kings, and you are the only half-Othali, half-human being alive in the entire universe. And you will live forever."

That was the end of the memory; Jaden found himself back in the dark fog of the prisoner's mind—*Abrax's* mind. He withdrew from his thoughts and explained to Melissa what he'd witnessed. Melissa stared at him in shock for a moment.

"That explains it..."

"Explains *what*?" asked Jaden.

"Nothing—when I first saw him, I thought for a second that he *was* Ashai. He bears a strong resemblance."

"So, in a way, he's my... half-brother?" asked Jaden.

"Yes, I guess you could say that," Melissa said with a frown. "I wonder who the woman was who performed the procedure to combine Ashai's DNA with his father's..."

"Hang on—do you know how old this guy is?"

"Roughly forty, why?"

"Did humans have that kind of technology back then? To edit genes and stuff?"

"Well, in vitro fertilization has been around since the 1970s, and modern gene-editing techniques first came into being in the mid-to-late-80s. So, the woman who did this must have been involved with one of those early teams—this would have been cutting-edge science at the time. I was aware of the technology back then but waited until it developed more before trying to bring you and your sister to life."

"That's pretty crazy," said Jaden. "I wonder why he doesn't have powers like us..."

"Yes, that is curious," Melissa agreed.

"It must mean that there's something special about *your* DNA, not Ashai's, right?"

Melissa considered this for a moment.

"I guess so," she said with a frown. "Jaden, what did Abrax's father look like—can you show me?"

"Sure."

Jaden reached out with his mind and penetrated Melissa's thoughts. He showed her Abrax's memory.

"I figured it had to be him," she said.

"Who?"

"Come with me," Melissa said, getting to her feet and walking out of the brig. Jaden followed her into the corridor. "Jaden, I didn't want to talk about this in front of him, but Abrax's father was Ervin Noorani—the member of the Sphinx who we killed in New York."

# Chapter Twenty-eight: Nephthys

Malia was lying on the floor of her chamber, desperately trying to think of some way out of this place, when she heard a soft buzzing sound. Sitting up, she realized the door to her cell had disappeared.

Rising quietly to her feet, she moved to the doorway. There was a corridor beyond, its walls the same gray stone as her room. The passage was narrower than the ones in the other Majestic compounds, and the ceiling was lower.

Malia crept out of her cell, keeping her eyes peeled for any sign of movement, but there was nobody out here. There was another door only ten feet or so from her room—Malia guessed that this must lead to the observation area. She tried to pass her hand through it, but it was solid, and she couldn't open it.

Reaching out with her mind, Malia realized that her powers worked now that she'd left her cell. She tried opening the door telekinetically, but it wouldn't budge. Next, she searched the area telepathically, thinking that maybe someone was using an emitter to remain invisible. But she found no one.

Malia walked farther along the corridor. It extended only about thirty feet or so before making a ninety-degree turn to the right. Keeping her back to the wall, she edged closer to the corner, fully expecting to find Lucifer or one of his hybrids waiting for her. But peering around the edge, she saw that the area was empty.

She rounded the corner and kept going, careful to be silent. What the hell was going on here? Who had let her out—and why?

Malia passed only two more doors, both solid and locked, before coming to a large storage room at the end of the corridor. It seemed like whoever had released her intended for her to go this way—the only other choice was to return to her cell.

Creeping cautiously into the room, Malia had a look around. The room was long and narrow—only a few times wider than the corridor. There were crates and barrels stacked up on one side, and shelving hosted various scientific equipment on the other. Malia scanned the room telepathically, but there was nobody here.

Suddenly, one of the barrels flew toward her head; Malia ducked in the nick of time. But as she straightened up, two more barrels came flying—reaching out with her mind, she stopped them in midair.

As she continued through the room, something shot off the shelf, hitting her in the shoulder and knocking her to her knees. Malia yelped in pain. Regaining her feet, she searched the area telepathically again but couldn't find anyone. She ran to the far corridor; one more barrel flew at her as she went, but she knocked it aside with her mind.

Around the next corner, Malia found two more locked rooms and then an open doorway. Creeping up to the opening, she peered through it. This was a hangar bay. It was much smaller than the ones she'd seen in the other Majestic compounds and hosted only one flying saucer. Beyond the doorway, observation windows provided a view of the hangar bay from the corridor.

Malia stepped inside, quickly scanning the area visually and telepathically. It seemed to be empty. She walked across the room, staying alert, and approached the saucer. Maybe she could get her implants to link to it... How had Jaden done it? Malia focused on the holographic images in her vision and chose the saucer icon. Suddenly a red outline formed around the edges of the saucer, and the word "Link?" appeared above it.

Malia's heart jumped into her throat. Could this actually work?

"Yes," she thought, almost leaping with anticipation.

But then the red outline around the saucer flashed twice, and the words "Access denied" appeared above it.

"Damn!"

"Surely, you didn't think I'd allow you to take my only saucer?" a voice drawled from behind her.

Startled, Malia turned but couldn't see anyone. The voice was Lucifer's; she was sure of it. She was about to search for him telepathically when some unseen force slammed her back against the wall, ten feet off the ground.

How was this possible?

*Anything is possible when you put your mind to it, Ms. Kwan.*

Lucifer had penetrated her mind. Malia expelled him but suddenly felt terrified—he was using telepathy and telekinesis against her. This shouldn't have been possible—he hadn't had these powers before.

She reached out telepathically and found Lucifer standing in the doorway. Penetrating his mind, she forced him to become visible before he could react. It worked, but he immediately ejected her from his head.

Malia fought his telekinesis, trying to counteract it with her own. Her body started to vibrate, and she recalled the time she and Jaden had battled for control of a boulder—that had shattered under the stress. She put more power into it and slowly began moving to the floor, but felt like the strain was physically pulling her apart.

This wasn't going to work—her body was going to break before she reached the floor. Malia's heart was beating a mile a minute; she could feel the adrenaline pumping in her veins. She was about to reach out telekinetically to throw Lucifer across the room when the realization hit her: she still couldn't tap into the Earth's magnetic field, despite being outside her cell's shielding. What the hell was going on here?

Suddenly, Lucifer let her go. Malia dropped the last few feet to the floor, stumbled a couple of steps, and then recovered her balance.

"How the hell did you do that?" she demanded. "You only had our healing powers before!"

Lucifer gave her a serene smile—nothing like his usual smirk. Then he transformed, and moments later, it was Durga standing there.

"Osiris is dead. But he brought me your DNA after injecting himself with it. And while it gave him only limited abilities, it conferred your full powers upon me, as you have now seen."

Malia was stunned; she had come to count on being the only one other than Jaden who possessed telepathy and telekinesis. If it worked on this Durga—or whoever she was—might it yet work on the hybrids? Had they tried it on them?

"So, Lucifer wasn't part of the Sphinx, after all? It was just you and Noorani?"

"There is one more," Durga replied with her smile, moving toward Malia now. "Osiris could have become a member at any time, had he wished. But he had no interest. No, Osiris shied away from that kind of leadership position. He preferred the independence that running his own compound afforded him.

Malia started walking around the far side of the saucer, trying to keep her distance from Durga.

"Then who else is part of the Sphinx?"

"Osiris was my lover," Durga said, ignoring her question and frowning for the first time. "And you took him away from me; you murdered him in cold blood. For that, you will pay, *Nephthys*."

Malia and Durga continued circling each other, the saucer between them, floating only a few feet above their heads.

"But you offered to make me a part of the Sphinx," Malia said.

"I'm afraid that was only a ruse," Durga replied, her smile returning. "Osiris told me you would never join us, but I wanted to find out for myself."

"So, you were lying about having an agent inside the Africa compound, too."

"Oh, no, I'm afraid that part is true. And they will murder your family to avenge my lover's death, and then you will know the depths of sorrow that you have inflicted on me."

Malia felt a stab of panic imagining Jaden and Melissa dying at the hands of a Majestic assassin. She was trapped here, with no way to escape or even to warn them...

"Why not just kill me? I'm the one who took Lucifer away from you—they had nothing to do with it!"

"An eye for an eye, young one. Killing you would not be just—you didn't kill me. No, you must live so you can endure the same pain that I have."

Malia was now on the side of the saucer closest to the door. She didn't see any other way out of the hangar, so she turned and ran out of the room and down the corridor. Though she heard no footsteps, she felt certain Durga was coming after her.

Running through the passages, Malia stopped to try every door again but could not get through them. Why couldn't she tap into the magnetic field here? Once she reached the storage area, she stopped, searching frantically for a place to hide.

But the room was so small; her options were limited. Finally, she ducked behind a stack of barrels. Reaching out with her mind, she monitored the corridor telepathically, waiting for Durga to approach.

Minutes went by, and nothing happened. Malia couldn't help thinking of Jaden and their mother, imagining the assassin murdering them in their sleep. Tears came to her eyes as she once again tried to think of how she could get out of this place or get a warning to someone at the compound.

Something pricked the very edge of Malia's awareness. It had to be Durga—she'd seen no one else here. Seemingly of its own accord, a plan suddenly formed in Malia's mind. If she could knock Durga unconscious, then she should be able to take her emitter and use her implants to access it. There had to be a scanner around here somewhere—then she could use that to get the woman's bioscan. With that, she could replace her—and then she should be able to access the compound's control systems to get a warning to her people. And she would be able to access the saucer, too... although the thought of flying that without any training was highly intimidating.

There she was, again—Durga was coming closer, now. Malia penetrated her mind, but Durga was ready for her. Before Malia could extinguish her consciousness, the woman expelled her from her mind. She was much more powerful than Lucifer had been.

Suddenly, Durga entered Malia's mind.

*"I do enjoy games, Nephthys, but I'm afraid you are no match for me."*

Malia ejected her from her mind, but it was too late.

"Ah, yes, that is a clever plan. Acquiring my emitter would indeed provide you with a means of escape. But I will never let you have it."

Malia couldn't see her, but judging by the sound of her voice, Durga had to be in the storage room now. Reaching out with her mind, Malia focused as hard as she could, then hurled every barrel and crate at the source of the sound. It all landed with a deafening crash, blocking access to the room in that direction.

Searching the area telepathically, Malia tried to locate Durga. If she could get in her head while she was stunned, then maybe she could knock her out before Durga expelled her. But Malia couldn't find her.

Emerging cautiously from her hiding place, Malia crept toward the pile of debris. She didn't see anyone underneath it, but Durga might still be invisible. Searching telepathically again, she still couldn't find her.

Suddenly, Malia felt an arm circle around her neck, pulling her back.

"Looking for me?" Durga's voice said in her ear.

Malia grabbed the woman's arm, trying to break free. But a moment later, she felt something prick her neck. Malia tried to penetrate her mind, but the sedative hit her system, and it took every ounce of concentration to stay awake.

Durga released her. As Malia turned, Durga became visible, flashing Malia her serene smile.

"Time to sleep, Nephthys."

Malia fought with all her might to remove the sedative from her bloodstream, but it was too much. The edges of her vision went black, and she fell to her knees, struggling to remain conscious. But it was no use: a moment later, everything went black.

# Chapter Twenty-nine: Hathor

Hathor set a course for Majestic's Australia compound, located in the mountains in the southeastern region of the continent. Upon arrival, she commenced her scans to find the hangar bay doors. There they were—embedded in the side of a cliff face. She set her vessel to hover a hundred meters out. Salvatore and Venus took up flanking positions, and they awaited the Othali warship.

But moments later, the hangar bay doors opened. Scanning beams flooded the area, and before Hathor could react, three saucers emerged, firing on her ship. They hit her with a volley of laser blasts, knocking her shield output down to twenty percent.

Hathor took off into the sky, but the three enemy vessels pursued. She returned fire, but their next round of shots took out her shields. Hathor engaged in evasive maneuvers but couldn't shake them.

"This is Hathor—I'm in trouble," she told the others through her implants.

"We're in pursuit," Salvatore told her.

But a moment later, another round of fire damaged her engines; output was down to fifteen percent. Finally, Salvatore and Venus fired on the enemy, and they fled. Hathor scanned the area looking for a place to unload the soldiers before she lost the engines completely.

There—she spotted an open space by a lake in central Tasmania.

Hathor navigated the ship into position and ordered the soldiers to disembark. But as the last of them left the ship, her engines failed. Firing thrusters, Hathor managed to steer the vessel away from the Othali below, but it crashed into the lake.

Inertial dampers had failed; the impact threw Hathor out of her seat in the cockpit. Internal controls were still functional; she dropped to the main level and then into the airlock. Taking a deep breath, she opened the portal. Water filled the chamber. Hathor swam out of the ship, cleared the saucer's edge, and headed up to the surface. Floating for a moment to catch her breath, Hathor spotted Salvatore swimming toward her.

"Are you alright?" he asked when he reached her.

"I'm fine. Let's get to shore."

Once they'd made it back to land, Salvatore said, "Venus is getting your soldiers onto the other two saucers. They'll be quite cramped, but I'd prefer not to leave them here. We'll leave your saucer here for now, then come back for it once we're finished with the compound."

Hathor nodded. She followed Salvatore to his ship; they boarded and moved up to the cockpit.

"They were ready for us, this time," Hathor noted.

"That's not too surprising," Salvatore replied. "Once we'd taken out Europe and Asia, they had to know we were coming for the rest."

They flew back to the compound. The Othali ship was in position, but the hangar bay doors were undamaged and left open.

"Strange," said Salvatore. "It seems they abandoned the compound. The warship reports that it has been maintaining an active scan since its arrival, but no other vessels have entered the area."

"It could be a trap," Hathor suggested.

"Perhaps," Salvatore agreed. "The compound's shields are inactive—scans show eighteen human life signs, but no hybrids."

"What about explosives? They could be planning to lure us in, then blow the place once we're inside."

"I'm not showing any."

"There could still be hybrids using their emitters to remain invisible—they wouldn't show up on our scans that way."

Salvatore nodded.

"We'll have to implement active scans once we're inside."

Salvatore and Venus moved their saucers into the hangar bay. Salvatore flooded the area with active scanning beams, but there was nobody here. Once the soldiers had disembarked, Hathor dropped to the flight deck with Salvatore. They assigned a team of soldiers to keep the hangar bay secure, then moved into the corridor.

"With the commander gone, we won't be able to gain access to the command systems," Salvatore observed.

"I'm connecting now—they wiped everything. The data's gone, and they removed the security."

Venus took half of the soldiers and moved down to level two. Hathor and Salvatore took the rest and went to work clearing the first level room by room. Hathor checked the command center, but the area was empty. They secured the rest of the level, posting guards by the entry points, and then moved down to the third floor.

By the time they'd reached abductee processing, they still hadn't encountered any hybrids. They went to work reviving and evacuating the humans. But as Hathor got to the elevator and opened the doors, laser blasts hit the group before she could run her scan. She flattened herself against the wall, firing her plasma cannon into the elevator. A hybrid became visible as she hit the floor.

Hathor scanned the carriage—it was empty, now. But checking the corridor, she spotted a second hybrid running into one of the abductee chambers. Hathor ran to the room, using her emitter to go invisible. Stepping inside, she found one human and two Othali soldiers passed out on the floor. She raised her scanner, but a laser blast hit her in the chest before she could activate it.

Hathor fell, struggling to remain conscious. She felt the hybrid moving past her legs and fired her plasma cannon, but the shot hit the ceiling.

"Salvatore, this is Hathor," she said through her emitters, her vision going black around the edges. "We've got one hybrid running loose in abductee processing."

"I'm on it."

Hathor lay on the floor, breathing deeply. Slowly, her vision cleared, and her strength returned. Regaining her feet, she went to check on the soldiers and the abductee. They were out cold. She managed to revive one of the soldiers, then moved out to the corridor. Soldiers were escorting the last of the humans to the elevator. Hathor grabbed three soldiers and instructed them to take care of the people in the room.

Moving toward the access tunnel, Hathor ran into Salvatore.

"Are you alright?" he asked.

"A little dizzy. Did you find the hybrid?"

"Yes, I took care of her," he replied, patting his plasma cannon.

Once they'd cleared the rest of the facility and moved the humans up to the saucers, Hathor went with Salvatore down to the bottom level. They planted two fusion grenades, then returned to the hangar bay.

Boarding Salvatore's saucer, they moved up to the cockpit. They followed Venus out of the hangar bay and retreated to a safe distance, and then Salvatore detonated the fusion grenades. A mushroom cloud erupted high into the sky.

"One more compound," Hathor observed.

Salvatore nodded.

"We'll drop off the humans at our compound and then head to South America. But I'd like Melissa to give you a quick check-up while we're there."

"That won't be necessary," said Hathor. "I'm fine."

"You crashed earlier and then took a laser blast. Humor me."

Hathor knew any further resistance would be futile; Salvatore was a very stubborn man.

# Chapter Thirty: Jaden

"So, this Abrax guy is the Sphinx's son?" said Jaden.

"Apparently," Melissa replied. "Jaden, if that's so, then he must have known who else is part of the Sphinx. Can you see if you can find anything about that?"

"I'll try, but someone suppressed his memories. It's like everything's dark in his head—Lucifer did this to some people we met in his compound."

"Something's not right," Melissa said with a frown. "I don't understand why they would do this to the Sphinx's son—or why they'd take him prisoner and torture him."

"Well, I'll see what else I can find. But it's gonna be tough."

Just then, Salvatore emerged from the access tunnel and walked over to them.

"Melissa, Hathor took a laser blast at close range as we were clearing the Australia compound. Could you take a look at her before we head out again? She insists she's fine, but I'd like to be sure."

"Yes, of course," Melissa replied.

"Thank you. How is it going with our prisoner?"

They brought him up to speed with what they'd found out so far.

"This is intriguing. I am eager to hear more."

"If you don't mind staying here with Jaden, he can continue while I look in on Hathor."

"Yes, of course."

Melissa headed off to the medical bay, and Jaden went back into the brig with Salvatore. They took the two seats facing the cell.

"Hey," Jaden said to Abrax, who was still sitting on the edge of his cot. "I'm gonna try to find more memories, alright?"

Abrax nodded. Jaden penetrated his mind, once again finding everything veiled behind a thick fog. He returned to the memory he'd seen before and focused on surfacing anything else that had to do with the Sphinx.

He heard faint sounds, like echoes of Noorani's voice. And fleeting images of his face flashed by, along with visions of a woman Jaden didn't recognize. But no matter how hard Jaden concentrated, he couldn't get the memories to surface.

Jaden had an idea. Focusing inside himself for a moment, he stimulated his adrenal glands. Within moments, he felt his heartbeat accelerate. Returning to Abrax's mind, he imagined shining a searchlight into the darkness, tapping into the Earth's magnetic field to channel as much power into the process as he could.

Finally, he found another memory floating up to the surface. Focusing on it, Jaden tried to immerse himself into the images. It worked. He was sitting in the cockpit of a flying saucer, and through the windows, he could see the Giza pyramid complex. Abrax's mind felt older now—this had to be at least a few years later than the previous memory. Jaden noted that sitting in the saucer felt commonplace to Abrax. And he had the neural implants this time; Jaden could see the familiar symbols around the periphery of his vision. Noorani was sitting across from Abrax.

"What are we doing here?" Abrax demanded.

"I told you that it was time for you to meet my partner," Noorani replied. "And this is where we will find her."

"Oshun lives in the Great Pyramid?" Abrax asked skeptically.

Noorani moved down to the main level without answering. Abrax followed him down to the airlock.

"We'll need to go invisible before we descend," Noorani told him.

Abrax accessed his emitter and activated his shield. His father vanished, his outline visible in red thanks to the implants. They dropped to the desert floor, landing near the front of the Great Sphinx. Noorani led him around behind the monument, walking toward the pyramids. But he stopped halfway there.

"Follow me," he said, suddenly stepping forward and disappearing into the ground.

It looked like there was nothing but sand, but Abrax knew this had to be a hologram. Stepping forward, he dropped into a long shaft, his descent controlled by a gravitational beam. Reaching the bottom, he found himself standing in a narrow tunnel.

"What is this place?" Abrax asked. "And how do you keep the humans from finding the portal?"

"The hologram covering the entry remains solid to anyone not wearing an emitter," Noorani explained, ignoring his first question.

Abrax followed him through the tunnel. Unless his sense of

direction was failing him, he was pretty sure they were moving *beneath* the Great Sphinx. Finally, they emerged into a large stone chamber. The walls were bare, and the room was empty except for two stone benches. There was a metallic door across from the tunnel entry.

"We're under the Sphinx?" asked Abrax.

"Yes," Noorani replied, deactivating his emitter. Abrax went visible, too. "Legend has it that there was a vast 'Hall of Records' beneath the monument that the people of Atlantis used to store important documents. Nonsense, of course; my people stored their data electronically. But they did use this chamber to house computer equipment. It was removed before the Athenians destroyed our colony."

"And we're meeting Oshun *here*?"

"This is only the antechamber. We'll be meeting her inside. But first, I wanted to tell you a little more about how *I* first met her."

Jaden could sense that Abrax had always been curious about this and felt his anticipation.

"I lived in the United States at the time, in a log cabin up in the Colorado Rockies, far away from anyone else. One night, I was driving home when I noticed a bright light in the sky. It wasn't an airplane, but it was following me. Even when I turned off the main road to go up my driveway, it stayed with me."

"Was it a flying saucer?" asked Abrax. "Like ours?"

"That's what it looked like, but I had never seen one before that day. My engine died, so I got out of the car and started running toward the house. But then a bright light shone down on me, and I found myself rising inside the craft. I lost consciousness, and when I awoke, I was inside a dark room, lying on an exam table.

"A man was looking over me, wearing a black suit and tie and sunglasses. He asked me where I was from. I told him that I'd moved there from New York a few years earlier, which was true. But he knew."

"He knew you weren't from Earth?"

"Yes. I told him about Othal and Atlantis. And he said that he needed to take me to his leader. They knocked me out again, and I woke up here, in this very chamber. The man in black escorted me inside, and I met Oshun."

"And she helped you create me," said Abrax.

"Yes. She was fascinated by the powers Tessa Gosher's children possessed and was eager to see if we could produce a being with those abilities. And she was also interested in acquiring Othali technology. We lost everything when we destroyed the colony, but I was an engineer, and I still possessed my knowledge. Oshun offered to make me a full partner in her organization if I agreed to help her create you and work with her to improve their technology. I agreed.

"The rest of the organization knows us only as the 'Sphinx.' None of them know our true identities."

Abrax knew that his father worked with Oshun but didn't know what they did and had never heard this part of the story before. Noorani had always been highly secretive about his work.

"Father, does your organization abduct people as they did with you? What is the purpose of that?"

"I'm going to allow Oshun to explain that to you," Noorani replied with a grin.

"Why can't *you* tell me?"

Noorani did not answer; he strode across the room and walked through the metal door. Abrax followed him. There was another tunnel here; they walked past several doors, finally entering a large chamber at the end of the passage. Ornate tapestries hung from the walls, and thick carpets covered the floor. Across the room, a Black woman was reclining on a bed of plush cushions.

"Oshun, this is my son, Abrax," said Noorani.

"Greetings," said Oshun, flashing Abrax a smile. Her skin was somewhat darker than Abrax's or Noorani's, and her head was bald. "Please, lie here next to me."

Abrax felt uncomfortable but did as she asked. As he lay back on the cushions, Oshun turned to face him. Noorani stood close by.

"Now that you have grown into manhood, your father and I would like you to work for our organization. However, I wanted to meet you first."

Oshun reached out to touch his forehead. But at that moment, the memory ended abruptly, and everything went black.

Jaden withdrew from Abrax's mind. He walked out to the corridor with Salvatore and told him what he'd witnessed.

"The memory ended there?" asked Salvatore. Jaden nodded. "We'll need to pay a visit to the Great Sphinx before we proceed to South America. But first, let's see if you can find out anything else. I have a suspicion, but I'd like more information about Oshun before we go."

"I'll see what I can do," Jaden said with a sigh. "But I'm not making any promises. His brain is fried—whoever did this to him did *not* want us to see any of this."

"Understood," Salvatore replied.

They returned to Abrax's cell and retook their seats.

"You need more memories?" Abrax asked warily.

"Uh, yeah, we do," Jaden replied. "Sorry about this."

Jaden penetrated his mind again. He sought any recollections that included Oshun, but Abrax's mind remained stubbornly dark. Instead, he tried searching for any other visits to the Great Sphinx. Glimpses of another encounter flashed in Abrax's mind along with faint echoes of Oshun's voice.

As before, Jaden drew power from the Earth's magnetic field and channeled it through his mind, forcing the memory to the surface. Finally, the images became stronger. Abrax was sitting in the control center of a Majestic stronghold. Jaden could sense that this was Africa—the very compound they were in now—and that Abrax was the commander. Abrax's mind felt somewhat older than it had last time, but this was still many years in the past.

Abrax received a message from the Sphinx through his implants. It was a summons. In the entire organization, only he and one other knew their identities. Abrax had kept their secret, as promised, but had not seen Oshun since their first meeting. What could this possibly be about?

He strode out of the command center and made his way up to the hangar bay. Once on board his saucer, he flew out of the compound and traveled to the Great Sphinx. He disembarked and entered the underground complex through the hidden tunnel. Inside, he found Oshun and his father in the reception chamber, reclining on their cushions, wearing their headdresses. Abrax took a knee before them.

"At your service, Your Majesties."

"Rise, Abrax," Oshun said, her tone giving no hint of her mood.

Abrax stood up, facing the two of them, his hands clasped behind his back. Apprehension rose within him, but he forced his features to remain impassive.

"You have done well," Oshun told him with a serene smile. "We gave you command of our most important facility, and you rose to the challenge. But there has been a development, and it is time to alter your role in the organization accordingly."

"Yes, ma'am," Abrax replied.

"The humans have made a discovery," Noorani told him. "They have found something I sought for many years."

"Sir?"

"We knew that Tessa Gosher fled Atlantis to take her children's DNA somewhere for safekeeping but could not determine the location. It turns out that she hid it inside a secret chamber beneath the Great Pyramid."

Abrax was stunned. He knew how desperately Oshun wished to acquire that material.

"Have you been able to acquire the samples?"

"We have chosen not to do so," said Oshun. "Osiris believes it would be best to let the humans bring these beings to life, and we agree."

Abrax felt himself flush with anger. They had reached the crux of the problem: Abrax had failed to learn of the humans' discovery, despite its location in *his* territory. Somehow, Osiris had managed to outshine him.

"Respectfully, Your Majesties, I do not see why we should allow the humans to carry out something so important. Allow me to retrieve—"

"These beings will be half-Othali, half-human, just like you, my son," said Noorani. "We do not believe our hybrids are compatible. These beings require a *human* surrogate to bring them to life. We will not allow any vile human to live among our people, so the humans must be the ones to do this."

"Fear not, Abrax," Oshun added. "Osiris will monitor their progress. If these beings manifest the same powers as Tessa Gosher's first set of children, we will acquire them when the time is right."

Osiris again.

"Yes, ma'am," Abrax said, bowing his head. "I apologize for failing Your Majesties."

"Failing us?" said Noorani, sounding puzzled. "How so, son?"

"I am in command on this continent; I should have been the one to learn of this discovery, not Osiris."

"Nonsense," Oshun replied. "It was an American team that found the chamber, and they kept the details of its contents to themselves. That placed the find within Osiris's jurisdiction.

"On the contrary," she continued with a smile, "you have served us admirably. And we feel that the time has come for you to assume your true calling."

"Ma'am?" said Abrax, confused now.

"You are descended from kings, son," said Noorani. "We would like you to join us as an equal member of the Sphinx. You have proven your mettle in leading our largest compound. Now it is time for you to take on the mantle of leadership for all of Majestic."

"Will you join us, Abrax?" asked Oshun.

Abrax felt overwhelmed with emotion. He had secretly hoped this might happen one day but had never dared to expect it. He took a knee once more.

"Your Majesties, you honor me. I humbly accept."

"Rise, Abrax," Oshun said with a grin. "You are one of us now; you kneel to no one."

"Thank you," he replied, regaining his feet. A bold impulse overcame him. "Might I know, now, where you come from? You have told me that you are not from this Earth, and though you resemble the Othali, I know that you are not one of them, either."

Oshun regarded him in silence for a few moments but continued to smile.

"Yes," she said finally. "You have earned the right to know the truth."

As Abrax watched, Oshun's appearance changed. Long black hair flowed from her head; her pupils became slits like a cat's, and her skin grew scales. Angry red scars appeared, starting on one side of her face, trailing down her neck, and disappearing below the collar of her robe.

"You are from Mars? But how can that be—I thought Osiris's brothers and sisters betrayed him? How did you come to be a part of Majestic?"

"Who do you think *created* Majestic?" she said, removing her emitter as if to show him that this was her true form. "I am Isis, the mother of our people, as Osiris is their father."

For a moment, Abrax was speechless. Isis was a figure of legend in the organization. But...

"I was told that the others murdered you—that Osiris assassinated three of them to avenge your death and that he hunts the others to this day?"

"They left me for dead; that much is true," she replied. "And though he has regretted it ever since, even Osiris believed me to be dead. He took me to a place he thought would be my tomb.

"But somehow, the smallest kernel of life persisted inside me. Though my heart had stopped, the life force within me refused to die. When I awoke, I was cold and alone. And death indeed would have taken me had I not summoned Osiris to me. He returned and nursed me back to health.

"And until this day, only your father and he have known that I still live."

Abrax considered everything she had told him.

"How did you survive when everyone thought you dead?"

"Long have I pondered that very question, and there can be only one answer: I am a god, as are you and your father and Osiris. And gods cannot die."

"But I thought your people were mortal?"

"True, the others are. But Osiris and I have altered our genomes. We will live forever, like you and your father. And together, we are ushering forth a new civilization to live on Earth and restore it to its true glory."

Abrax heard her words, and though they sounded fantastical, he knew them to be true. They were immortal and creating a new people. Truly they were gods.

Abrax's memory ended there, and everything went dark again. Jaden withdrew from his mind, backing away from the cell. Abrax was smirking at him now; Jaden knew that he still retained the memory he'd witnessed.

"Uh... we need to talk," Jaden said to Salvatore. They returned to the corridor, and Jaden told him what he'd seen and heard. Salvatore's expression grew graver with every word.

"You are certain it was Isis?" he asked. "It wasn't simply another holographic projection?"

"She removed her emitter," Jaden told him again. "It was her, man. I saw Isis."

"Can you show me?"

Jaden nodded. Reaching out with his mind, he showed Salvatore the woman he'd seen.

"Yes. That is Isis," said Salvatore, taking a deep breath. "And we are holding a member of the Sphinx in our brig."

"This is crazy," Jaden replied. "What the hell happened with them—why did they put him in prison and torture him?"

"I do not know, but neither do I trust this," said Salvatore. "For now, I want you to stay out of the brig. I must take the others and go to the Great Sphinx."

# Chapter Thirty-one: Salvatore

Salvatore headed up to the medical bay and asked Venus to meet him there. Melissa was just finishing with Hathor when he arrived; Venus walked in moments later.

"How's our patient?" Salvatore asked.

"She's in good shape," Melissa replied. "I would recommend some rest after trauma of this nature, but—"

"No time for that," said Hathor.

"Indeed," Salvatore replied. "We need to add an emergency stop to our itinerary."

"Oh?" said Venus.

Salvatore told them what Jaden had seen in Abrax's memory.

"That's impossible," Venus said when he was done, waving her hand dismissively. "Isis cannot be alive—we stunned her with a blaster, stabbed her in the heart, and tossed her off a cliff."

"I know," Salvatore replied with a sigh. "I'm the one who stabbed her."

"But our scans confirmed she was dead!" said Hathor. "They must have planted this memory in the prisoner's brain somehow. It cannot be."

Salvatore shrugged.

"Jaden showed me his memory of her. It was Isis."

"Well, we should certainly pay a visit to the Great Sphinx, regardless," said Venus. "And whoever the Sphinx might be, we need to capture them alive and download the data from their system. As much as I'd prefer to skip all of that and blow the place off the map..."

"Yes, agreed," Salvatore replied. "And if they do have another chariot in service, there's a good chance we're going to encounter it there. I'll notify the warship that there's been a change in plans. We should depart immediately."

Salvatore went up to the hangar bay with Venus and Hathor, and Hathor linked to a new saucer. Once they'd boarded their ships with their soldiers, they left the compound and headed to the Great Sphinx. The trip took very little time.

Upon arrival, Salvatore flooded the area with active scanning beams but detected no enemy vessels. Next, he scanned the space beneath the Great Sphinx. He'd expected the site to be shielded, but it was not. There was indeed a tunnel complex down there, but no life signs or energy emissions of any kind.

"This is Salvatore," he said to the others through his implants. "I've completed my scans, but I'm not showing any evidence of Majestic activity here."

"We should still go down and check it out in person," Venus suggested.

"Agreed," said Salvatore. "I'll go with an armed escort. The rest of you should remain on your ships in case this is some sort of trap."

"What about the tourists?" asked Hathor.

"They're in for a show," Salvatore replied.

Salvatore dropped to the main level, collected his plasma cannon and scanner, gathered three Othali soldiers, and descended to the desert floor behind the Great Sphinx. Some of the humans in the area spotted them and took photos of them with their phones. Salvatore ignored them. He scanned the ground between the monument and the pyramids but found no access tunnel and no holographic projection to indicate where the entry might be.

Checking the scans from his saucer, Salvatore found what looked like an access tunnel with an entry point on the top of the monument. He flew up to the top of the Great Sphinx and remotely accessed his saucer's gravitational beam to move the soldiers up with him.

Behind the head, Salvatore found a metal hatch; his scans indicated there was a shaft beneath it. The hatch was locked—it appeared that this was something added to the structure very recently. Salvatore hoisted his plasma cannon onto his shoulder and blasted the hatch out of the way.

Inside was a shaft barely wide enough for a man to pass. There was some sort of blockage partway down, roughly level with the ground. But his scans showed that the passage did continue beyond that. Salvatore aimed his cannon into the shaft and fired to clear the obstruction. He stationed one of the soldiers to stand guard at the opening and then dropped into the passage. It was narrow enough for the other two soldiers to clamber down behind him.

Salvatore reached the bottom; it was utterly dark here, and he had to shine a light to see anything. He found himself standing in a low stone chamber, with a tunnel extending in one direction. Once the soldiers had reached the bottom, they proceeded into the tunnel.

The passage sloped gently downward. At the bottom, they came to a much larger space. Salvatore scanned the entire area, but there was nobody here and no technology. Moving through the complex, they found half a dozen chambers of varying sizes connected by tunnels. But the entire thing was empty.

More than that, Salvatore could find no evidence of any activity here in an extremely long time. They might have been the first people to enter this complex in thousands of years. Salvatore contacted Venus, Hathor, and the warship to let them know what they'd found.

"So you're telling me the Sphinx was *never* here?" asked Venus.

"Correct."

"If anyone were operating there, they'd have to have some sort of power supply," said Hathor. "Hang on a moment." After a pause, she added, "I'm not detecting any kind of geothermal system or power lines leading to the complex."

"Majestic must have implanted those memories in our prisoner's mind, somehow," said Salvatore.

"Or altered them," Hathor pointed out. "It's possible the content was real, but they changed the location."

"This is disappointing," said Salvatore. "We're returning to the surface."

Salvatore returned to the entry chamber with the soldiers. He positioned his saucer directly above the shaft, then engaged the gravitational beam to take them back up to the ship. Once on board, he moved up to the cockpit. Accessing the control system for their satellites, he positioned one in geosynchronous orbit directly above the Giza complex and set it to record all activity here. He did not believe Majestic was utilizing this complex, but now they'd have conclusive evidence if they were.

# Chapter Thirty-two: Hathor

Hathor set a course for the South America compound. Majestic had constructed it in the Andes mountains of Argentina, not far from the border with Chile. She engaged her engines, then sat back, staring out the cockpit windows.

Initially, word of Isis's survival had rocked Hathor to her core. She'd watched the woman die and had had no reason to question that death since. Isis had revealed herself to be a megalomaniac when she unveiled her plan for the global conquest of Earth. And now that Hathor reflected on the matter, Majestic's extermination plan did seem like it could be Isis's brainchild. Isis being the Sphinx *made sense*. Hathor had tried for years to identify Majestic's leaders with no success whatsoever. Discovering Noorani had surprised her—she'd never had any reason to suspect another Othali colonist had survived the destruction of Atlantis.

But Isis *shouldn't* have surprised her. They were using her DNA and Lucifer's to create all the hybrids. That seemed like precisely the kind of thing Isis would do. Creating an entirely new species in her image? Yes, this had Isis's fingerprints all over it. Hathor should have seen this earlier.

And yet now their failure to find any evidence that Isis had ever operated beneath the Great Sphinx called the legitimacy of the prisoner's memory into question. Perhaps they'd simply altered the location of the memory to throw them off. They certainly would have expected that Jaden would use his powers to interrogate the prisoner. Could they have altered the Sphinx's identity as well?

If it *wasn't* Isis, then who else could it be? Hathor could think of no one else who fit the bill as well as she.

When they arrived at the South America compound, Salvatore ran his active scans but detected no other ships in the area. The Othali warship moved into position and destroyed the blast doors. Hathor guided her saucer into the hangar bay right behind Salvatore's and Venus's. There were no hybrids in the area, although scans did show far more life signs inside the compound than she would have expected. Hathor disembarked with the soldiers and met up with Salvatore and Venus.

"No greeting committee, this time," Venus noted.

"And no saucers," Salvatore added, "which is quite odd. Based on the number of hybrids inside, I would speculate that this is where they took the personnel from the Australia compound."

"The personnel, but not the saucers?" said Hathor.

Just then, they received a signal from the Othali.

"This is the warship. We are under attack. Six enemy saucers arrived and engaged us at point-blank range."

"Do you require assistance?" asked Salvatore.

"Negative. Commander Anhur just wanted to apprise you of the situation."

"Understood," Salvatore replied through his implants. "Let's proceed," he added out loud to Venus and Hathor.

But at that moment, two of the enemy saucers flew into the hangar bay and opened fire on the soldiers. At the same time, dozens upon dozens of hybrids disembarked from the ships. Hathor accessed her saucer and fired its weapons at the newcomers, as did Salvatore and Venus. But once the enemy ships had unloaded their passengers, they took off again.

An intense firefight broke out between the Othali soldiers and the hybrids. Salvatore flooded the hangar bay with active scanning beams to make sure any invisible hybrids could be seen. Venus ordered half of her team to establish a blockade at the entrance to the corridor to make sure the hybrids inside couldn't come to the aid of those in the hangar bay.

The hybrids could fly, and soon, the air was full of them as they tried to gain superior positions on their Othali opponents. But the soldiers formed knots of three or four, standing back to back to defend against attackers from any angle. Hathor, Salvatore, and Venus formed a knot of their own, picking off hybrids with their plasma cannons.

For several minutes, chaos reigned, and it seemed for a time that the hybrids would overwhelm them. But they managed to turn the tide, and some of the hybrids fled, flying out the ruins of the hangar bay doors. The ones who remained refused to surrender, and they ended up killing every last one of them. But the battle had cost them dearly: they'd lost more than half of the Othali soldiers.

Salvatore checked in with the warship. They reported that they'd destroyed two of the enemy saucers, and the other four disengaged and disappeared.

"They didn't stick around to assist their people here?" said Hathor.

"They'll be back," Venus replied. "It would seem they're making their last stand here. We need to move."

"Agreed," said Salvatore.

They assigned twice as many troops as usual to keep the hangar secure and then proceeded into the compound with the rest. Salvatore and Venus headed down to the lower levels. Hathor took a group of soldiers to the command center. The commander was a man named Levar; Hathor brought up his bio on her implants and studied his photo.

But when they reached the command center, they found that the door was inoperative—they couldn't get through. One of the soldiers blew a hole through it with his plasma cannon.

Laser fire greeted them through the opening; it hit two of the soldiers before they could get out of the way. The other soldiers returned fire through the door before climbing through. Hathor assigned two men to guard the entry, then followed the others in. A couple of dozen hybrids had holed up in here; Hathor checked their faces as she fired her plasma cannon but did not see the commander among them.

Levar could be using his emitter to remain invisible, but Hathor had no chance to use her scanner with the barrage of weapons fire. Instead, she planted herself in the doorway—at least this way, he'd have to go through her to leave the room.

Suddenly, a laser blast hit Hathor in the leg. She hit the floor, screaming in pain, but had no trouble staying alert. An instant later, she felt something hit her foot but saw nothing. She suspected someone invisible had gone by. Scrambling to her feet and favoring her injured leg, she stumbled back into the corridor. The soldiers she'd stationed out here were unconscious on the floor. Pulling out her scanner, Hathor checked the area. Someone was moving toward the elevator.

Hathor took to the air, flying down the corridor and firing her plasma cannon as she moved. A man's voice yelped in pain, and there was a crashing sound just as the elevator doors opened. Hathor flew into the elevator, smashing into whoever this was. Invisible hands grabbed her weapon, wrenching it out of her grasp, and then a fist connected with her jaw.

Hathor saw stars but grabbed onto the man and slammed him to the floor. Straddling him, she held onto his shoulder with one hand and punched him repeatedly in the head with the other. Finally, she knocked him unconscious, and he became visible. This was the commander.

Hathor pulled out her scanner and ran a full bio-scan. Then she extended her claws and stabbed him through the heart.

Getting to her feet, she found the elevator door was still open.

She hobbled back toward the command center, taking on Levar's appearance as she moved. Interfacing with the control system, she assigned herself, Salvatore, and Venus command-level access. Next, she returned to her true appearance and locked out Levar and his people. Then she contacted Salvatore and Venus to let them know they had control. Returning to the command center, she found that the soldiers had taken out the hybrids and secured the area. Salvatore's voice came through over the speakers, announcing that any hybrids wishing to seek asylum should immediately report to the hangar bay.

But as Hathor walked toward the soldiers, one of them shot her with his plasma cannon. Hathor looked down in surprise at the hole in her stomach. The other soldiers apprehended the shooter; one of them disarmed him while another scanned him—there was a distortion. The soldier smashed the butt end of his cannon into the shooter's temple, knocking him unconscious. As the shooter hit the ground, his appearance changed: this was a hybrid. He'd replaced one of the fallen Othali.

Hathor fell to the floor, her vision going dark. Just before losing consciousness, she managed to use her implants to warn Salvatore and Venus that there could be more hybrids using their emitters to replace Othali soldiers.

# Chapter Thirty-three: Salvatore

Salvatore had just finished securing the bottom level of the compound when Hathor told them that they had taken over the control systems. He made his announcement over the intercom system and then had another transmission from Hathor.

"This is Hathor. I'm hit... Hybrid took an Othali soldier's appearance. There may be more..."

"This is Salvatore. Message received. Are you alright?"

There was no reply.

"Hathor?"

Using his implants, he checked the control system; she was in the command center. Salvatore flew to the end of the corridor and up the access tunnel to the top level. Running into the command center, he spotted Hathor lying in the middle of the room, a group of Othali soldiers gathered around her. There was a hole in her abdomen.

Salvatore dropped to one knee by her side and used his scanner to check her vital signs. Hathor was dead. Closing his eyes, he gave Venus the bad news.

"Shit," was her only reply.

His heart heavy, Salvatore initiated a data transfer from the compound's systems to the saucers'. Then he flew down to the lower levels and helped Venus and her troops escort the last of the hybrid children and their mothers up to the hangar bay. He left her and the soldiers to get all the evacuees aboard the saucers, then returned to the bottom level. Once he'd planted two fusion grenades, he ordered the rest of the soldiers up to the saucers and returned to the hangar bay himself.

As usual, they ran active scans on everyone boarding the saucers but found no more unexpected hybrids. Salvatore ran one last scan of the compound interior to make sure they weren't leaving anyone behind, then boarded his ship and moved up to the cockpit. He took control of Hathor's saucer remotely and then followed Venus out of the hangar bay with both vessels. Once they'd reached minimum safe distance, he detonated the nukes. A giant mushroom cloud filled the sky.

Salvatore set a course back to their compound and engaged both ships' engines. He reflected on their progress during the trip over the Atlantic. They'd successfully destroyed all the known Majestic compounds but paid a heavy price. Dozens of Othali soldiers had sacrificed themselves along with Hathor and Malia. And while they'd finally discovered the identity of the last member of the Sphinx, they still had no idea where to find her. Their losses might yet prove to have been for naught.

Once they'd reached the compound and docked the saucers, Salvatore chose one of the soldiers at random. He scanned her to verify her identity, then handed her the device and assigned her to the airlock to check everyone else as they disembarked. Next, he went over to Hathor's ship and did the same there. Salvatore met Venus, and they waited off to the side while the soldiers took care of taking the human abductees and hybrids to the appropriate levels for processing.

"So, it's just Bastet, you, and me, now," Venus commented. "And apparently, we got Isis back."

Salvatore heaved a long sigh.

"Yes. I'd hoped to save more. Hathor should have remained here for that last run. She needed more recovery time."

"Short of knocking her out, there's no way you could have kept her here. We're talking about the woman who infiltrated Majestic's ranks and replaced their North American commander, for heaven's sake."

Salvatore nodded.

At that moment, Jaden came running into the hangar bay.

"I heard you were back. Do you need me to figure out which hybrids are legit resistance members?"

"Yes," Salvatore replied. "But it'll have to wait. I'm going to convene a quick meeting to apprise everyone of our progress and plan our next move. You can get started after that if you'd like."

"Alright. Hey, where's Hathor? Didn't she go, too?"

Salvatore took a deep breath.

"I'm sorry, Jaden. Hathor didn't make it."

Jaden stared at him for a moment, confusion in his eyes.

"No—you mean they *killed* her?"

"One of the hybrids replaced an Othali soldier and took her by surprise," Venus explained. "Plasma shot to the abdomen."

Jaden's eyes filled with tears. He closed them tight, pressing one hand to his forehead, and said, "Aw, man..."

Salvatore tried to pull him into a hug, but Jaden ran out of the hangar bay.

"He's taking it harder than I would have expected," said Venus.

"Hathor went to find him when he flew off the other night. It sounds like they bonded."

Once the soldiers had finished moving the evacuees out of the hangar bay, Salvatore contacted the key people to arrange a brief meeting. An hour later, he met everyone in the conference room. Venus, Melissa, Brian, Sydney, Miguel, Bastet, and Jaden were there, and Anhur, Bukhari, and Shurani were patched in via hologram. Salvatore updated everyone on their progress that day with the other compounds and the prisoner interrogation and broke the news about Hathor.

"I'm sorry for your loss," said Anhur. "This is a heavy blow. Was there any information in Majestic's systems regarding the true location of the Sphinx?"

"We'll need some time to conduct a thorough analysis, but a quick search has not produced any results," Salvatore replied. "The scans of Antarctica are nearly finished, and so far, nothing has turned up there, either."

"So they gotta be underwater or in outer space," said Miguel.

"The warship still has to check Antarctica with active scans," said Venus, "but I still doubt we'll find anything. It could take months

KEN WARNER

to search the oceans. And although we can tell there's nothing of significant mass orbiting the Earth, it could take years to scan the rest of the solar system. I'm sure Isis will release her virus and decimate humanity long before that."

"What about that extra equipment we found in the Othali power station?" said Brian. "The one in Puerto Rico. There was a cube made from the same material as the pyramid but much newer. We know that Noorani was part of the Sphinx, and the age of that object would put it in the right timeframe to have been constructed by Majestic. Could they be using that somehow to power the Sphinx's compound?"

"That's a good question," Salvatore replied. "I hadn't considered that, but it could well be. We should return there and see if we can trace any power lines running out of that station.

"But we need a contingency plan in case we don't find Isis in time to stop her from releasing the virus. Are we any closer to determining the mechanism giving Sydney and Miguel their immunity?"

"Unfortunately, not," said Melissa. "But I've also started researching vaccination strategies. If we can't find Majestic's vaccine, we'll have to produce our own."

"I'd like to help you with that," Venus told her. "I became an arms dealer on Earth, but medicine was my field in another lifetime."

"I'd appreciate it," Melissa replied.

"I think that concludes our business for this evening," said Salvatore. "It's getting late, but I'm going to go have a look at that power station."

"Very well," said Anhur. "Let us know if you find anything; we'll begin the active scans of Antarctica immediately."

The meeting broke up. Brian approached Salvatore as he walked out to the corridor.

"Mind if I join you?"

"Not at all," said Salvatore.

They made their way up to the hangar bay. Once they'd boarded Salvatore's saucer, they moved up to the cockpit. Salvatore opened the hangar bay doors and guided the ship out of the compound. He lay in a course for the Puerto Rico power station, and they shot into the sky.

"It's interesting that Abrax remembered meeting Isis beneath the Great Sphinx," said Brian. "I knew Lucifer could suppress memories but had no idea they could *alter* them."

"Indeed," said Salvatore. "If this excursion doesn't lead anywhere, I'd like to have Jaden interrogate him one more time. The answers we need are locked inside his mind. We need only to find them."

When they arrived in Puerto Rico, Salvatore moved the ship directly over the power station's location. He initiated a full scan of the area.

"Fascinating," he said. "There are power lines running from the mystery cube up to a tower on the surface."

"A tower?" asked Brian. "What kind of tower?"

"Let's go take a look," said Salvatore.

The tower was in a clearing in the middle of a heavily wooded area near the shore. Salvatore took the saucer in low over the clearing, then he and Brian went down to the ground. In the center of the clearing was a metal structure that stood more than a thousand feet high. There were roughly two dozen circular objects attached to the upper half of it.

"Those look like microwave antennas," said Brian. "And they're all pointed skyward. They must be using them to transmit power to something in orbit."

"Yes," Salvatore agreed. "But the system is inactive, and based on the level of deterioration, I would estimate that it hasn't been used in at least thirty years."

"It is curious that they wouldn't have used solar power," Brian observed.

"Agreed. Although, solar arrays require significant surface area to collect sunlight. Microwave receivers are much more compact. They already had access to the Othali power station, so installing a microwave transmitter would have been an easy alternative."

"Good point," said Brian. "So, it would appear they had some sort of orbiting station at one point in the past, but no longer?"

"That would seem to be the case," Salvatore agreed. "I'm afraid this is a dead end."

They boarded the saucer and returned to the compound. Salvatore went to find Jaden. He was in the conference room, interrogating one of the hybrids. Salvatore waited until he was done.

"You look exhausted," Salvatore noted.

"Yeah, breaking into so many minds is tiring," Jaden said, then yawned. "It was easier when... well, when there were two of us to split the work."

Salvatore nodded.

"Take a break for tonight; you can finish tomorrow. But I'd like to try one more thing with Abrax if you're feeling up to it?"

Jaden agreed. Salvatore told him about the microwave transmitter as they headed to the brig.

"So, you think Abrax's memory is real, but it just happened on a space station instead of under the Great Sphinx?"

"Probably not the space station—Abrax's age would seem to eliminate that possibility. But somewhere other than the Sphinx," Salvatore confirmed. "And we think Majestic might have found a way to alter certain aspects of his memory, in addition to suppressing it. I'd like you to examine that recollection once more and see if you can detect any such forgery."

"Alright, I'll try."

"And while we're at it, let's see if you can unearth any other memories pertaining to Isis or her whereabouts."

"Okay."

"And... try to find out why they imprisoned and tortured him. If he'd turned traitor somehow..."

"Salvatore, this isn't exactly just 'one more thing,'" Jaden said with a grin.

"I'm sorry. It's just that our time is running out, and we're short on answers."

"I know, man. I got you."

They arrived at the brig and took their usual seats outside Abrax's cell.

"Is it true?" he asked them.

"Huh?" said Jaden.

"That memory you found last time. The Martian woman said I am a god. Is this true?"

Jaden chuckled.

"Nah, I don't think so. If you were a god, how could you be trapped in here?"

Abrax scowled at him.

"You still don't remember anything?" asked Salvatore.

"Only what the boy found."

Salvatore nodded.

Jaden stared intently at Abrax, deep in concentration. Minutes went by, and Salvatore waited. Before long, Salvatore noted beads of sweat forming on Jaden's brow and guessed that he must have been tapping into the Earth's magnetic field.

Finally, Jaden sat back, taking a deep breath. Glancing at Salvatore, he nodded. The two of them stepped out to the corridor.

"What did you find?" asked Salvatore.

"Well, the parts of his memories that are *outside* the Great Sphinx are definitely different than the stuff that happens *inside*."

"How so?"

"Like when his dad told him about being half-Othali, and the two times he met with Isis, he was *excited*. I mean, that stuff made him feel special. It's like those were his fondest memories, you know?"

"Yes, go on."

"Okay, so with the stuff leading up to those memories—traveling to the Great Sphinx and all that—there's basically no emotion at all. Which is weird, right? I mean, when Isis summoned him from the compound here, that was only the second time he was ever going to meet her. And when he gets the summons, there's nothing. He's not excited or scared or anything. It was almost like... he watched a movie about those parts instead of actually *being there*."

"Fascinating. Those parts of the memories must have been manufactured somehow."

"Yeah, I think so. I feel like those three memories were so important to him that he could never forget them. Even when they wiped his mind, they couldn't totally get rid of them. So instead, they had to change the parts leading up to them to make sure we couldn't see where they really happened."

Salvatore nodded.

"But the rest of those memories are real."

"Yeah, I'm pretty sure."

"And the meetings with Isis took place somewhere with stone walls? It wasn't on a vessel or space station?"

"No way. It was underground somewhere."

"Were you able to uncover any other memories with Isis?"

"Nah. But they're there... Like I could feel that she was someone super familiar to him, but only those first two times he met her were special enough to survive."

"Any luck finding what caused them to imprison him?"

"No. And that's weird, too. You gotta figure that getting caught as a traitor and being kicked out of the Sphinx and all that would be crazy emotional. But there's nothing. Everything else is completely gone."

Salvatore considered this for a moment.

"Thank you, Jaden. This has been very helpful. We should go get some sleep."

"Salvatore, Abrax seriously believes that he's a god. And Isis, too. That memory woke up that feeling in him, and it runs deep. We've gotta find a way to stop them. For Malia. And... for Hathor."

"We will, Jaden. We will."

# Chapter Thirty-four: Nephthys

Malia woke with a start—something had pricked her neck. She struggled to open her eyes—her head felt like it was stuffed with cotton. The sedative was still in her system. She was lying on the floor of her cell, staring at the stone wall across from her. But the doorway was open. Sitting up, Malia heard a soft noise behind her. Turning, she spotted Durga standing over her.

"Feeling it yet?" the woman asked, flashing her serene smile. Malia realized she was holding something in her hand—a syringe.

Malia focused inside of herself, trying to identify what Durga had injected into her veins. There was something; she couldn't tell what it was, but it was spreading fast. It didn't feel like a drug...

Malia gasped.

"You gave me the virus?!"

Durga smiled at her.

"It will attack your central nervous system. The early symptoms include dizziness and confusion, followed by partial paralysis."

Malia concentrated with all her might on removing the virus from her veins. But she realized that something in her body was already neutralizing it. Were her healing powers able to counteract the virus? She didn't think that was it—there was something else in her bloodstream that didn't belong. It didn't seem like a chemical; Malia couldn't tell what it was.

"It's not affecting me..."

"Correct. You see, we have taken measures to protect our people, you and your brother, and those with DNA compatible with our own. We've reached a critical threshold, but we need to continue harvesting their sex cells to produce more hybrids.

"But I'm afraid that for the rest of Earth's people, the time has come. I have released the virus. It will be a matter of only a few weeks before billions of humans take their last breaths."

"Liar!" Malia yelled. "Salvatore and the others will stop you. They found your virus samples in the Africa compound—they'll create a vaccine!"

"It's too late for that. We have hybrids living among the humans in every major city all over the globe—thousands of them. They reside in their communities and work in their largest buildings. And each one of them had in their possession a special device designed to release the virus on our command. We have now issued those orders.

"Even if your people had a vaccine ready to go today, there is no longer any way to stop what we have put in motion."

Malia stared at her for a moment in shock and disbelief. But there was nothing in her tone to make her think Durga was lying. She knew this had been Majestic's plan all along, and now they'd finally executed it.

"You're a monster..."

Malia felt panic and rage surging inside of her. She had to find a way out of here to warn the others what Durga had done. Maybe there was a chance they could save some people if they acted quickly—or, at least, save themselves.

Gathering every ounce of power she could muster, Malia reached out with her mind and slammed Durga into the wall. There was a horrible cracking sound when her head hit the stone, and Durga looked dazed for a moment, but she fought back. Her power was incredible; despite Malia's best effort, she could feel Durga counteracting her and slowly inching back toward the floor.

Malia knew what she had to do. Durga was stunned, and if Malia acted quickly... Malia released her hold on Durga, immediately penetrating her mind with the full force of her will. Concentrating with all of her might, she extinguished the light of Durga's consciousness. She could feel the woman struggling against her, fighting to stay awake. But Malia had the edge.

Durga slumped to the floor, leaning up against the wall. Malia didn't relent; she pushed Durga's mind as deep into darkness as she could. Slowly, the woman slid down the wall until she was lying on the floor.

And suddenly, Durga's appearance changed; Malia realized her emitter must have gone offline. Her headdress remained, but a skintight black jumper replaced the sari, and scales appeared on the skin of her face, neck, and hands. There was a scar running down the side of her face and into the collar of the jumper.

Malia gasped: this woman was a Martian. And it could only be one person. But Salvatore told them that they'd killed Isis ages ago...

There was no time to solve this riddle now. Malia removed the Isis's emitter; she was able to access it through her implants. But she'd need the woman's bio-scan to replace her and gain access to the control system.

Malia dashed into the corridor and made her way to the storage room. She searched through all the equipment and checked inside the crates but couldn't find a scanner. Doubling back, she tried getting through the doors but couldn't get into any of the rooms. She ran beyond the storage room, but the rooms here were secure, too. Finally, she ended up in the hangar bay, but there was nothing here but the saucer.

Malia found one more doorway beyond the hangar bay, and this one let her pass. She ran into the chamber beyond, stopped short, and gasped. The far wall was built entirely of glass. Staring through it, Malia discovered that this compound had been built into the rim of a giant crater. And looking upward where the sky should have been, she could see only the blackness of outer space.

This compound was not on Earth. Whether she was on the Moon or one of the outer planets' satellites, Malia couldn't tell. Neither the Sun nor any planet was visible from this vantage point. If this was the Moon, she must have been on its far side; otherwise, she would have been able to see the Earth.

What was she supposed to do, now? Without a scanner, she had no way out. There was only one thing she could do. She would have to try accessing Isis's memories without awakening her. Her only hope was that there was a scanner in one of the areas she could access.

Malia ran back to her cell. But she skidded to a stop as she moved inside: Isis was gone. Malia could have kicked herself—she should have done more to incapacitate her before leaving the room.

Reaching out with her mind, Malia tried to find her telepathically—maybe she'd grabbed another emitter and used it to go invisible. But the cell was empty. Malia crept back down the passage again, slowly this time so that she could check every area with her mind. But Isis was nowhere to be found.

Suddenly a clanking sound echoed through the corridor, followed by a buzzing noise. Throwing caution to the wind, Malia ran toward the source of the noise. She found that the entry to the hangar bay had been sealed; through the windows, she could see that the bay doors were opening.

"Farewell, Nephthys," a voice said over the intercom; Malia froze. "I must return to Earth to take my rightful place as the ruler of the world. Sadly, you will die a slow, miserable death here, utterly alone. And then my Moon base will become your tomb. But I want you to know that in the meantime, I will personally slaughter every person you love—your mother, your brother, and Salvatore. I had considered inviting Jaden to join me, but I am sure he is just as stubborn and stupid as you. And killing him will give me my vengeance for Osiris. An eye for an eye, yes? Perhaps I will send you images of his broken corpse through your implants when I am done."

Malia watched the saucer exit the hanger and shoot off into space. Then, as the bay doors closed again, Malia screamed in despair and sank to the floor with her back against the wall.

# Chapter Thirty-five: Abrax

Abrax's eyes snapped open. He was lying on the cot in his cell and had been sound asleep. What had awakened him? Sitting up, he listened intently. But there was no noise here beyond the quiet hum of the force field barring his only exit.

Turning toward the corridor and sliding his legs over the edge of the cot, he gazed through the barrier. The lights were dimmed; it had to be the middle of the night. He could see one soldier by each edge of the force field but knew the other two were probably still out there, too.

Suddenly, his implants accessed the compound's control system—seemingly of their own accord. No, that wasn't accurate—the system had initiated contact with his implants. What the hell was going on here?

The control system had triggered something—the words "Restoring... Standby" appeared in red across the top of his vision. The next moment, it felt like fire was splitting his head open. The pain was unbearable, and Abrax had to clamp his jaw shut to keep from screaming—somehow, he knew that he couldn't let the guards realize that anything was amiss.

Images flashed before Abrax's eyes—a flood of them as if a dam inside his mind had burst. They were his memories. Everything was coming back to him, all in a rush. His entire body shuddered as the veils of darkness were lifted from his mind.

Finally, the pain disappeared; Abrax let out a long sigh. He felt suddenly lightheaded and nearly blacked out. But it passed quickly.

Now he remembered why he was here: he had but one mission.

Isis had suspected that the enemy would attempt to take one of their compounds. She'd doubted they would be bold enough to target Africa, but just in case, they had a plan. Isis had planted a rogue process in the control system. The program did nothing unless it detected her or Abrax inside the facility—but then, at midnight, it would access their implants and grant them command-level access.

Once Africa had fallen, they put the rest of their plan into motion. Isis inflicted wounds on Abrax's body to make it appear that he'd been tortured. Then she suppressed his memories but left a restoration protocol encrypted in his implants. If he were to connect to any compound's control system, the routine would restore his memories.

They had initially planned to have a lone hybrid deliver Abrax to Africa and then implement his fake tooth before being interrogated. But after the enemy had infiltrated and then destroyed the compound in Europe, they knew they'd be coming for the others. And the softhearted fools were rescuing the mothers, children, and resistance members. So they'd planted Abrax in the Asia compound's brig.

And everything had gone exactly according to plan.

Abrax accessed the control system and confirmed that he

had command. Then, he shut out all other users and assigned Isis command-level access. Next, he checked the personnel assignments and identified the four soldiers guarding his cell. He sent a transmission to three of them, ordering them to the production facility to investigate a "security breach." Once they'd left the brig, Abrax got to his feet and lowered his cell's force field.

"Hey!" the lone soldier shouted, pointing his plasma cannon at him.

Abrax grabbed the barrel of the weapon, pointing it away from himself just as the soldier pulled the trigger. The plasma shot hit the opposite wall. Abrax smashed the soldier's temple with his elbow, grabbing the cannon out of his hands as the man hit the floor.

Hoisting the cannon over his shoulder, Abrax walked to the exit. He'd seen two soldiers guarding the access tunnel on his way here. Stepping into the corridor, he shot one of the guards, then the other before she could react. They both fell to the floor with holes in their abdomens.

Abrax hurried into the access tunnel and flew down a few levels. When he emerged into the corridor, he shot the two soldiers standing guard. At the far end of the passage, he found one of the equipment storage rooms. He retrieved three emitters; clipping one to his belt, he accessed it through his implants and made himself invisible.

Returning to the access tunnel, he flew up to the level where they kept the mothers and children. Stepping into the corridor, he shot the two guards, then hurried along. Accessing the control system, he found the room the two pregnant hybrids were sharing. The door was locked, so he used his command access to override it. Inside the quarters, he moved into one of the bedrooms and awakened the first woman, covering her mouth to make sure she didn't scream.

"The Sphinx sent me here to get you," he told her. "Here, put this on, and go invisible," he added, handing her the emitter.

Abrax hurried into the second bedroom, awakened the other mother, and gave her the last emitter. Once they were ready, he led them into the corridor and down to the access tunnel.

They flew up to the top level. Abrax told the women to wait in the shaft while he moved into the corridor and shot the two guards. Then, he summoned the women and guided them to the hangar bay.

Inside the observation area, he spotted half a dozen soldiers guarding the flight deck. One of the saucers had its exterior compartments open. That was strange. They must have been doing maintenance, but there was nothing in the system logs about it. This made him uneasy.

Accessing the control system, he flooded the hangar bay with active scanning beams. He had a feeling one of the Martians might have been using an emitter to go invisible, but there was nobody there. Nothing to worry about, then.

Abrax accessed one of the saucers through his implants and took control. He used the ship's weapons to mow down the guards. Then, he led the two women into the hangar bay and guided them to the saucer. They floated up into the airlock and moved to the main level. Abrax left them there and ascended to the cockpit. Accessing the control system, he opened the hangar bay doors, then moved the saucer out of the compound and shot into the sky.

# Chapter Thirty-six: Venus

Venus spent a few hours tossing and turning, but it was no use: she couldn't sleep. The recent losses of Malia and Hathor weighed heavily on her mind. And the fact that they had no idea where to find Isis and no way to stop her from releasing her virus.

Getting out of bed, Venus headed up to the hangar bay. She needed to work on something to get her mind off of everything, and she had the ideal project in mind. Once she'd checked in with the soldiers standing guard, she accessed her saucer and opened the exterior compartments. She wanted to upgrade the weapons with high-output plasma cannons, but there hadn't been any time. And she still needed to fabricate the new equipment. But in the meantime, she could at least tweak the existing weapons to increase their yield.

She started opening the panels and disconnecting the power couplings, but she'd need tools for the rest of the job. Heading back out to the corridor, she made her way to the elevator and moved down to the production facility. But when she arrived, she found three Othali soldiers standing around looking confused.

"What's wrong, boys?"

"We were standing guard in the brig, but then we received orders to come here to investigate a security breach," the leader told her.

Venus looked around the area.

"What security breach?"

"I don't know, ma'am. Everything was secure when we arrived."

"Well, who gave the order?"

"I'm not sure—it sounded automated."

"Hmm," said Venus.

She tried accessing the control system to investigate but found that she'd been shut out.

"What the hell?"

"What is it?"

"I'm locked out of the control system."

The soldier's expression showed suspicion.

"Ma'am, could this have anything to do with our prisoner?"

Venus knew it must.

"I'm sure it does. Come with me!"

She led the three soldiers out to the corridor and ran to the elevator. But they were locked out.

"Damn!" Venus shouted. "Give me your weapon!"

The lead soldier handed her his plasma cannon. Leaving the guards behind, she flew to the other end of the corridor, using her emitter to go invisible as she went, and raced up the access tunnel to the top floor. Stepping cautiously into the passage, she spotted the two guards for this level lying dead on the floor.

"Shit."

Venus crept into the hangar bay's observation area. As she watched, one of the saucers moved through the open doors and flew into the night. She flew back down the access tunnel and went to the brig. Sure enough, the lone guard was dead, and Abrax's cell was empty.

"Salvatore, this is Venus. Are you awake?"

A moment later, he replied, "I am now."

"We've got a security situation. Can you meet me in the hangar bay?"

"Yes."

Venus flew back up to the hangar bay. She closed her saucer's compartments but found she could no longer access the ship's control systems.

"Dammit!" she shouted as Salvatore hurried into the area, wielding a plasma cannon.

"What is it?"

Venus explained.

He focused for a moment, then said, "I can't access my ship, either. We should alert the Othali."

Venus nodded.

"Othali warship, this is Venus."

"Go ahead, Venus," a voice replied.

Venus had her put Commander Anhur on the line, then explained the situation to him.

"Understood," he replied. "Moments ago, we detected a gravitational engine signature leaving Earth's atmosphere. That must have been your rogue saucer."

"And if you could detect it, that means they were accelerating to escape velocity. Where was that ship headed?"

"Its course when we lost contact would take it to the Moon," Anhur told her.

"That must be where Isis's base is located," said Venus. "They've locked us out of our ships—can you intercept?"

"Affirmative," Anhur replied. "We're on our way."

Venus relayed her conversation to Salvatore.

"They must have planted Abrax in the Asia compound so he could infiltrate this facility," he said. "But why? Just to shut us out of the control system?"

"That's a significant blow," Venus pointed out. "We're locked out of the system, and except for the warship, we have no vessels."

Salvatore considered this for a moment.

"They could have retaken the compound this way, but they didn't. Why?"

Venus shook her head.

"If they're releasing their virus, they wouldn't *need* the compound anymore! Isis could be executing her plan to take over the planet. They could hole up on the Moon until the virus runs its course and then set up shop at any lab in the world to continue their hybrid production."

"It's also possible that they're completing some higher priority first before returning to retake the compound in force," said Salvatore. "We should alert the others. But let's also check the rest of the compound to assess the situation and see what else Abrax might have done on his way out."

Venus and Salvatore returned to the corridor and moved down

to the next level. They checked the entire floor one room at a time, rousing everyone from sleep as they went. Bastet and Brian Kwan each got dressed, armed themselves, and joined them to search the rest of the compound. They found dead guards on one more level—the floor that hosted the hybrid asylum seekers, children, and mothers. After a room-to-room search, they discovered that the two pregnant hybrids were gone.

"That's why they sent Abrax here," said Salvatore. "They wanted Malia and Jaden's clones."

Venus nodded.

"And once they've secured them, they'll probably come back to retake the compound. We need to prepare."

# Chapter Thirty-seven: Nephthys

Malia forced herself to calm down, taking deep, steadying breaths. Getting to her feet, she moved back to the observation area. Reaching out with her mind into the blackness of space, she tried to find someone—anyone who might be out there. Maybe Salvatore and the others had sent saucers to look for her... But it was no use. There was no one out there.

Instead, Malia tried once more to reach someone back on Earth. But she simply lacked the power here to communicate across such a vast distance. Without the Earth's magnetic field, her telepathy wasn't strong enough.

Malia tried the doors to all the rooms again—there must have been food and water here somewhere. Isis couldn't have survived here without them. But Malia couldn't get into any of them. She returned to the storage area, searching for a weapon or anything she could use as a tool to force one of the doors open. But there was nothing.

Returning to the observation area, Malia found herself sinking into despair as she gazed out into space. There was no way out of here; Isis had left with the only saucer. And Malia hadn't been able to get her bio-scan, so she had no way to get into the other rooms.

A tear slipping down her cheek, Malia realized that she truly was going to die here.

But at that moment, something caught her eye. Something was moving high above the surface—it was only a pinprick of light, traveling slowly across the sky. It looked like a satellite. Did they have any satellites orbiting the Moon? Malia didn't know of any. It could be a ship.

Reaching out telepathically, she tried to sense if there were any people up there. And there were—hundreds of minds, all of them Othali. This had to be the warship. Malia felt her excitement rising, but she needed to focus. She had to alert someone on that ship to her presence down here. Nadia. Malia knew Nadia's mind better than anyone else's on the warship. The vessel was almost out of view. Malia searched for Nadia's mind, finally finding her.

*"Nadia—can you hear me?"*

A moment passed.

*"Yes! Who is this?"*

*"Oh, my God—it's me, Malia! I'm down here on the surface of the Moon. Isis is alive—and she has powers like Jaden and me. She has a base in the side of this crater. I think it must be on the far side because I haven't seen Earth. I'm trapped—"*

*"I thought you were dead?"*

*"No—Isis made it look that way, but she took me here! I need your help! I have no way out!"*

*"Understood. Hang tight, Malia—I'm going to notify the commander. Stay with me, okay? In case I need to talk to you."*

*"I will."*

Malia sank to the floor, crying tears of relief.

# Chapter Thirty-eight: Shurani

Ensign Shurani took his saucer in low, directly above the Burj Khalifa in Dubai. His shields were up, so none of the humans below would have any idea he was here. Next, he set a course for the Grand Canyon in Arizona and engaged the engines. The vessel shot into the sky.

He couldn't help grinning ear to ear. It was astounding how fast these saucers were. And how maneuverable—they could stop almost instantly, taking off again in a different direction after only a fraction of a second. These craft put the Othali shuttles to shame.

But the vessel's ease of operation was easily its most impressive feature. Learning to control it would hardly be challenging, even for someone who had never flown any kind of aircraft before—the thing practically flew itself. The only tricky part was getting used to these neural implants and the capabilities of the saucer. But Shurani found himself becoming more fluent with its operation every time he went out like this.

No sooner had he arrived at the Grand Canyon than he received a transmission from the warship.

"Commander Anhur wants you back here, immediately. We've got a situation."

"What is it?"

"They'll fill you in when you arrive."

"Understood."

Shurani set a course back to the warship. He reached it only minutes later and docked in the hangar bay. Once he'd disembarked, he hurried up to the bridge. Commander Anhur glanced at him.

"Ensign. The Africa compound reports that their prisoner has escaped. He locked them out of their ships, took the two pregnant hybrids, and commandeered one of their saucers. At last contact, they were headed to the Moon. We're in pursuit."

"Sir, let me go with the saucer. It's faster."

"Negative. You're not cleared for combat flights on that thing."

Shurani bit back his protest.

"Yes, sir."

This was frustrating—it would take the warship almost ninety minutes to reach their destination. Shurani could get there in a fraction of that time with the saucer. But the commander did have a point: if it came to a firefight, he'd be in trouble.

Letting out a long sigh, Shurani took a seat at an empty console along the rear wall. They had the Moon on the main viewscreen; it grew ever larger in the display as they approached. Anhur checked with the science station periodically, but they had no further contact with the enemy vessel, despite running active scans of the lunar surface as they drew closer.

"Sir, we're on final approach," the navigator said, finally.

"Very well, Ensign. Put us into orbit."

"Yes, sir."

The warship entered lunar orbit, and they continued scanning the surface.

"Sir, I'm detecting something at the L2 Lagrange point," said the science officer.

"What is it?" asked Anhur.

"Unknown," the officer replied. "It's shielded."

"Give me an active scan," said Anhur.

"Yes, sir."

"Sir, that must be where they're constructing the new chariot," said Shurani. "L2 is the location where the centrifugal force of the orbit perfectly offsets the gravitational attraction of the Earth-Moon system. It would be the perfect construction site. They'd need only minimal course corrections, and the Moon would block detection from the Earth."

"Active scans would seem to support that hypothesis, Commander," said the science officer. "The structure I'm detecting has the same dimensions as the vessel we engaged over New York, but only a fraction of the mass."

"Any other vessels in that area?" asked Anhur.

"Yes, sir. Eight saucers."

"One of those will probably be our quarry," said Anhur. "Navigation, let's complete one orbit then set course for that construction project."

"Yes, sir."

At that moment, a voice came in over the intercom.

"Commander, this is the medical bay. Lieutenant Bashandi is on her way up to the bridge. Could you please order her to return here when she arrives?"

"Would you care to explain what's going on, Ensign Fareed?"

"I wish I could, sir. She said she needed to contact you. I asked her what it was about—she hasn't been cleared to return to duty yet. But she refused to tell me and got up and walked right out of medical."

"Understood," Anhur said with a sigh.

Only a minute later, Nadia strode onto the bridge.

"Lieutenant?" said Anhur.

"Sir, Malia Kwan is *alive*!"

Anhur stared at her as if she'd sprouted a second head.

"How do you know this?"

"She contacted me telepathically—just now," Nadia told him. "Isis faked her death and took her to her base down on the Moon. And, sir... Isis has the same powers as the twins."

"Do you know where the base is?" asked the science officer. "We haven't detected anything yet."

"Malia says it's embedded in a crater wall, and she thinks it's on the far side."

"Can you find out if she's safe?" asked Anhur.

"Yes, give me a moment," said Nadia. A few seconds later, she added, "Yes, she says she's fine, just scared and alone."

Anhur sighed.

"Navigation, keep us on course for that construction project," said Anhur. "Lieutenant, please let Malia know we will be coming for her very soon."

"Yes, sir."

Shurani watched as the warship completed its orbit of the Moon and then shot out toward the Lagrange point. The science officer put the active scan of the area on the main viewscreen. Visible only in artificially generated red outlines was the framework of a large saucer. Several smaller vessels were stationed nearby.

"Sir, we're moving into weapons range," said the navigator.

Anhur nodded.

"Target the chariot and fire," said Anhur.

But at that moment, the warship shook violently; Shurani had to hold onto the console to stop himself from falling out of his seat.

"Report!" said Anhur.

"Sir, we're under attack," said the tactical officer. The viewscreen changed, showing the red outline of another chariot—one that looked complete. "Second chariot off our port bow. It came out of nowhere, sir."

"Return fire!" said Anhur.

The viewscreen showed several laser blasts hit the chariot. The vessel hit them with several more shots, then moved away before the warship could return fire.

"Take out the unfinished one," Anhur ordered.

The viewscreen changed back to the construction project. A moment later, their laser blast hit it, blowing it up in a fiery explosion.

"Sir, the remaining chariot has disengaged," the tactical officer reported. "They've moved out of range. The smaller saucers have moved off as well."

"What was their course?" asked Anhur.

"They were headed to Earth when we lost them."

"Alert the Africa compound that they're probably about to have company," said Anhur. "Warn them that Isis possesses the same abilities as the twins. And... let them know that we've found Malia alive and are initiating a rescue mission."

"Yes, sir."

The warship headed back to the Moon.

"Sir, I've located the Majestic compound," the science officer reported minutes later. "Sure enough, it's embedded in the rim of a crater."

"On screen," said Anhur.

A lunar crater appeared on the viewscreen. Structures were outlined in red on the far wall. Shurani could make out what appeared to be hangar bay doors.

"Any chance we can access the control system?" asked Anhur.

"No, sir," the science officer replied.

"We'll have to cut our way in," said Anhur. "Ensign Shurani, prepare the saucer. It's time to rescue Malia."

"Yes, sir," said Shurani, getting to his feet. "Can you let her know I'm on the way?" he added to Nadia on his way out of the bridge.

Nadia nodded.

"Good luck out there."

Shurani headed down to the hangar bay. When he arrived, he

found Malik, the chief engineer, waiting for him, a metal, square-shaped apparatus leaning against the wall next to her.

"So, you've used an EAL before, yeah?"

"I've trained on it," said Shurani. "But this saucer is nothing like our shuttles, so I'll have to improvise a little."

The EAL was an emergency airlock. If a vessel's built-in airlock system was inoperative, the EAL could provide safe egress for its passengers without venting the atmosphere to space.

"Never in a real rescue?"

Shurani shook his head.

"Alright," Malik replied with a sigh. "Our hand lasers won't be able to get through those blast doors. We'll be cutting out an opening with the ship's weapons, which means the atmosphere *will* vent through the hole. Now, chances are that their system will try to repressurize the hangar bay. So when you plant this thing over the opening, there's going to be some outward force acting on it as that air vents. You'll need to apply a little more pressure than normal to get that seal to form."

"Right," said Shurani. "So, you wanna go with me and take care of that part of the mission?"

"You'll be fine," she said with a reassuring smile.

Malik headed back to engineering. Shurani walked into the makeshift locker room they were using until the docking port could be reconstructed. He found his spacesuit and changed into it. Then he grabbed a plasma cannon and a spacesuit for Malia and returned to the corridor. He moved the EAL out to the dock; the thing wasn't very heavy, but it was nearly as tall as he was, making it awkward to carry.

Once he'd reached the saucer, he activated the gravitational beam, transporting himself and the EAL into the airlock. Shurani moved up to the cockpit, dropped the plasma cannon and extra spacesuit on the floor, and contacted the bridge.

"We're ready when you are," came the reply.

"Understood. Departing the hangar bay now."

Shurani moved the saucer out of the docking port. The warship was hovering inside a lunar crater near the rim. Shurani could see nothing but rock through the cockpit window; he had to activate the holographic imaging system to see the blast doors. He positioned the saucer off to one side.

"*Shurani, is that you?*" asked a voice in his head.

"*Hey, Malia—yes, it is. They're going to cut a hole in the hangar bay doors so we can get you out of there. Just to be safe, why don't you go as far away from that area as you can?*"

"*Alright, I'm heading there, now.*"

"*And stay in contact—I'll let you know when it's time to come back.*"

"This is Shurani; I'm in position," he reported to the warship.

Moments later, they fired their laser, cutting a square hole in the blast doors. The instant they finished, the interior pressure blew the cutout into space.

Shurani turned the saucer sideways, taking it in close over the opening. Once it was in position, he headed back down to the airlock. Holding onto the EAL, he activated the gravitational beam. He landed on the blast door, next to the opening. With the artificial gravity still active, it felt like he was standing upright on a metal floor.

He unfurled the EAL, opening it up to a cube, then placed it over the opening in the blast door. Sure enough, he had to press it against the surface harder than usual to get it to form a seal. Once that was done, he reversed the saucer's gravitational beam and went back up to the ship. He grabbed the extra spacesuit and plasma cannon from the cockpit, then disembarked again.

This time, he landed on top of the EAL. Opening the outer hatch, he climbed inside, pulling it closed again behind him. Once he'd pressurized the EAL, he opened the inner hatch and moved into the hangar bay. Shurani became disoriented for a moment as the direction of gravity changed by ninety degrees but recovered quickly.

Shurani took in his surroundings. This hangar bay was relatively small, and there was only one entry to the rest of the compound. Shurani tried the door, but it was sealed shut, and without access to the control system, there was no way to open it.

*"I'm inside the hangar bay,"* he reported to Malia. *"But I'm going to have to blast my way through the door. Stay where you are while I do that."*

*"I will—but isn't that going to suck the air out of the compound?"*

*"No, we've set up an emergency airlock over the opening we created. The hangar bay is fully pressurized."*

Shurani hoisted the plasma cannon over his shoulder and fired at the door. It blew a hole through the metal, but he had to fire a second shot to create an opening large enough for him to fit through. Climbing inside, he reached out to Malia again.

*"I'm in—where are you?"*

She didn't reply, but suddenly, he heard footsteps running toward him. Moments later, Malia came running around the corner, grabbing him in a bear hug and nearly toppling him over.

"Oh, my God! Thank you! I was afraid I was going to die in here!"

"Now, we couldn't let that happen," Shurani replied with a grin. Once she'd released him, he handed her the spacesuit and added, "Go change into this, and let's get out of here."

Malia ran off. She returned a minute later wearing the spacesuit, her clothes in hand. Shurani helped her seal it up, and then they climbed back into the hangar bay. The two of them moved into the EAL, and Shurani closed the inner hatch.

"I'm going to depressurize the compartment, then open the outer hatch," he explained. "Then I'll reverse the ship's gravity beam, and we'll float right up to the saucer."

Malia nodded, and Shurani proceeded. They flew up to the saucer's airlock and then moved up to the cockpit.

"Alright, let's get back to the warship," said Shurani.

"No," said Malia. "Isis is going to try to kill my mother and brother—the warship will take way too long. I need you to take me there in the saucer."

# Chapter Thirty-nine: Jaden

Jaden woke up to the sound of banging. What the hell was going on? Sitting up in bed, he listened intently, but the sound had stopped. But then he heard it again. Alert now, he got out of bed, pulled on his pants, and crept out of his bedroom. But a moment later, he heard voices—his mother was talking to someone. Walking into the living room, he found Salvatore conversing with Melissa.

"What's going on?" he asked, rubbing the sleep from his eyes.

"Abrax has escaped," Salvatore explained.

"We should go after him!" said Jaden.

"We can't at this time. Somehow, he locked us out of the control system—and out of the saucers. But we've alerted the warship, and they're in pursuit."

"So... what do we do, now?" asked Jaden.

"Stay here, both of you," Salvatore replied. "We're checking the rest of the compound to see what else Abrax might have done on his way out. I'll return when we know more."

Salvatore left, and Jaden went back to his room to finish getting dressed. He sat down in the living room but felt extremely impatient now and couldn't sit still. After a few minutes, he wanted to find Salvatore and see what was going on, but Melissa refused to let him leave.

"Salvatore told us to stay put," she said. "So, just relax. He'll be back."

Jaden felt like the anticipation was going to kill him. But finally, Salvatore returned.

"I'm afraid Abrax took the two pregnant hybrids," he told them.

"You mean the ones with our clones?" said Jaden.

Salvatore nodded.

"And we believe Majestic forces will be arriving soon in force to retake the compound. We are gathering everyone in the hangar bay to discuss preparations."

Salvatore left to inform some of the others. Melissa and Jaden headed up to the top level. The elevator was no longer functional, so Jaden had to use his powers to fly Melissa up the access tunnel. They arrived in the hangar bay to find dozens of Othali soldiers arranging stacks of storage containers. The hangar bay doors were open, the night sky visible beyond.

Sydney and Miguel arrived a minute later, then Brian and Bastet soon after. More Othali soldiers showed up, and finally, Salvatore and Venus strode into the room.

"Could I have everyone's attention, please," Salvatore shouted over the din. Everyone stopped what they were doing and turned to face him. "The warship just informed us that they found two more Majestic chariots out beyond the Moon. One was still under construction, and the warship destroyed it. But the other one is fully operational and headed toward Earth. We have reason to believe they will show up here with their remaining force of hybrids to retake this compound."

There was much murmuring among the crowd.

"There is more. We also believe that Isis, a member of the Sphinx, will be leading the attack herself. And we have learned that Isis possesses telepathy and telekinesis, just like Jaden and Malia Kwan. She may share their healing powers as well, although we have not been able to confirm this."

"What the hell?" Jaden asked Melissa as the room erupted in vocal reactions to this news. "How did she get our powers?"

"She must have injected herself with your DNA, just like Lucifer did," Brian suggested. "Only she had better success."

"Settle down, please," Salvatore called out over the chatter. "We are unable to access the control system, and we have lost the use of the saucers." Jaden gazed at all the ships just hovering there, utterly useless to them. "As you can see, the hangar bay doors are open, and Majestic will be able to fly their saucers into the compound to unload their hybrids.

"We are setting up the storage containers to provide some cover. The hybrids will undoubtedly use their emitters to go invisible, so we will need to use handheld units to flood the area with active scanning beams. We'll have several soldiers stationed at key points to do this, but should they be overtaken, you may need to use your own scanners.

"The warship is on its way but will take much longer to get here than the Majestic forces. We will have to face this threat on our own. They could be here at any minute, so let's take up arms and get into position!"

A cheer went up from the crowd as everyone rushed around to prepare for the attack. But as Jaden set out to find himself a plasma cannon, Melissa grabbed him by one arm.

"Not you," she said. "You're coming with me back to our quarters."

"*What*?! No way, Mom! You heard what Salvatore said—Isis has our powers, now. I *have* to stay and help!"

"Jaden, no!" Melissa screamed. "I can't bear to lose you, too! You will come with me immediately!"

"And do what? Hide under my covers and hope they don't find us? Isis will walk all over these people if I'm not here to help! I'm the only one who can counter her powers!"

Salvatore walked over to them then. Jaden figured he'd probably heard his spat with his mother.

"Can you two come with me, please?"

"Sure," said Melissa. "Maybe you can help me talk some sense into my son!"

He collected Brian, Sydney, and Miguel, then led them all out to the observation area.

"I have some more news that you should hear before the others," he began, taking a deep breath. "Malia is alive."

"*What*?" Jaden blurted, not sure he'd heard him correctly.

"It seems Isis directed her forces to fake Malia's death. She's been keeping her in her compound on the Moon. Malia could not reach us telepathically over such a great distance but contacted Nadia when she saw the warship go by.

"One of the Othali soldiers has rescued her, and they are on their way here. I'm afraid Majestic had a head start, however, so they will arrive first."

Melissa covered her mouth with both hands, tears streaming down her cheeks. Brian pulled her into a hug.

"This is terrific news!" Sydney said, smiling and crying at the same time.

"Mom, you *have* to let me help, now," said Jaden. "If I can hold Isis off for just a few minutes, then me and Malia together can kick her ass!"

"Jaden, *no!*" said Melissa.

"Melissa, I am sorry to say this, but I fear we are doomed without Jaden's help," said Salvatore. "He is the only one here who can counteract Isis's powers. Without him, she will be able to disarm all the soldiers, and we will be unable to resist the hybrids."

"I *will not* risk losing him!" Melissa insisted. "I can't go through that again! Jaden and I will wait in our quarters—"

"They will find you when they're done up here," said Salvatore. "And then you will face Isis and her hybrids alone."

"Then we'll *leave*! Right now—Jaden can fly us somewhere safe."

"No, I won't!" said Jaden. "You can't force me to leave!"

Melissa stared at him for a moment, then sobbed.

"Melissa, Salvatore is right," Brian said. "I'm sorry to say so—I don't want to endanger Jaden any more than you do. But it's true; he is the only one who can go head-to-head with Isis, now."

Melissa calmed herself, taking a deep breath.

"Well, it seems I don't have any choice. But you must promise me that you will do everything in your power to protect him! Isis will target him!"

"We will," Salvatore assured her.

Melissa regarded Jaden for a moment, then sighed and hugged him.

"You listen to Salvatore. And come back to me safe and sound."

"I will, Mom. Don't worry."

They left the observation area in time to see Venus directing a group of soldiers out to the corridor.

"What's going on?" asked Jaden. "Why are they leaving?"

"They're the backup," said Salvatore. "If the initial wave of hybrids takes out our troops in the hangar bay, we'll have these soldiers in reserve."

Melissa and Sydney headed out to the corridor. Jaden and Salvatore moved into the hangar bay with Brian and Miguel. Salvatore took Jaden to the rear-left corner, introducing him to two Othali soldiers and handing him a plasma cannon.

"These two have implants and emitters," Salvatore explained. "I want all three of you to go invisible. Jaden, we would like you to concentrate on using your powers to overwhelm the enemy. Disarm as many of them as you can. But you will also need to focus on neutralizing Isis. We have no way of knowing *when* she will join the battle, but we are confident that she will. Whatever she tries to do with her powers, you will be our primary defense against her. Stay invisible. Use your telekinesis to stop any plasma shots that come your way. And stay behind these men—they will shield you from laser blasts."

"I got it," said Jaden. "But if we're invisible, they're not gonna aiming at us anyway."

"Don't count on that," Salvatore warned. "They'll be able to flood the area with active scanning beams."

"Oh, damn. I forgot about that."

Salvatore squeezed his shoulder, then went off to join another group of soldiers. Jaden focused. Stimulating his adrenal glands, he formed a bubble of stillness around him, extending it to encompass the two soldiers. Then, he hoisted the plasma cannon onto his shoulder, pointing it toward the open blast doors, and waited.

The hangar bay grew eerily silent as everyone waited for the attack; minutes dragged by, but there was no sign of the enemy. Jaden could feel the power coursing through his veins; he was ready.

Suddenly, their own saucers opened fire on their soldiers. Screams filled the air as laser blasts incinerated the storage containers, along with many of the people taking cover behind them. What the hell? Isis must have taken control of the ships remotely.

Gathering his energy, Jaden focused on the saucers, hurling them out of the hangar bay. Moments later, several large objects arrived, their presence observable only by the shimmering effect they caused in the scanning beams.

"Enemy saucers!" a voice shouted.

The next moment, the beams showed dozens of hybrids disembarking from the saucers. The remaining Othali opened fire on them. As the hybrids hit the flight deck, they formed ranks, returning fire. Reaching out telekinetically, Jaden disarmed the hybrids, tossing their weapons out the hangar bay doors. The Othali mowed them down, but new arrivals from the saucers quickly took their places. Jaden disarmed them, too.

This process repeated itself a few times, and it started to seem like the Othali might win the day. But suddenly, a group of Othali soldiers flew through the air, slamming into the far wall. Jaden heard horrible crunching noises as they impacted, then fell to the floor and didn't move.

Isis must have arrived. Jaden searched the area telepathically but couldn't locate her. Another group of Othali went flying into the wall. The remaining soldiers' weapons flew out of their hands.

"Shit!" Jaden shouted.

Finally, he found her—he could sense a powerful mind hovering near the top of the hangar bay doors. But at that moment, Isis hurled another group of soldiers into the air. This time, Jaden managed to arrest their progress before they hit the wall; he set the soldiers down on the flight deck.

Next, he penetrated Isis's mind, immediately forcing her to become visible. She ejected him from her mind, but not before he pointed her out to his two protectors. Aiming his plasma cannon, Jaden fired at Isis at the same time as the soldiers. But the plasma shots came to rest inches before impact—Isis must have created a bubble of stillness around herself.

Suddenly, Isis entered his mind.

"*Nice try, little boy,*" she said as she forced him to become visible.

Jaden could now see the two soldiers, too. A second later, all three of their plasma cannons flew out of their hands.

Isis floated down to the floor, striding forward. With a wave of her arms, the storage containers all shot out of the hangar bay, exposing the remaining soldiers. Invisible hybrids fired their weapons; laser blasts and plasma shots took out the Othali.

Jaden reached out with his mind, grabbed Isis, and hurled her into the near wall, twenty feet off the floor. But she penetrated his mind again, trying to extinguish his consciousness. Jaden had to devote his full attention to staying awake, and Isis returned to the floor. He managed to expel her from his mind, but then Isis disappeared again.

The second wave of Othali hurried into the hangar bay, using their scanning beams to locate and fire on the hybrids. But as the firefight broke out, Jaden found himself flying into the rear wall, over the observation area windows.

"*Your sister murdered my lover. Now, I will kill you to avenge his death. Say goodbye, little boy.*"

Jaden struggled against Isis's telekinesis, trying to return to the floor. But suddenly, one of the enemy saucers came hurling toward him. Jaden brought his full strength to bear on stopping it; it came to rest inches from his chest. Drawing in all the power he could from the magnetic field, he focused on pushing the ship away from him.

But then he felt Isis's power surge, too, and knew she must have been doing the same thing he was. The saucer inched toward him, finally connecting with his chest. Jaden struggled mightily to push it back, but it began compressing his chest. He found it difficult to breathe and thought his ribs would crack.

Jaden screamed with the little breath he had left, fighting back with one last surge of power. But it was no use; the saucer was crushing him, and his vision started going black.

But a moment later, the saucer flew away from him, smashing into the side wall and shattering. Jaden didn't understand how that had happened. But now, he floated down to the flight deck. And when he landed, he spotted a figure standing at the edge of the hangar bay doors, silhouetted against the first light of dawn, a plasma cannon on her shoulder: Malia had arrived.

# Chapter Forty: Nephthys

"Show yourself, Isis!" Malia shouted once she'd set Jaden on the floor.

"*You little bitch. So, you managed to escape your tomb, after all,*" a voice said in her head. "*That's fine. A quick death for you, then.*"

Malia felt an unseen force toss her out of the hangar bay. She flew back inside, searching telepathically for Isis. Several plasma shots hit her bubble; Malia spotted the hybrids in the scanning beams and disarmed them before returning fire, blowing holes through their abdomens.

Isis penetrated her mind, trying to knock her unconscious. Malia fought back, ejecting her from her mind. But suddenly, an unseen force flung her high in the air, pinning her against the ceiling. Malia fought with all her might, slowly moving back toward the floor.

"*I found her!*" Jaden's voice said in her head.

Isis appeared out of thin air, hovering by the rear wall, several feet above the flight deck.

"*Try to knock her out,*" Malia said to Jaden.

He must have been doing it because Malia found herself free of Isis's telekinesis. Reaching out with her mind, she hurled one of the enemy saucers at Isis. But Isis flew out of the way in the nick of time;

the ship smashed into the wall and fell to the floor.

Malia dropped to the deck, frantically trying to spot Isis again. Jaden ran over to her, plasma cannon in position, and the two of them stood back-to-back, ready for anything.

Isis appeared out of nowhere, directly in front of Malia. Malia tried to fire her plasma cannon, but Isis used her powers to rip it out of her hands.

"Jaden!" she shouted, reaching out with her mind to control Isis.

Jaden turned, and Isis disarmed him, too. But together, Malia and Jaden hurled Isis into the far wall, up near the ceiling. At the same time, Malia penetrated her mind, trying to force her unconscious. But Isis ejected her from her mind and flung Malia and Jaden into the opposite wall.

"*Hold her, Jaden!*" Malia told him.

"*What do you think I'm doing?*"

Malia refocused her telekinesis on resisting Isis's; it worked— Isis had to devote her energy to fighting off Jaden's control. Malia dropped to the floor and went invisible. She spotted a plasma cannon across the hangar bay and made it fly into her hands. Aiming Isis, Malia fired, but the fireball stopped in midair before hitting her— her bubble was still intact. She needed to make the woman lose focus.

Malia rushed to a fallen soldier and found his laser blaster. Aiming at Isis again, she fired, hitting her in the shoulder; Isis shrieked in pain. Malia shot her with the plasma cannon again, this time blowing a hole through her abdomen.

Isis looked down at her wound, a surprised expression on her face. Then, her eyes closed, and she fell to the floor.

"Quick—shoot her in the head before she heals!" yelled Jaden, running over to her.

Malia aimed at her skull, but Isis disappeared. Malia fired anyway, but her shot blew a hole in the deck.

"Shit!" Jaden shouted. "Where did she go?"

Venus and Salvatore appeared by their sides.

"She must still be here," said Salvatore. "Stay alert!"

"I got her bio-scan while you two were fighting her," Venus told them. "I've retaken the control system—I'll flood the area with scanning beams."

The beams activated, and Malia spotted someone rising into one of the enemy saucers—someone with long hair and a scar down the side of her face.

"There she is!" Malia yelled. She fired her cannon, but it was too late.

The saucer moved out of the hangar bay.

"Malia, fly!" yelled Jaden, taking to the air and chasing Isis's saucer.

Malia complied but didn't understand—they couldn't hope to keep up with her this way. But a moment later, Jaden's saucer flew up from below. Malia followed him into the airlock, and they moved up to the cockpit as the ship shot into the sky.

"I've set it to follow Isis's saucer," Jaden told her. "We were close to it, so I think the saucer's tracking her engine output..."

"Great—so fire weapons!"

"Oh, right..."

Several laser blasts hit Isis's ship. She returned fire, the laser blasts impacting their hull.

"Uh... looks like our shields are down to seventy percent."

Jaden fired again, but Isis's saucer flew erratically, dodging the shots. She fired several more direct hits in retaliation.

"Shields are down to forty-five percent," Jaden reported. "And uh... the little antenna icon in my vision went gray. I think maybe we lost communications."

"Mine's gray, now, too," said Malia. "Salvatore, this is Malia. Can you hear me?" There was no reply. "Well, fly like Isis did so we don't get hit again!" Malia told him.

"I don't know how! Why don't you use your powers and knock her out of the sky?!"

Malia reached out with her mind but then realized they were flying over water. Using her implants, she accessed the saucer's control system and checked the map. They were over the Mediterranean, flying fast toward the European coast.

"Not yet," Malia said to Jaden. "I've got an idea—just don't lose her!"

"What's your idea?"

"You'll see."

"I hate it when you do that," Jaden muttered. "Hey, she's increasing speed—she's going over the limit that Salvatore always says not to cross!"

"We can make an exception this time," said Malia. "Stay on her!"

"Alright, but if Salvatore and them chew me out for this, I'm blaming you!"

Minutes later, they reached land. And as Malia had anticipated, Isis led them into the Alps, weaving insanely fast between snow-covered peaks.

"Holy shit!" said Jaden. "This is the wildest ride I've ever been on. She's trying to lose us between the mountains—that's why she took us here!"

"Right, so don't lose her," said Malia, tapping into the Earth's magnetic field and augmenting her powers.

"I won't—this thing's basically on auto-pilot, anyway."

But at that moment, Isis's saucer made a sudden turn between two peaks, and Jaden's ship blew right past her.

"Jaden!"

"It's not my fault—the ship did it, not me!"

"Well, find her again!"

"Looks like it's still tracking her—hang on."

They rounded the next peak, and Isis's saucer came into view again, a little farther ahead of them, now. Reaching out with her mind, Malia focused on slamming Isis's ship into a passing mountaintop. She managed to shift Isis's course, but not enough—it skimmed the surface, blowing a wave of snow into the air, but didn't crash.

"Can you shoot her, please?" Malia demanded, gathering her strength for another attempt.

"Oh, right," said Jaden. Several blaster shots hit Isis's ship as they wound low through a valley.

But then, Malia noticed that Isis was starting to pull away from them.

"What's happening?"

"I dunno—it's like something's pushing against us. We won't be able to track her if she gets much farther ahead."

Reaching out with her mind, Malia could sense Isis using her telekinesis to hinder their progress. She found Isis telepathically and penetrated her mind, trying to knock her out. Isis expelled her quickly, but Malia hadn't expected this to work—she only wanted to stop her from slowing them down.

"Did you do something?" asked Jaden. "We're going faster again."

As they passed a nearly sheer cliff face, Malia gathered her strength again. Concentrating with all her might, she pushed Isis's saucer toward the mountain. The edge grazed the rock, and her saucer began wobbling. Malia gave it another burst of energy; Isis's ship hit the cliff again, and this time began spinning end-over-end. It spiraled out of control and hit the snowy slope far below.

Jaden's saucer overshot the crash site. He circled back, and they watched Isis's wrecked saucer slide down the mountainside, finally falling over another cliff and crashing far below.

"Yes!" shouted Jaden.

"Let's go," said Malia, getting to her feet.

"Go—where?" said Jaden. "We got her. That's it!"

"We need to be sure," Malia replied, dropping down to the main level.

They each grabbed a plasma cannon and a scanner from the

storage compartment and then dropped into the airlock. Using their emitters, they went invisible, then dropped out of the saucer. Malia gasped as they flew down toward the crash site; it was bitterly cold here. They landed near the saucer, weapons pointed toward the wreckage. Malia reached out telepathically, trying to sense Isis inside, but couldn't find her. The ship was destroyed; there were two significant fractures in the hull, and Malia could see flames within.

"Let's go inside," she suggested.

"What for? She's dead—there's no way she could have survived this. And the scanner's not showing any life signs in there."

"I don't sense anything, either, but we need to be sure," Malia insisted. "They thought she was dead last time, too, and look what happened."

Jaden shook his head but followed her in through one of the cracks. They were on the main level; Malia didn't see anyone here. She checked the area with an active scanning beam but still couldn't find Isis.

"Let's check the cockpit," she said.

The ship was resting at a steep angle, so they had to fly up to the top level. But the cockpit was empty.

"I don't get it," said Jaden. "Where did she go?"

"Airlock," Malia suggested. "Let's go."

They dropped back to the main level, scanning it once more to make sure Isis hadn't moved into the area. But when they reached the portal to the airlock, they realized that the impact had crushed

THE RIDDLE OF THE SPHINX

it. Malia checked with her scanner just to be sure, but there was no room for a person in there.

"Shit!" yelled Jaden. "How the hell did we lose her?"

"I don't know," Malia replied, creeping out of the fissure in the hull.

Jaden followed her out. Malia scanned the surrounding area and searched telepathically, too, but couldn't locate Isis anywhere.

"Uh-oh," Jaden said, gazing above them.

Malia followed his stare and spotted a vessel clearing the top of the peak. It was huge—this could only be the chariot.

"We'd better get out of here," said Malia.

"Yeah," Jaden agreed.

But as they took to the air to return to their saucer, the chariot fired on it with three rapid-fire laser blasts. The saucer went up in a massive explosion.

"Oh, shit!" said Jaden.

The chariot flooded the valley with active scanning beams.

"Fly!" yelled Malia.

The two of them raced through the air as the chariot fired on their previous position. Malia didn't understand how they were going to escape—they couldn't outrun this ship.

But an instant later, something out in front of them fired on the chariot. The ship was cloaked behind its shields, but from the small area Malia could see when it fired, she knew it was the Othali warship. The shots hit the chariot, and it reversed course, shooting off into the sky.

The warship became visible, and Malia and Jaden flew around to the docking port. But before she moved inside, Malia heard a voice in her head.

"*You have eluded us for now, Nephthys. But we still won: Humanity is extinct. There is nothing you can do to stop it.*"

It was Isis. Malia tried to reply, but she was gone.

Malia and Jaden flew into the warship and met Nadia on the docking platform. She gave them each a hug, then escorted them up to the bridge. Commander Anhur greeted them when they arrived, shaking their hands.

"Well done, both of you."

"Commander, we have to get back to the compound!" said Malia. "Isis released the virus!"

# Chapter Forty-one: Venus

Venus watched as Isis's ship left the hangar bay, and then the twins flew after her. What the hell were they thinking? But then Jaden summoned his saucer; they boarded and shot into the sky after Isis.

Venus summoned the remaining saucers back inside the hangar bay. But just as the last one cleared the doors, the chariot appeared, firing several shots into the compound. They hit some of the saucers; the force of the explosion threw Venus across the hangar bay. She was unhurt, though, and sent the command to close the blast doors. The chariot's weapons could probably get through them, but it would take some time; the first chariot's blasters had been significantly weaker than the Othali warship's.

The compound shook as several more shots hit the structure. Venus accessed the external optical sensors through her implants in time to see the chariot take off after the twins. She tried reopening the doors, but something was jammed. The chariot hadn't been trying to get *through* the blast doors—their goal had been to disable them.

"Dammit!"

Salvatore hurried over to her.

"Are you hurt?"

"No—but Malia and Jaden went after Isis, and we're stuck here."

"Why?"

"The chariot damaged the blast doors," she explained. "Malia and Jaden, this is Venus. Are you there?" There was no reply. "I can't reach them."

Salvatore concentrated for a moment, then said, "Neither can I."

Venus accessed the compound's control system.

"We can track their transponder—they're pursuing Isis toward the sea. The chariot is going after them but falling behind. Engine output for all three vessels is well beyond the detection threshold."

"What about the Othali?"

Venus nodded.

"Othali warship, this is Venus."

"Go ahead, Venus."

She explained the situation and asked for their location.

"We're about ten minutes out. Commander Anhur says we can intercept."

"Very well. I've restored your access to our control system—you can use that to track their transponder."

"Understood. Warship out."

There was nothing more they could do from here. Venus assigned a crew to get to work repairing the blast doors. The rest of them started moving the injured soldiers down to the medical bay. Not too much later, the warship contacted them.

"We've recovered Malia and Jaden and are en route to you, now."

"What about Isis?" asked Venus.

"The twins forced her saucer down, but there was no sign of her at the crash site. We briefly engaged the chariot before they fled. Isis may have been on board. Also... Malia reports that Isis has released the virus."

Venus let out a long sigh.

"Understood."

Venus relayed the updates to the others, then checked the internet for news about the virus. Sure enough, all the major outlets were reporting an outbreak of a mysterious neurological disease. Thousands of people were showing up at hospital emergency rooms worldwide complaining of hallucinations and partial paralysis.

Venus and Salvatore awaited the warship's arrival in the hangar bay with Bastet, Brian, and Miguel while Melissa and Sydney continued tending to the wounded. The mechanics managed to get the blast doors working again by the time the warship reached them. Venus was about to send a saucer for the twins, but they flew into the hangar bay on their own.

"Isis released the virus!" Malia told them. "What are we going to do?"

"I'm afraid there's nothing we can do," Salvatore told her. "It would take us weeks to months to develop a vaccine, and... it will be too late."

"No!" said Malia. "Isis gave me the virus, but it had no effect! They already have a vaccine—we just have to find it!"

Brian shook his head sadly.

"Your mother found the virus in Sydney's system and Miguel's. It had been neutralized, but she found no evidence of a vaccine. We don't know how Majestic stopped it."

"Well... a vaccine just teaches your immune system how to fight the virus, right?" asked Malia. Brian nodded. "Then it wasn't a vaccine. I could feel something in my bloodstream neutralizing the virus, but it *wasn't* my immune system—I know what that feels like. And it didn't seem like a chemical or drug, either. Whatever it was... it seemed like it had a mind of its own."

Salvatore fixed Venus with a stare.

"Nanobots."

Venus nodded.

"It must be."

She pulled out her scanner and checked Malia.

"Yes. She's got nanobots in her bloodstream." She checked Jaden next. "He's got them, too."

"Isis told me they've 'taken measures' to protect all the humans with Martian-compatible DNA," Malia told them. "She said that they still need those people to produce more hybrids."

"Wait a minute," said Brian. "This doesn't add up. They've abducted countless thousands of humans over the decades, but only a fraction of the people with compatible DNA. How could they have injected the rest of those people with the nanobots?"

Venus scanned Brian.

"You've got them, too."

"But *I've* never been abducted."

"Unless... the nanobots must function as a virus," Salvatore suggested. "They must be self-replicating."

"Isis must have released them into the wild," said Venus. "If they programmed the nanobots accordingly, then they could spread exactly like a virus. They could have released them months or even years ago."

"I ain't so sure this helps us, though," Miguel pointed out. "It'd probably take you folks even longer to reverse engineer them things than it would to create a vaccine, no?"

"If we could find where they manufactured the nanobots, then we wouldn't *have* to reverse engineer them," Brian suggested.

"Well, it wasn't here," said Venus. "There's nothing in the database about this, and I've seen nothing in the production facility to suggest they've been working on nanotech here."

"What about the Moon base?" said Malia. "There were a bunch of rooms up there that I couldn't get into. That was the Sphinx's compound—they could have made the nanobots there."

"We need to find out," said Venus. "I've got Isis's bio-scan, so I should be able to get us in there. Let's go!"

Bastet remained behind to guard the compound while the others boarded one of the saucers. Venus went up to the cockpit with Salvatore, Malia, and Jaden. She moved them out of the hangar bay and took off into the sky.

"Could you two darlings give us a little kick in the ass, so we can stay under the radar, so to speak?" Venus said to Malia and Jaden once they'd left the atmosphere.

"Sure," Malia said with a grin, and Jaden nodded.

They focused for a minute and propelled the saucer well beyond the velocity needed to escape the Earth's gravity. Venus reversed the engines in time to put them into orbit around the Moon. Malia described the location of the compound, and Venus found it on the far side. She took them into the crater and hovered the saucer outside the blast doors.

"Now, don't be alarmed—I've got to transform to get us inside," she warned the twins, then used her emitter to take on Isis's appearance. Next, she used her implants to access the compound's control system. There was no sign that anyone had returned here since Malia's rescue. Venus checked for any "back door" processes on the system but found none. She assigned herself, Salvatore, and Bastet command-level access then returned to her normal appearance. Once she'd accessed the system as herself, she revoked Isis's privileges along with Abrax's and Noorani's—there were no other users registered in the system.

Finally, she opened the blast doors and moved the saucer into the hangar bay. Once she'd closed the doors again, she pressurized the area.

They disembarked and moved into the compound. Venus opened all the interior doors. After a quick search, they located a lab and a production facility.

"This is it," Venus told the others. "They've got the equipment here to construct and replicate nanotechnology."

"We need the source code for the nanobots," said Brian.

They moved back to the lab, and Venus searched the database.

"I've got it," she told them. "Yes. They released the nanobots in major cities around the world months ago. It looks like the nanobots' transmission rate is even faster than the virus's."

"So chances are they were just waiting for the delivery rate to reach something close to 100% before releasing the virus," Brian suggested.

"Yes," Salvatore agreed. "But now we have another problem. Building and programming our own nanobots could take quite some time."

"Not if we just modify theirs," said Brain. "Can I see the source code, please?"

Venus brought it up on a holographic display.

"Of course, this isn't a language I know," said Brian.

Venus walked him through the program.

"Alright, so these nanobots check the host's chromosomes for certain genetic markers that indicate possible compatibility with Martian DNA," he said when she was done. "And if they find them, then they remain active and on the lookout for the virus. Then, when they find it, they neutralize it. But if they don't find the markers, then they go dormant, allowing such a host to become infected with the virus."

"Yes, correct," Venus confirmed.

"Then this is simple. Just remove the qualifying condition. Delete the part of the code that checks the genetic markers, then recompile the program and install it on a new batch of nanobots."

"And those will remain active regardless of the host's DNA and neutralize the virus no matter what," said Salvatore.

"Exactly," Brian replied.

"We're not going to have time to run any tests," Venus pointed out. "The virus is already spreading like wildfire down there. So, we've got one shot at this."

"Majestic has already done all the testing for us," said Brian. "We're reproducing the same agent, minus one section of code. It'll work."

Venus took a deep breath.

"We're going to need to compile the new code and fabricate a new set of first-generation nanobots. Why don't you two take care of the code, and I'll get to work on the hardware?"

Salvatore nodded.

Venus hurried back to the production facility. Accessing the equipment through her implants, she found the schematics for the latest run of nanobots and loaded them into the system. The nanobots consisted of an exterior housing embedded with a microscopic integrated circuit. She had the equipment ready to go by the time Salvatore and Brian finished the code. Venus checked their work, then loaded it into the system. Next, she located the distribution devices Isis had used to spread the last nanobots around the world. These were thin metal wafers, roughly half the size of a typical cell phone.

Venus ran some quick calculations. Twelve of the fourteen Othali pilots trained on the saucers had survived. Add herself, Salvatore, and Jaden, and that made fifteen saucers that could travel around the world to distribute the nanobots. Figuring in their transmission rate compared to the infection rate of the virus... and the time that had passed since the initial release... 1,080. That was the optimum number of distribution sites they would need to visit to have any chance of stopping the virus. Beyond that, they'd move well past the point of diminishing returns—adding more sites would have only a negligible impact on the nanobots' effective transmission rate.

Venus set up the equipment to produce 10% more than they needed just in case some were damaged in transport, then started the production. Twenty minutes later, their new set of first-generation nanobots were ready to roll.

They loaded the devices into a metal crate and moved it up to the saucer's airlock. Once everyone had boarded the saucer, they all headed up to the cockpit. Venus depressurized the hangar bay, moved them out of the compound, and closed the doors again behind them. Then, she set a course back to Earth and engaged the engines.

"I'll alert the compound to have the remaining pilots ready to go upon our arrival," she told the others. "We'll save a lot of lives today. But these nanobots will not help people who were already infected with the virus before receiving them. The damage to their neurological systems will already be done."

"Right," said Brian, heaving a deep sigh. "But it's the best we can do."

"How many people are still going to die?" Malia asked, her eyes welling up with tears.

"There's no way to tell at this point," Salvatore replied. "We'll have to wait and see."

# Chapter Forty-two: Nephthys

Malia disembarked with the others the moment the saucer arrived inside the compound. Venus took the crate of delivery devices down to the flight deck with her. The Othali soldiers, including all the remaining pilots, were gathered in the hangar bay, waiting for them. Salvatore addressed the crowd.

"As you've heard by now, we have prepared nanobots programmed to neutralize Majestic's virus regardless of the makeup of the host's DNA. Venus has calculated the optimum number of distribution sites and selected them using an algorithm that takes population into account, as well as geographical proximity to other urban centers.

"For example, in a situation where two cities are connected by significant urban sprawl, we need to release the nanobots in only one of the urban centers for them to spread to the other. On the other hand, a city with a smaller population surrounded by a large rural area will need its own delivery.

"Venus has assigned each pilot a partner and a geographical territory. She has already selected the drop points for each area. Bear in mind that this is the same method Majestic used to release the original nanobots and the virus. Once they realize what we are doing, there is a chance that you will encounter hybrids at your drop points trying to hinder your efforts.

"It's unlikely that our algorithm is identical to theirs or that they would have any way of knowing the precise drop point we've selected within each city. And we have randomized each route to add an extra layer of unpredictability. But you should remain alert, just in case.

"We have chosen buildings with high traffic for each drop point. Like the virus, the nanobots will achieve their highest transmission rate indoors, so you will need to enter each location and activate the delivery mechanism inside the structure. Depending on the time zone at your location, some of your buildings may not be open. In that case, use your weapons to break in and release the nanobots anyway. They will remain active and airborne until people arrive.

"Any questions?" No one responded. "Very well; let's proceed. Venus will transmit your assignments to you through your implants momentarily."

The room erupted in noise and chaos as people got to work.

"You're with me," Jaden said to Malia. "We've got North America."

Malia nodded.

Venus had soldiers divvying up the delivery devices and moving them to each saucer while Salvatore addressed the group. So Malia and Jaden ran over to his new saucer and flew up to the airlock with their cargo. They hurried up to the cockpit. Jaden moved them out of the hangar bay, and they took off into the sky.

"Hey, uh... I just wanted to let you know I'm glad you're alive,"

Jaden said with an awkward grin as they flew over the desert. "I never realized how much it would suck without you till I thought you were dead."

"Thanks," Malia replied, smiling in return. "For a while, I was pretty sure I was gonna die, too."

"And... I'm sorry for trying to kill you that day back in Fiji."

Malia giggled.

"I'm sorry, too. But I think maybe we should refrain from any more training sessions like that."

"Yes," Jaden agreed.

"Bastet won't be too happy about that. It seemed like she was enjoying herself."

"Yeah, well, she'll get over it."

They reached their first stop in Philadelphia and Jaden hovered the saucer over the street. Malia moved down to the main level, grabbed a plasma cannon and one of the delivery devices, and then dropped to the ground. It was the middle of the night here, and there weren't too many people around.

Venus had selected the Reading Terminal Market. The building was closed at this hour, so Malia used her plasma cannon to blow a hole in the glass doors. There was a burglar alarm, and the siren sounded immediately. A couple of passersby gawked at her but didn't try to stop her as she entered the building. Malia activated the delivery device, then tossed it farther into the market.

Police sirens blared in the distance as Malia returned to the street and flew back up to the saucer. She reached the cockpit as

Jaden engaged the engines and took off for their next destination.

They worked through the night, with stops ranging from San Diego to Anchorage, Boston to Mexico City. The continent crossed into daylight, and still, they continued, stopping in one city after another.

Malia encountered a little trouble in San Antonio. Venus had selected a crowded mall across from the River Walk. It was early afternoon by the time they'd arrived here, so getting inside was no problem. Malia activated the delivery device and set it down on a counter in the food court. But as she headed toward the exit, someone came up behind her and grabbed her by the shoulder.

"What are you doing here, Ms. Kwan?" the man asked as Malia turned to face him. It was no one she recognized. But he gave her a smirk, and suddenly his eyes changed—his pupils were slits.

"Hybrid," she muttered, turning and running toward the exit.

The mall was crowded, so she hoped that maybe he'd leave her alone. But she had no such luck; the hybrid took to the air, flying over the heads of the crowd and landing in front of the exit. He drew a laser pistol, but Malia used her powers to send him flying into the ceiling before he could fire.

Several people screamed, and the crowd began running toward the exits as the now-unconscious hybrid hit the floor. Malia hurried out the door and flew back up to Jaden's saucer before any more hybrids could show up.

They didn't have too many stops left, and Malia didn't see any other hybrids. Once they'd finished their last delivery, they flew back to the compound. It was nighttime in Algeria by the time they'd arrived.

About a third of the teams had completed their runs, and they were gathered by the rear of the hangar bay, watching a holographic display of a newscast. The program featured nonstop coverage of the mysterious pandemic that had spread across the world, seemingly out of nowhere. Millions of people had checked into hospitals and clinics complaining of dizziness, hallucinations, and partial paralysis. Some had shown brain-swelling and fallen into comas. The news anchor reported that doctors had not yet been able to identify the source of the disease, much less find a cure.

People had started dying from the illness. The death toll was low so far, but Malia knew it would get much higher before long. She could only hope that the nanobots would overtake the virus before the situation grew catastrophic.

# Chapter Forty-three: Jaden

Along with everyone else living in the compound, Jaden spent the next several days compulsively watching news programs, tracking the progress of the Majestic virus. Salvatore had alerted world leaders to the situation—and their efforts to combat it. Most world governments had mandated shutdowns of all schools and businesses and instituted lockdowns. But still, the virus spread faster than any other in human history.

Salvatore had explained that having thousands of distribution points had accelerated the expansion in addition to the virus's extreme infectiousness. Most viruses had been initially introduced to humans at a single source.

For the first few days, things had gone relatively well. The death count worldwide had climbed into the hundreds of thousands, but the world's citizens complied with the lockdown measures. But then the tally rose to a million deaths, and only a few days later, ten million. And at that point, the fundamental underpinnings of civilized society began to break down.

The news programs reported that the major world economies were collapsing. Civil unrest broke out in hundreds of urban centers around the globe as people protested against the containment measures. And as a result, the death count continued to accelerate; it topped one hundred million after only ten days.

Jaden began to question whether the nanobots were working at all. Salvatore assured him that they were and that it would probably be only a matter of a few more days before they caught up with the virus. They had released the nanobots inside the compound that first day, and nobody here had become ill.

The most densely populated areas of the world broke down into anarchy as civil unrest evolved into revolt. People were growing increasingly angry, afraid, and desperate as civilization itself continued to break down. The basic supplies necessary for survival became scarce; food was difficult to find. Starvation began adding to the already catastrophic death toll. Hospitals were no longer accepting new patients, the morgues were overflowing, and the dead began piling up on the streets, spreading other diseases in addition to the virus.

By the morning of the fourteenth day of the pandemic, the tally had risen to one billion dead. But then it happened. The world reached some sort of tipping point as the nanobots overcame the virus. The death rate fell off a cliff. For the first time since Majestic released the virus, the news programs began expressing optimism that perhaps the nightmare would come to an end.

Salvatore called a meeting for the following evening. Jaden had been dreading this. He knew the Othali had hung around to see how things developed with the virus. But now that the outcome seemed assured, they'd be making preparations to leave Earth forever—and

Jaden, Malia, and Melissa would be going with them. Jaden asked Melissa if he could skip the meeting.

"Why?"

"It's too depressing. I don't want to leave."

"Come on. Commander Anhur specifically requested our presence."

"Ugh," Jaden replied.

He headed to the conference room with Malia and Melissa. Brian, Sydney, and Miguel were already here, as were Salvatore, Venus, and Bastet. Much to Jaden's surprise, Babcock was here, too. Last Jaden had known, he was living on the Othali warship with his granddaughters.

Jaden sat down between Malia and Sydney. Moments later, holograms of Commander Anhur, Lieutenant Bukhari, and Ensign Shurani appeared at the head of the table.

"Good morning, everyone," said the commander. "Thank you for joining us. I understand there has been a significant development?"

"Yes," Salvatore confirmed. "Our nanobots have finally overtaken the virus. There have been roughly 1.1 billion deaths as of this morning, but the rate of new deaths has plummeted."

"Still, so many dead," said Sydney. "It's difficult to comprehend…"

"Yet it could have been so much worse," said Venus. "It would have been double that had our response taken only one additional day."

"The damage to the world's civilizations has nevertheless been catastrophic," Brian pointed out. "It's going to take a long time to rebuild."

"Has there been any sign of Isis or Abrax?" asked Anhur.

"None," said Salvatore. "They must be sorely disappointed in the outcome."

"What about all them hybrids?" asked Miguel. "They had thousands of them living all around the world, right? What are they doing now?"

"We don't yet know for sure," Salvatore replied. "I have been in touch with government leaders in the United States and Europe and provided them with the identities and locations of all the hybrids in their countries—we collected the data from the Sphinx's Moon base. They've had their hands full responding to the virus, but their preliminary investigations have come up empty."

"Meaning what?" asked Anhur.

"The hybrids are gone," Salvatore replied with a shrug. "Isis had plans to establish new cities in the aftermath of the pandemic, once the virus had finished its work. But with nearly seven billion humans surviving, I'm sure they've had to alter their plans. I suspect most of them have simply taken on new identities and will begin integrating back into society as people rebuild."

"Well, you can count on Isis hatching a new scheme for global conquest," said Venus. "It may not be a virus this time. They spent decades developing the first one, and the nanobots' code is broad enough to stop any variants. Isis is nothing if not patient, so it may take decades more, but we *will* have to contend with her again eventually."

"Yes," Salvatore agreed. "But the Malor may prove to be a more imminent threat."

"*What?*" said Sydney; several others voiced surprise at this remark as well.

"What are you talking about?" asked Brian. "I thought they'd rounded up all the stragglers at Gitmo?"

"They did, but the virus hit the base hard," Salvatore explained. "President Mendoza tells me that the Malor managed to overpower the surviving guards and escape. Their whereabouts are currently unknown."

"Well, this brings me to some news we'd like to share," said Anhur. "My staff and I have been debating the matter for some time now, but we have decided not to seek out that new planet, after all. We had feared that humanity is not ready for the ongoing presence of an alien race. But in light of recent events, it seems they do not have a choice—whether the Othali remain or not.

"Helping defend the humans from Majestic has infused our people with a sense of purpose that they have not felt since our homeworld was destroyed. And at this point, the people of Earth need all the help they can get."

"Wait," said Jaden, suddenly brimming with excitement. "You're telling me that you're *staying*?"

Anhur considered him with a grin.

"That is indeed what I'm telling you."

"*Yes!*" Jaden yelled, pumping his fist in the air.

"Well, we would very much appreciate the opportunity to extend our alliance," said Venus. "My team and I have spent the last couple of weeks improving our fortifications here and upgrading the weapons systems on our saucer fleet. But knowing your warship is nearby, too, will certainly put my mind at ease."

"I agree; this is great news," Brian said, flashing a smile at Jaden and Malia. "It would have broken my heart to say goodbye to my niece and nephew again. But I have a proposal. With the hybrid threat still present, I believe it's safe to say that the humans at the table would like to continue residing here, for security purposes?"

"Damn straight," said Miguel. "I don't fancy waking up in the middle of the night in my trailer staring down the barrel of a hybrid plasma cannon."

Sydney nodded her agreement.

"You bet your sweet ass we're staying here," said Babcock. "Lucifer may be gone, but I have no doubt any one of his people would be happy to make good on his promise. My granddaughters aren't happy about it, of course, but this is the only place in the world I can keep them safe."

"Right," Brian continued. "Yet at the same time, I think all of us would agree that permanent confinement underground or in orbit is hardly desirable. So, I've taken the liberty of purchasing Bastet's little island in Fiji."

"*My* island?" Bastet asked with a note of surprise.

Brian chuckled.

"I would like to build a retreat center there. Our people here and on the warship could use it as a getaway for a week or two at a time. Get some R and R, enjoy the outdoors for a while. Maybe we could hire Venus's former staff to come back and work there. Those chefs of yours were top notch."

"Oh, I'm sure I could arrange it, darling," said Venus. "I've missed my old crew."

"We'll need to keep a few saucers stationed there for security purposes," Salvatore pointed out. "The hybrids could attack us there if they learn of it."

"Absolutely," Brian agreed.

"I have another concern," said Venus. "We're still housing the last of the human abductees from Majestic's compounds here. Once things get back to normal in the rest of the world, we can return them to their homes. And the hybrids we've identified as resistance members are welcome to stay here or take their chances elsewhere as they wish.

"But what about the rest of the hybrids? The ones loyal to Majestic. Are we keeping them imprisoned here indefinitely?"

"We must," said Salvatore. "We certainly can't release them."

"That wasn't the alternative I had in mind..." Venus muttered.

"No, no," Sydney said with a frown. "We're *not* executing them. They've all been brainwashed by Majestic from a very young age. It's very similar to a cult in that respect. There are specialists out there who can help them."

"Are you willing to take charge of that?" asked Venus.

"I am," Sydney said with a nod.

"There's one more matter I'd like to address," said Anhur. "Isis's Moon base. What will we be doing with that?"

THE RIDDLE OF THE SPHINX

"We should destroy it," Salvatore replied. "I have retrieved the equipment and data housed there. If it remains vacant, Isis or Abrax could retake it."

"I'm a little surprised she hasn't tried to return there already," said Venus.

"When she left me there to die, it didn't sound like she had any plans on coming back," Malia told them.

"Perhaps, but her failure with the virus might have changed her mind," Brian pointed out. "I don't think any of us wants to live on the Moon. Destroying the base would be best."

"Very well," said Anhur. "We will take care of that today. And I believe that should conclude our business for this morning?"

"Actually, I have one more announcement," said Sydney, holding out one hand and turning red. "Miguel and I are getting married!"

Jaden spotted an engagement ring on her finger.

"Congratulations!" said Melissa, getting up to hug Sydney.

"*Where* did you get that diamond?" asked Malia. "It's *huge*!"

"Venus helped us out," Miguel said with a grin.

"It was no problem at all, dear," Venus replied. "I had to stock up for the weapons systems, anyway."

Jaden joined the others in congratulating Sydney and Miguel. They officially adjourned the meeting, but Salvatore held Jaden back as the others left the conference room.

"I found something that Hathor left for you," he said.

"Seriously? What is it?"

"It's an address," said Salvatore. "Somewhere in Texas."

Jaden was confused. He had no idea what this could be about. "Uh... what's there?"

"I'm afraid I have no idea. You'll have to go have a look to find out."

"You're gonna let me go there? What if it's dangerous?"

Salvatore shrugged.

"If it were, then I doubt Hathor would have left this for you."

Jaden could hardly contain his curiosity. He ran up to the hangar bay, boarded his saucer, and set a course to the mystery address. Leaving the compound and shooting off into the sky, he wondered where Hathor was sending him.

When he arrived at the address, he found a mobile home sitting on a plot of land by a lake, far from any neighbors. There was a beach, and a girl was lying on a reclining chair, sunbathing in her bikini.

"No way," Jaden muttered, his heart jumping.

He brought up a holographic image of the girl in the center console. Sure enough, he knew who this was. Sending a silent *thank you* to Hathor, he dropped down to the ground to meet the girl.

Somehow, Hathor had tracked down Savannah.

*Here ends the Majestic series.*
*Jaden and Malia's story will continue...*

Made in the USA
Coppell, TX
08 August 2021